I0787980

LORDS OF THE ENDLESS PLAINS

CORSAC FOX
BOOK 3

BLAZE WARD

KNOTTED ROAD PRESS

Lords of the Endless Plains
Corsac Fox, Book 3
Blaze Ward
Copyright © 2024 Blaze Ward
All rights reserved
Published by Knotted Road Press
www.KnottedRoadPress.com

ISBNs:
Paperback: 978-1-64470-403-5
Hardback: 978-1-64470-406-6

Cover art:
Jay O'Connell https://www.jayoconnell.com/
Illustration 108050035 © Raffaele1 | Dreamstime.com
Illustration 22850687 © Seamartini | Dreamstime.com

Cover and interior design copyright © 2024 Knotted Road Press

Reviews
It's true. Reviews help. Even a short one, such as, "Loved it!" So please consider reviewing this book (and all of the ones you've read) on your favorite retailer site.

Never miss a release!
If you'd like to be notified of new releases, sign up for my newsletter.

http://www.blazeward.com/newsletter/

Buy More!
Did you know that you can buy directly from the Knotted Road Press website?

https://www.knottedroadpress.com/shop/

ALSO BY BLAZE WARD

The Jessica Keller Chronicles

Auberon

Queen of the Pirates

Last of the Immortals

Goddess of War

Flight of the Blackbird

The Red Admiral

St. Legier

Winterhome

Petron

CS-405

Queen Anne's Revenge

Packmule

Persephone

First Centurion Kosnett

Encounter at Vilahana

Consensus at Aditi

Hegemony at Dalou

Princes at Ewin

Empire at Gloran

Domain at Yaumgan

Additional Alexandria Station Stories

The Story Road

Siren

Two Bottles of Wine With A War God

The Science Officer Series Season One

The Science Officer

The Mind Field

The Gilded Cage

The Pleasure Dome

The Doomsday Vault

The Last Flagship

The Hammerfield Gambit

The Hammerfield Payoff

The Bryce Connection

The Science Officer Series Season Two

Alien Seas

Buried Among the Stars

Captain Navarre

Last Stand

Lost Dreams

Ghost Towns

Games People Play

Prophet and Loss

Dandelion

Emergency

Warchild

Moot

Doomsday Girl

Princess

The Coven

Preacher Man

Captain Daring

Revoked

Returned

Reborn

The Lazarus Alliance

Escape

Return

Rebellion

Revolution

Liberation

Retribution

Alliance

Shadow of the Dominion

Longshot Hypothesis

Hard Bargain

Outermost

Dominion-427

Phoenix

Princess Rualoh

CONTENTS

FOX

LORDS OF THE ENDLESS PLAINS

WARLORD

TRAVELER

RAIDER

For Harald and Gibbitt and Esko

FOX

ONE

"All hands to action stations," the call came over the speaker.

Captain Ulysses Fortier—Uly—was already on duty, listening to his own voice echo around his bridge as everyone hyped up to that next level.

Combat imminent.

For a moment, he wondered how many stories started that way. As a professional pirate hunter, a great deal of his usual workload involved quietly seeking information about pirates, long before looking for the men and women themselves.

And only then hunting them down.

Like today.

As folks around him dug out emergency spacesuits and put them on, Uly supposed that he should consider it a mark of his success that those folks were getting harder and harder to find.

Pirates, that was.

Criminal gangs were quietly packing up and moving elsewhere. Or settling for the kinds of smuggling that Uly really didn't care all that much about. If your people really wanted something bad enough that they were willing to turn to crime to import it, that spoke to problems of governance and culture beyond his power to fix.

License it. Regulate it. Tax it. Humans drank ethyl alcohols in concentrations that frightened other species. At the same time, every species had some interesting chemical they ingested in order to relax, or hallucinate, or something.

The Khet had a particular species of mushroom that they consumed in order to take fantastical hallucinatory voyages, that did nothing for anybody else. Weren't even that good to cook with, as they tended to be too woody in taste.

But it worked for them. And they had to import it illegally.

And thus, crime flourished on the Khet world of Z'Gosza. Worse, the massively wealthy oligarchs complained that nobody was paying taxes on such things, which might be the single highest insult they could throw at one another.

Somebody else getting rich by cheating.

Unacceptable.

Uly looked around his bridge as folks were settling. Not bad. Sixty seconds from the moment he'd been sure that they could do it.

Now, for the dangerous parts.

TWO

Uly studied the plot. Because they had previously found a nice, quiet place to hide the cargo vessel *Wren*, he had all of his top crew with him today.

Human teenagers who had been midshipmen on *King Hewitt II* when he'd captured it originally, with most of the adults aboard having been killed by the only shot that had hit the vessel. But Uly had subsequently helped shape them into the sorts of young officers that he needed. Wanted.

Demanded, for this sort of work.

"Sailing Master, call the cadence," Uly said firmly.

Drew Roscoe. Civilian, who had been training as a pilot under Mistress of Sail Hylda Hobbs, still the only officer anybody who had served on *King Hewitt II* missed. Or had anything nice to say about.

"We have a track, Captain," Drew replied. "Been following it clean, so I think we're chasing our target to his base, but he might be about to pounce on someone else. Or maybe he's found a place to lair while he waits."

"Either suits me, Roscoe," Uly said. "Gunner, stand by your weapon systems."

Lieutenant Sterling Huff. Formerly a Midshipman and

Astronomer's Mate. Gifted stellar cartographer who had also discovered a great facility for understanding alien cultures.

Both of those men had once belonged to the *Combined Crowns of Danumash*, the so-called Seven Kingdoms, while Uly had once been their archfoe as a member of the *Institutional Republic of Batyr*. Aristocracy versus meritocracy.

Sterling hadn't known there were aliens out there in the wider galaxy, save that *King Hewitt II* had been transporting a group of alien slaves when *Batyr* had captured the vessel and Uly had liberated them.

And ended up with all three crews accepting him as commander. Collecting more people as they went. Heady, but disconcerting at times, to have so many alien faces looking to Uly to lead.

"Sir, I'm studying the charts that Z'Gosza updated for us," Huff replied. "Cultural, rather than merely geographical. I think that our target is leading us down into another place like Lacium. Not as dangerous or well-armed, but still something of a pirate den. Maybe a small station where folks can come for some quiet rest and recreation. Possibly a few fences and shops. Maybe folks who used to deal with Z'Gosza."

He nodded over to the only Khet on the bridge, Administrator Rabiu Khadijan, who was still technically their liaison to the Z'Goszan government, even though he had functionally changed sides to sail with Uly and the *Corsac Fox*.

"A threat to the ship?" Uly asked.

After all, they'd gone after Lacium with the help of the Z'Goszan government and a lot of military intelligence ahead of time. Plus surprise.

And the fact that Humans tended to be militantly aggressive in ways that other species didn't comprehend. Even in their worst nightmares.

"Negative on threat, sir," Huff said. "Ionization trail suggests that we're tracking a smaller vessel. Ultra-Bomber or Armed Probe. We cannot, however, determine who will be in the moorage until we drop out. Alternatively, we could assume our destination and cut our sail short, sneaking up on them."

Uly considered it.

"Roscoe, your thoughts?" he asked.

Uly had known too many officers who assumed that they were right all the time. Then gave orders based on that assumption, blaming underlings for whatever failures inevitably occurred.

Uly led because these folks had elected him to lead. Expected him to lead. This was no longer a military organization, save that he was building something to replace what all of them had lost along the way.

Most of his crew had been civilians who had been swept up in his riptide. And had still chosen to remain aboard *Corsac Fox* when given the chance to depart.

"I think Huff's got it, sir," Roscoe replied, looking up from his boards.

Uly caught Sterling's deep blush. Second-youngest crew member, only older than Lieutenant Solomon Wyndham, who was the Security Officer for the ship at the ripe, old age of sixteen.

But Solomon had Dan, Uly's Second-in-Command and Right Hand, training him. And he was learning.

"Roscoe, go ahead and slide us a little off the target's track and drop the ship out a few light-minutes from Huff's predicted coordinates," Uly ordered. "Huff, do a quick optical scan of what you can see from that distance, then we'll either move in and pounce ourselves, or back off. Questions?"

"Negative, sir," both men managed in harmony.

Uly nodded and let himself relax a little. He looked over at Dan and caught her smile.

THREE

Dan noted the way Uly was turning into the sort of commanding officer she'd always wished she could have had, back on *Marshall Castillon*. Captain Savatier had only been the most recent of them, but all had been hard, mean bastards. Didn't help that they had all been pale Euros from good families, and she'd been the Afro-Siberian grunt from the wrong side of the starport.

Almost all of the officers she'd ever known on *Marshall Castillon* had been punks.

Almost.

Then Uly came along and reset all her expectations of what an officer could be.

Then the silly goose had made her his Second-in-Command. *Commander* Sheridan Chastain.

Dan smiled at him when he looked over. Noted how much calmer he was these days, but they were all getting used to life as something of a police gendarme. Pirate hunters, because that was a far more ethical solution to being broke and never wanting to return to the tiny Human regions over in *Auga* Imperial Sector Seventeen.

"I should go roust my boarding parties," she said, eyes locked with Uly.

She could see him wanting to stop her from going. Hold her back, here on the ship. But they were too thin in crew, even today, when Z'Gosza had only started to let them recruit broadly.

That, and a few pirates who her current crew were willing to speak up for.

The *Corsac Fox*—the ship and not the man everyone was now referring to by that name—could hold a lot of troopers. Pirate ship, intending to board and storm.

Uly had rightly said that they would add crew slowly. Carefully. Vet them, then socialize them into the family, as it were.

The results were exceptional, but none of the people she'd had were ready to lead their own assault. Not yet.

Another year, and Solomon would be ready. Perhaps two for Nasrin Monfared—the Mazhin dancer turned scholar of violence—and Anari Supasei—Sabre School Emro that the foolish *Auga* had demanded must be Moss School, because she was too smart to be a mere warrior.

Nasrin had a head start on Anari. Anari was closing the gap quickly. Both would be formidable warriors in not too long.

"Go," Uly said simply. "Be safe."

Dan nodded and keyed her general comm.

"Boarding teams report to the arsenal for equipment," she ordered. "Security Team, you'll have the ship shortly."

Solomon Wyndham, a kid turning into a giant and a soldier.

Gennady Travers, who'd been with her for years. Long-limbed and skinny like ancient legends of trolls. About as pretty to look at, too.

Emil Beranger, Gennady's short, squat sidekick whose cybernetic replacement shin wasn't invisible, but didn't slow him down either.

Those three, plus a few others, would hold the ship, while Dan took her mishmash of Mazhin, Emro, Ononguli, and newly recruited Khet soldiers to see about those other pirates.

Dan smiled once more at Uly, then locked herself into Boarding Lead mode and scowled at the universe.

FOUR

Nasrin's sensory tentacles let her track far more information around her than eyes and ears allowed the others. Even scent, because most of them had less than a few square centimeters of olfactory capability.

A Mazhin had square meters.

Everyone was keyed up. Adrenaline, or whatever their biology's equivalent was. Emil and Gennady were checking out weapons to folks as they came through the line.

Nasrin could have cut ahead, because Dan treated her as an officer these days, but she chose to follow the others sequentially.

Emil handed her the omnibow without asking, adding a bandoleer of munitions for it. Painspheres and Firespheres. Psychological warfare that got your attention, fired or not.

Nasrin added the bandoleer over her boarding armor, then stepped well off to one side. Not a lot of women with this force, though there were some. Two Emro women, Anari and Yanouk, the former being Sabre School, with the latter having a dancer's sensibilities similar to Nasrin's, when it came to violence.

Katya Zehlennko, one of five Ononguli women aboard, all of them engineers, but Katya had started to join the inner ring of advisors that the Emro Exemplar of the Arts Suka Kuri had caused to come into being around Dan. All of them female. All of them body-guards to Uly.

All of them dangerous.

Nasrin had caught snippets of conversation between Suka Kuri and Dan, suggesting that they should specifically recruit some Thogin women as well as Khet, merely to drive home to a largely sexist and male chauvinist galaxy that the Corsac Fox—Uly, and not just this ship—trusted women to make decisions. Surrounded himself with them, though it was not a harem.

Dan had never crossed that final line, though Nasrin suspected the two Humans had come close.

And Uly was made up of charisma, boiled down and distilled. More than one of the other folks had mentioned how he could get you to *believe*.

Nasrin did.

The two Emro women stepped close, armed and ready. Katya joined them a moment later.

Dan came through the hatch and stepped around the line of men drawing weapons, but she kept her Heavy Exoripper pistol and Icemace in her quarters.

Nasrin preferred not complicating her personal space with violence. She was known by much of the crew as *The Songbird*.

She supposed hawks also sang.

"Update," Dan called, her voice carrying to all corners of the large ready room. "Uly is dropping us out a little short of what might be a station or small pirate base. Scouting, then he'll make the call to attack or withdraw."

Nasrin noted the spike of energy that ran through the crowd by the way their scent changed. None of the other Mazhin chose to accompany Nasrin into war. And only Haydar and Piruz served in any sort of position of authority. Not counting Vahid who was training folks to cook while feeding the officers.

Dan stepped close and surveyed her women officers. The three Human men would stay behind and guard the ship, but Nasrin and her tribal kin had all made it a point to interview and spend time around potential recruits.

No hint of treachery or ambiguity was allowed, and some folks had been turned away merely on her hesitation.

The crew was solid. And getting better. Bigger, as Uly allowed more folks from Z'Gosza and Lacium to join, though they weren't even half full yet.

Getting there.

In the meanwhile, the Corsac Fox was hunting down pirates and making the galaxy a better place, though she did laugh inside, when she considered what the Mazhin and Ononguli of her current family had done before meeting Uly.

FIVE

Uly studied the scan results that Haydar had thrown onto his side screen.

Data Officer, which meant that he could take what Sterling's sensors could gather, and turn it into information by washing out all the garbage and such.

Solid, actionable intelligence.

Except that one of the ships in harbor had a star next to it that Haydar obviously wanted Uly to see. To ask about.

He lifted his eyes to Haydar's tentacles, noting that the man seemed to be laughing quietly from the way they maneuvered.

"*Ahmadi*?" Uly asked, just because Haydar seemed intent.

"A *Mazhin* vessel," Haydar stressed, his eyes getting huge and his eyeslits snapping out before snapping back.

Mazhin?

Uly would say a long ways from home, but the Mazhin didn't seem to have a home world. Most of them, according to his handy local experts, lived on board starships, traveling endlessly as merchants, tourists, and, occasionally, pirates.

"Will that be a problem?" Uly asked.

Haydar's tentacles fluffed in every direction.

"Tell them you *Speak* for this Convocation," the Mazhin data nerd replied with an immense grin. "Watch them freak completely out."

Uly supposed so. They had elected Haydar, as the ten Mazhin on this ship had originally come from at least five different vessels.

Then they had decided that Uly would *Speak* for them.

"What about the ship we were chasing?" Uly asked, sidestepping all things Mazhin for now.

"*Ironhorn*," Haydar nodded with his entire upper half. "A weird Ononguli design. It appears to be an armed Probe, with a triple turret forward holding what look like 2dm tubes, and a single 2dm tube aft. Good for overwhelming light freighters, but not capable of going tentacle-to-tentacle with any sort of warship, to say nothing of us."

"And the others?" Uly asked.

"Even smaller and less threatening," Haydar scoffed. "Minnows that will likely scatter at the first provocation. Even the station looks harmless enough, from what I can tell from here."

"Excellent news," Uly decided, then opened the general comm so all of the ship could listen, including all the engineers aft who just minded hardware. "All hands, we're about to drop in for tea. There might be combat, but I doubt it. More likely, we'll be taking a few hostages against good behavior while chatting. Boarding teams, stand by for orders."

He cut the line and turned to Drew and Sterling, looking back for the words.

"Take us in," Uly ordered.

SIX

Uly watched the screen as *Corsac Fox* blinked briefly into warp, then back out. Drew Roscoe had chosen to drop them almost exactly at the center of a triangle connecting the station, *Ahmadi*, and *Ironhorn*, meaning that both ships were currently trapped here, inside the zone *Corsac Fox* was generating with the Variable Pulse Spatial Generator, even dialed down.

"All vessels, this is the Z'Goszan warship *Corsac Fox*," Uly announced on a common frequency. "You will surrender immediately for customs inspection. Or be destroyed. Station, you will stand down or we will open fire on you as well."

Not exactly sporting, since he was in a severely upgunned Interceptor, with firepower comparable to even larger ships. A light Striker-class ship, for instance.

These were civilian ships that had a few wavebolt launchers added. Nothing that was a threat.

And he had surprise.

"Forward battery, I have lock on *Ironhorn*," Sterling Huff announced. "Defensive gunners, you will intercept if *Ahmadi* fires anything. Do not wait for the order if they put wavebolts into space."

Uly nodded. By the book. He'd trained Sterling to that level of professionalism, back when he'd expected to turn the young man over to some future *Danumash* captain.

Sterling was staying put. And growing more professional and expert with every passing day. And his confidence.

Ironhorn was the pirate they'd been chasing. *Ahmadi* was a Mazhin ship that happened to be in harbor. The station was one that dealt with pirates routinely, but still enough under the table that Uly didn't feel the need to capture it and remove the crew like he'd done at Lacium.

"Roscoe, what's everybody doing?" Uly asked as the message wavefront reached other vessels.

"Probably tying their tentacles in knots," Drew replied, drawing chuckles from Haydar as well. "The Ononguli ship might start bashing their horns on a bulkhead, but they have to move to shoot at us. I might have done that on purpose, coming in low behind them like this."

"And excellent flying, Drew," Uly reminded him.

Drew Roscoe was older. Hell, most of his crew was older than Uly, but he'd been three years out of school and a mere Ensign, before he'd been sent on what had turned into the mission of a lifetime.

He still assumed that Captain Savatier had expected him to die or be captured in the process.

Drew nodded and blushed the same as Sterling had. They were all growing into roles bigger than they'd ever expected.

"Haydar, do you feel like overriding *Ironhorn* and letting me talk to their captain?" Uly asked, referring to the secondary communications systems that all Ononguli hulls had.

One Haydar had reprogrammed so that nobody could do that to him again.

Cackles greeted his question.

"Ready when you are," Haydar replied.

"*Ironhorn*, this is Captain Ulysses Fortier, commanding *Corsac Fox*," Uly said, knowing that it would echo through that ship's bridge. "You can surrender and talk. Or fight me and die. Your choice. I have news from the Lords of the Endless Plains."

Captain Chayka had taught him that phrase, back before *Compass*

Rose and *Scavenger Angel* had returned to the Ononguli Sphere with news of a previously unknown species of star travelers.

Humans.

And the Corsac Fox.

Uly cut the line and watched the screen. All those folks would need time to react to their reaction, rethinking their immediate plans.

An *Auga* Imperial Customs warship would have landed and immediately opened fire. Before demanding surrenders.

Even Lukyan Chayka, Conductor of *Compass Rose*, had noted with surprise and concern how Humans were even more dangerous than the *Auga*.

The galaxy was safe while Humanity was confined to a small, back corner of Imperial Sector Seventeen.

However, Uly still intended to stop the *Auga* from eventually conquering the entire galaxy, as was their current, methodical plan.

"Haydar?" Uly asked a few moments later.

"I'm sending subtle signals to *Ahmadi* that there are Mazhin aboard as part of the crew," Haydar replied. "More freak out on their part, but hey, I didn't get up this morning and choose to be a pirate."

Uly grunted, rather than say anything. Different kind of pirate, maybe. Haydar had occasionally mentioned his youth, and some of the things he'd done at Uly's age.

Not a man given to scholarly pursuits and ascetic lifestyles then. Not until much more recently.

"*Corsac Fox*, this is Conductor Illya Tkachuk, aboard *Ironhorn*," a male voice came over the line. "I'm not familiar with your ship, but my systems show you as the Ononguli vessel *Iron Wasp*?"

"Formerly, *Ironhorn*," Uly replied evenly. "It's my ship now and Adrian Sobol might have been traded home by the *Auga* by now. Do you need to satisfy your honor first?"

"Curiosity, *Corsac Fox*," Tkachuk replied. "We're standing down."

Uly nodded and turned to Haydar.

"*Ahmadi*, this is Haydar Ramezani, aboard *Corsac Fox*," Haydar said loudly. "Stand by for the *Speaker of my Convocation*, the Human Ulysses Fortier."

He cut the line and snickered. Must be some terrible practical joke. Hopefully, Uly would be able to get the story out of him later.

A male Mazhin face appeared on Uly's screen, tentacles all askew and getting worse.

"Speaker?" the man asked, incredulous.

"That is correct," Uly nodded carefully. "I have several members of your species aboard my vessel. They elected me to *Speak* for them."

"Okay, I gotta hear this," the man said. "*Speaker* Jamsheed Abbasi, standing by for your orders, *Corsac Fox*."

Uly nodded and muted the line.

"What's the station doing?" he asked.

"Frantically trying to surrender on channel seven," Haydar chuckled. "I told them to wait their turn. How do you wish to play this?"

Uly smiled and considered his options.

"Let's put Dan and her folks on the station," he decided. "Then every commanding officer can come aboard the station with exactly one aide, for a conference. They obviously haven't gotten the news around here yet. We need to rectify that."

Several folks snickered, including Rabiu Khadijan.

"Rabiu," Uly said. "None of these folks were dealing with your Factor or Directors, correct?"

"Correct," the Khet nodded. "Somebody else, far across some distant org chart. The Factor suggested this area because of geography, rather than score-settling."

Uly nodded. Rampant capitalist oligarchs, controlling an entire planetary economy with a strict bureaucracy of papers and power. Uly still didn't understand how it worked, but Ethir Ewen, the leader of his small mob of Thogin miscreants, assured him that it did, then offered insights on how to make it work for Uly.

Rabiu had also been seduced into helping.

And here they were.

"Good enough," Uly said. "Get them surrendered. Get the warships moved out of our way, and we'll move close to the station to put Dan and hers aboard."

"And then, sir?" Sterling asked.

"Then we'll chat," Uly nodded.

SEVEN

Dan had landed with a large team of armed killers, issuing orders for the station bosses to meet her in the landing bay, nobody armed but her folks.

She'd seen some of Huff's scans suggesting that the *Fox* could have annihilated this station at their leisure, were they of a mind, so she hadn't expected any trouble. Hadn't been any.

Helped, having a pair of armed Emro babes on her flanks, plus a Mazhin and Ononguli. All female. The men coming up behind that had just been the hammer that drove the nail home.

Khet bureaucrat in charge would have rolled onto his back, but they only did that when they needed to start floating. He wasn't dead yet.

"Your orders, Mistress?" he stammered weakly as he processed the vast number of weapons pointed at him.

"You've surrendered honorably," Dan replied. "We're going to make sure your guns are not loaded, then all the captains and conductors around here who want to talk can meet. Lead me to your command space."

Not exactly polite, except by tone, but Dan didn't really care.

"What's your permanent population?" she asked as the man staggered into motion, two Khet aides looking like they were ready to catch him if he fell over suddenly. "And how much of that is staff?"

"About one thousand, Mistress," one of the aides replied. The sharper looking of the two, though that wasn't saying much. "Staff and crew amount to about one hundred. Maybe a little less, depending."

"Anybody going to give my women trouble?" she asked.

Dan liked the way they had to crane their heads back to look up at the two Emro women, both well over two meters tall. And broad in the shoulders like that species was. Strong. Big.

Intimidating.

"No, Mistress," the boss managed.

Dan nodded and followed.

"One team holds the bay," Nasrin yelled back. "Second team ready for engineering, with third for life support if it is somewhere else."

Eventually, Anari would give those orders as second nature, but she was still getting used to being Sabre School, when they'd made her give up those dreams and follow the Moss for engineering.

Dipshit *Auga* were sexist pigs, but that was fairly common in this galaxy.

Dan couldn't fix everybody, but she was going to correct all the ones she met.

Boots followed her through the first airlock. Lots of boots. Heavy tread.

Idly, Dan wondered if the men were intentionally stomping on the deck to make the hull ring. Hell of an announcement that trouble was coming.

She approved.

Command Deck, when they got there, wasn't much larger than the *Fox*'s bridge. Nice three-sixty view, like a conning tower, from diamond sheets curved to the space. The *Corsac Fox* was just visible as the closest, with two others nearby and the rest backed off.

Most of them had decided that maybe they could stick around and learn what Uly had to say, rather than merely run for their lives and hope they escaped.

You'd have to run a long ways to escape Uly, if you did that.

"You sit," she ordered the boss. Then she pointed at the dumber of the aides. "Lead this woman to the gun deck."

"This way," he said, nodding to Anari.

Dan wanted Anari getting the most comfortable being intimidating. The other two were tough, but artists first. Sabre School meant to be a warrior. A scholar and artist of violence.

She took a team and went. Nasrin had moved off to one side and was casually pointing a Painsphere at the room.

That had the crew's undivided attention.

"Engineering?" Dan asked the sharper aide.

"One deck below us, and then three decks of equipment," he said carefully.

"Yanouk, that one is yours," Dan said.

Again, Anari was the trained engineer, but there was a method to Dan's madness.

And Nasrin had her omnibow.

A second team departed with the other Emro woman.

"Is there going to be any trouble?" Dan asked, hand negligently resting on the butt of her pistol.

"No, Mistress," the boss Khet said. "None whatsoever."

"Good," Dan smiled at him. "Let's keep it that way."

EIGHT

Dan had turned things over to a couple of her male leads, with instructions to shoot first then call for help. And she'd said that in front of the various Khet minding the Command Deck, watching them pale and their gill slits flap rapidly with nervousness.

Dan didn't figure they'd cause any troubles.

She was back down on the flight deck as the first shuttle arrived.

Ironhorn's boat. Professional pilot bringing it in, then rotating in place to point the bow out as the airlocks lined up. Only needed to extend her airlock walls about two meters to get a seal.

Dan was willing to be impressed. Even for Ononguli sailors, that was pretty sharp work. And it gave her a better understanding of the conductor aboard, one Illya Tkachuk.

She was on the other side of a clear portal watching, with her women around her. Tkachuk emerged from the airlock when it cycled, staggering a step when he saw his welcoming committee.

Younger-looking Ononguli, now that she'd spent enough time around them to have a feel for the species. Taller horns than most, but not by much. Darker red skin. Brighter eyes, maybe.

He carried himself with a wary confidence, like a smaller dog intruding on somebody else's yard, but not willing to back down from the challenge.

"What...?" he started to say.

"Human," Dan replied. That was always the first question. "Commander Dan Chastain. First Officer of *Corsac Fox*, and your host today."

Sharp boy. He processed that quickly and nodded.

"Host?" he asked carefully.

"I've taken control of the station," Dan said simply. "Everyone is under safe conduct to come hear what the Corsac Fox has to say."

"That's really him?" Tkachuk asked. "All the way out here?"

"That's right," she said. "This way."

She turned and drew the Ononguli man with her. Time to get everyone settled, then Uly would lay down a new law.

Dan was smiling in anticipation.

NINE

Nasrin had taken point for the second shuttle to arrive. A Mazhin vessel, off a Mazhin ship.

It had been years since she'd seen any cousins save the ones she lived with today.

She wasn't sure how she felt about it, but Dan had asked her to take charge of the strangers. Put them at ease, because Haydar had tricked them into really wanting to know how a Human came to *Speak* for a Convocation.

They'd figure that out soon enough.

Such thoughts put a smile on her tentacles as Speaker Abbasi from *Ahmadi* stepped through the airlock, scents and communications layered deep in ways that nobody but her and those two Mazhin could follow.

Well, she suspected that Uly, for all he had little true sense of smell, could follow. He was like that.

"Nasrin Monfared," she introduced herself with words, while conveying much of the history of the last several years to the newcomers.

"Wild Rose," Abbasi bowed, speaking the true meaning of her name in Spacer. "You tell a most interesting tale."

From the way his eyes flickered to the others, Abbasi was expecting the others to be confused that he knew so much, so quickly.

"The galaxy is even larger and stranger than one might expect," Yanouk spoke up, defying the man's expectations. "But you will come to believe, as well."

Nasrin nodded. They all believed, her included.

All the while, subtle scents and wild tales floated back and forth. Nasrin simply turned and nodded Abbasi and his aide to follow her in silence. Utter silence, which caused the two Mazhin to grow nervous.

They didn't expect outsiders to understand her kind. Who did?

The Corsac Fox. And that spoke volumes.

TEN

Uly stepped off the shuttle and into the airlock with Rabiu, Ethir, and Piruz. Haydar had flat refused to come, saying that the other two could convey what was needed.

Dan smiled at him, standing alone, so presumably all the others were off guarding the outsiders. Guarding might be too strong a word, but adequate.

Nobody in his right mind challenged a Sabre School Emro, and they would assume he had two such women handy, though Yanouk was Moss learning violence, in the manner that Sabre often learned dance.

A useful skill in your toolbox.

Uly smiled at Dan.

"All good?"

"Pregnant with anticipation," she chuckled. "I almost asked if Suka Kuri wanted to act as tea master today, but thought that such a thing might be utterly rude."

"Worse, she might enjoy it," Uly laughed. "You need to consider adding that team to your boarding parties, if we're going to keep doing this."

"What's the next step beyond gobsmacked?" Ethir asked in his birdlike voice, standing next to them.

Thogin might be physically small and slight, but the man was smart. And sneaky. Arrested too many times for petty crimes, because the authorities could never pin anything heavier on him and his three cousins.

"Beyond?" Dan asked.

Ethir laughed loudly.

"Ain't nobody ever seen nothing like Uly," he reminded them. "Gobsmacked won't cover it soon."

Uly laughed with him. The Corsac Fox was a role he played, but he had to remind all of them that they were part of that legend. That he couldn't do any of this without such a team.

"Wait until he gets introduced as Factor Fortier," Rabiu inserted devilishly. "Or better, Governor Fortier. That's when things get crazy."

Uly rolled his eyes at the trio.

"Let's do this thing," he said before they could really get going.

Dan nodded and pivoted in place. He fell in on her flank, rather than following her.

He was here because she had believed in him. The others had all come later.

Uly needed Dan in ways nobody else understood. And appreciated her beyond that.

She took him through a few short corridors to a hatch guarded by her men, who nodded crisply as the group approached, opening the door without words.

These Khet had been troopers who had gone to Lacium with him, then hired on in a more permanent manner later, having been vetted by his experts.

Uly nodded back and entered into an auditorium that would have held eighty easily, so the twenty-some seated rattled around a bit.

There was a lectern down front, with rows of seats going up. It reminded him of Third Year Orbital Mathematics, which was one of those classes that washed out a quarter of the folks that had survived that long, turning them into enlisted crew with good training, instead of officers leading.

Dan moved off to one side. Uly noted that she, Yanouk, Anari, Nasrin, and Katya were standing behind him, facing out, while all the male troopers were watching from sides and rear.

Heavy, but a solid communication even the most foolish captain could grasp.

And Speaker Abbasi's tentacles were going full speed with some conversation that included both the Mazhin male next to him as well as Nasrin.

She smiled when he made eye contact, so it must be good. Or at least noncontroversial.

"I am the Corsac Fox," he announced when he came to rest in front of these men.

All of them were men. Most pirate operations tended to be eight to one male at best. Sometimes one hundred percent.

Uly kept his growl inside and a neutral smile on his face.

"Previously, piracy was allowed to run rampant through this region, ceasing only when *Auga* vessels came this far out on some unknown mission," Uly continued, watching each of the men in turn. "That is going to change."

"Lacium," Conductor Tkachuk spoke.

"Correct," Uly nodded. "I captured the moorage, changed the governance model of the system, and will not tolerate piracy. Z'Gosza has hired me to clean things up. And they have come to see the value of a little more law and order than they had previously intended."

"The more profit, maybe," a Khet male spoke up from the back.

One of several such captains, mostly focused more on smuggling than banditry, from the sizes of their hulls.

"Much more profit," Uly agreed. "And they have begun hiring former pirate vessels to assist. Vessels like *Khile Heavy* and *Wereshark* might be names you know. Sometimes, crews had a change of heart and joined as well, but I've simply captured a few and sold the hulls on."

"What happens to us?" that same Khet asked.

"I don't care about smugglers," Uly announced. "If that's your business model, try not to get caught later, but I won't be sharing your vessel names with the authorities at Z'Gosza. And, one presumes, the folks at Lacium might already know who you are. I'm standing here to answer your questions first, before moving on to private conversations with Conductor Tkachuk and Speaker Abbasi once the rest of you have had your chance. How can I get you to see the light on this topic?"

ELEVEN

Rabiu simply didn't understand *how* Uly did it, but he'd seen the Human do it enough times to understand that he *could* do it.

Most of the captains had accepted things at face value, promised to behave, and departed for their own ships. Two others had pressed pretty hard on Uly in ways that let Rabiu know how many outstanding warrants for arrest they faced if they ever got as far as Z'Gosza. And Uly undoubtedly saw it as well.

Rabiu had warned his bosses—former bosses, but nobody had made anything official yet.

Uly got shit done. Now, rather than after a quarter year of committee squabbling and chops from several departments that had to sign off on every little thing to show you how important they were.

Dan had escorted the others one by one back to the flight deck and metaphorically kissed each of them on the forehead and sent them off, like guppies going to school in the morning.

Rabiu studied the two remaining captains. One Ononguli pirate. One Mazhin merchant. Or explorer. Something.

Didn't help that most of their language involved smell. Khet had very little olfactory sense. Exceptional taste buds, but licking someone for information right now would probably be rude.

Might be necessary, but the Mazhin woman seemed to have everything under control.

And she absolutely had Uly's back.

"You *Speak* for a Convocation of Mazhin?" Abbasi asked now that everyone unimportant had left.

"He *Speaks* for a Convocation of Human, Thogin, Emro, Ononguli, and Khet," Nasrin interrupted. "And Mazhin."

"How is that possible?" Abbasi demanded.

Asked sharply. One didn't demand anything around here, without the risk of getting one's headcrest bopped flat.

Nasrin laughed. It chilled Rabiu, even though he understood.

Uly got shit done.

"He is the Corsac Fox," Dan spoke up now. "The others have each chosen to join the crew when possible, and have remained many times when they might have opted to leave. Uly *Speaks* for all of us."

That poor Mazhin chap was out of his league, but that was a feeling Rabiu had almost a year's head start on understanding. Didn't get much better, but if you had to settle for second place, Uly was the best person to lose to, fins down.

And you were going to lose.

"And you really intend to end piracy?" the Ononguli conductor spoke up finally.

"I have already begun," Uly replied with that Human smile that seemed so little, yet yielded such devastating results. "Lacium has changed. This place will change, or I will come back and *fix* it. Ships that do not leave the region and choose to remain threats are being hunted down and ended as threats."

"Including *Ironhorn*?" Tkachuk pressed.

Rabiu watched Uly shrug. Another devastating motion, yet so simple.

Such complex emotions that Humans could convey non-verbally.

"When I last spoke with Lukyan Chayka, he and Maks Sobol, cousin of the terrible Adrian Sobol who once owned my ship, were headed back to the Ononguli Sphere with a message from me to the Lords of the Endless Plains," Uly said. "Those men demanded that my having a partial Ononguli crew, and a former Ononguli warship, meant that I was beholden to the Sphere. I am not, but that might change, depending on what those Lords decide and convey back to me later. As an Ononguli vessel, I can convey to you my strong suggestion that you move on. Or change occupations after you leave here."

"And we get to leave, just like that?" Tkachuk asked, obviously unbelieving.

"That is correct," Uly verbally harpooned the poor sod right behind his blowhole. "What you do tomorrow will be your choice from a position of knowledge, when previously you operated from ignorance. How you choose to use such knowledge is up to you."

"You could have blown us out of the water," Tkachuk pointed out.

"What would that have taught you?" Uly asked, adding a second harpoon.

Maybe a third. It was hard to keep score. Rabiu considered counting on his fingers, but didn't want to draw attention to himself.

"Sir?" Conductor Tkachuk asked.

"I could have destroyed you," Uly agreed. "You would have learned nothing. Now, you can make better choices. Perhaps return to the Ononguli Sphere and help keep the *Auga* at bay. Eventually, I will take my war to them."

"You're a single Interceptor, Corsac Fox," the conductor said. "What could you do to the Empire?"

"I was Adrian Sobol's prisoner aboard *Iron Wasp*," Uly said simply. "I escaped from the *Auga* and stole his ship. Now, I'm here."

Rabiu really wasn't sure how many harpoons that was.

Still, stunned silence. Better, everybody—and not just Rabiu—had to slam their mouths shut when they'd fallen open.

Not Dan and her women, though. Or Ethir. They'd all seen it coming.

Rabiu understood better how Uly could negotiate with Trade Factors on an even footing.

Ononguli conductors from the middle of nowhere didn't stand a chance.

Rabiu had an idea so ludicrous that he snortled under his breath before he could contain it.

Broke the spell. EVERY EYE turned his way, except the killers around the outside of the room.

Uly looked at him expectantly.

Rabiu stood up.

"Perhaps Z'Gosza should open formal trade and diplomatic channels with the Ononguli Sphere, Uly?" he asked. "Should the Factors see about possibly hiring *Ironhorn* to transport an ambassador and a proposed trade treaty?"

Good, everybody else got to close their own mouths for once.

Rabiu pasted his most careful and non-threatening smile on his mouth and waited.

That next step beyond gobsmacked? This was probably it.

Ethir was certainly grinning. Piruz, too.

Then Uly smiled.

Oh, crap.

LORDS OF THE ENDLESS PLAINS

TWELVE

Lukyan Chayka had followed Maks Sobol and *Scavenger Angel* all the way home, both of them dropping out of warp on a regular schedule, with *Compass Rose* trailing the *Angel*'s Variable Pulse Spatial Generator pulse-wake while making sure nobody snuck on the both of them.

Compass Rose was at the top end for an Ultra-Bomber. Two decks, but a pig with a large flight deck aft carrying a single, big, cargo shuttle. Used to work in tandem with the Khet Armed Probe *Legend of Ymnan*, and the Ugothan Seeker *Spirit of Iniquity*, because they had sensors and cargo capacity respectively to go with his firepower.

Scavenger Angel was a Seeker or maybe Rescue Cutter that had been stolen or bought from a wrecker and refurbished. Not a lot of crew. Lots of storage space, currently filled up with most of the belongings of *Iron Wasp*'s former crew, forwarded on by Uly.

Now Lukyan and Maks were almost home. For what it was worth.

Worse, it was a Tuesday.

It had all started on a Tuesday, and Lukyan had made it a careful practice not to taunt the gods of karma about ever being bored on a Tuesday again.

Compass Rose was in the van today, leading Maks as they cruised to a point where notes expected an Ononguli force to be parked, looking for incursions from the *Auga* probing for a soft flank, or anybody trying to sneak by. Lukyan didn't know when someone would pick them up, but he also wasn't the least bit surprised when the warp bubble popped around them, dropping *Compass Rose* into real space.

"Halt and be identified," all the speakers roared, which was just someone being a punk, since they obviously knew he was an Ononguli ship, to have sent that message on the private network.

Then Lukyan got a good look at the ship harassing him, and wasn't surprised.

Wardog Charlie had a reputation as wide as the Sphere itself. Bulldog of a ship, with single 6dm turrets fore and aft, and a willingness to go for the throat at the slightest provocation.

Fortunately, *Scavenger Angel* had been trailing close, because they dropped out right then, plus a second ship.

Big bastard, too.

Tanis Dragon.

Tanis Dragon?

What the hell had Lukyan done to warrant this kind of attention?

Or were the *Auga* getting pissy again?

Lovely, just the right time to come home, on top of everything else, including having to deal with his brother Bohdan.

What, exactly, was the mathematical square of a Tuesday?

"Guardships, this is Lukyan Chayka, aboard *Compass Rose*, acting in argosy with *Scavenger Angel*, commanded by Maks Sobol," he announced, keeping the growl out of his voice, as much as it wanted to creep in. "I carry diplomatic materials for the Lords of the Endless Plains."

There, let them chew on that.

"Lukyan, I'm getting a private signal from *Tanis Dragon*," Oskar spoke up from his Gunner spot. "DJ Gross is still Conductor."

Because of course he would be. You'd need someone like that to keep *Wardog Charlie* and Conductor Avhust Holub on a short leash, wouldn't you?

Lukyan considered his Tuesday, then rose.
"I'll take it in my office," he said.

41

THIRTEEN

Lukyan settled behind his desk with some fresh tea and took a deep breath before he opened the line. DJ Gross was a big name in the Sphere. And the fleet.

Hardass conductor, but an honest one. Lukyan wasn't sure he could say the same about Avhust Holub. Probably why the guy commanded *Wardog Charlie*.

"Diplomatic messages?" he said without preamble, but that fit his rep.

Lukyan had never worked with the fellow. Or for him. Only heard the stories.

"Indeed," Lukyan replied. "There's some stuff happening over on the far edge of Imperial Sector Fifteen. The Lords of the Endless Plains need to know about it."

"Can't be more important that the *Auga*," Gross replied disdainfully.

"They getting feisty again?" Lukyan asked, feeling a good, solid Tuesday sneaking up on him somewhere.

"Something riled them up," Gross nodded. "Maks's cousin seems to be involved, but I'm too far removed from the center of things to know more than that. Warn the kid, because some of it might roll downhill on him."

"Hell, if that's the case, it's probably going to land on my horns first," Lukyan replied.

"You weren't involved with Sobol, were you?" Conductor Gross asked, eyes narrowing.

"Tangentially," Lukyan said, letting the grimace show.

He was home, dealing with his own kind. They could see. Shit would be public soon enough.

"Tangentially?" Gross pressed.

"The messages I'm carrying to the Lords of the Endless Plains are from the guy who stole Adrian's ship and commands it these days."

"No shit?" Gross asked, impressed.

"No shit," Lukyan nodded. "Worse, he's got a heavily mixed crew, including a chunk of Adrian's folks, none of whom wanted to come home with me given the chance. And *Scavenger Angel* is hauling all of the old crew's personal effects."

"The Horde going to have to send a warfleet over there to hunt the punk down?" Gross growled.

"Honestly?" Lukyan asked, waiting for the man to nod before speaking. "I think me or somebody else might be hauling an ambassador back over there to do a deal with the guy. New species nobody here has ever heard of, from somewhere on the back side of Sector Seventeen, if I understand it. Violent and dangerous folks."

"The Horde doesn't need outsiders," Gross snapped.

"That's where you might be wrong, Conductor," Lukyan said honestly. "His name is Uly Fortier, and his mission is to stop the *Auga*."

"**Stop** the *Auga*?" Gross replied, disbelieving.

"Yeah," Lukyan nodded. "Worse? He might be able to."

FOURTEEN

Maks rather enjoyed being a conductor, even if *Scavenger Angel* wasn't exactly his vision of a warship. And since Uly had sold the ship to him for *one Imperial Guilder and certain other considerations*, he could turn around and sell it or trade up to something else, once he off-loaded the cargo.

Maks was pretty sure the families would all chip in for a haulage fee for him bringing home this stuff, even if most of it was crap.

Personal crap, which mean priceless in some ways.

And he got all the good karma for hauling it. That was fortunate, because Lukyan had explained how ugly some of the conversations were likely to get when folks around here didn't understand Uly. Thought they could issue that man orders and make them stick.

Or worse, went over there and tried to *make* Uly do something.

Maks was almost looking forward to watching Dan and her ladies break someone's horns off at the forehead when they got pissy at the Humans.

Maybe they'd hire him to haul someone? Or lead a force they thought was sufficient to corral Uly?

Bring a lot of ships if you decide to get stupid.

If folks back home were nice to him, Maks might even suggest a number, but he didn't figure anyone would listen.

Not the first time, anyway.

He was on his bridge, reveling in the feel of a command chair under his butt.

His command chair.

Stepan was monitoring sensors and gun turrets today, while Oleksandr flew.

Or would fly, as soon as Lukyan was done with the goons lurking over them today. Lot of firepower for this frontier. Shit must have gotten out of hand again.

Happened regularly enough.

Stepan caught Maks's eye.

"Ping from *Compass Rose*," he said simply.

Maks considered it.

"I'll take it in my office."

Maks moved to his office.

His. Not Lukyan's that Maks was keeping warm while the boss ate or slept.

Maks's.

Still kinda awesome.

Then Lukyan appeared on the screen and Maks felt his stomach clench.

"Good news, you're gonna be a hero," Lukyan said simply.

"Bad news?" Maks replied.

"They traded most of your cousin's crew home, but kept the top ten or so," Lukyan nodded. "Pretty sure you can name them without a lot of effort. Keeping those folks. And demanding the Sphere do something about Uly."

"WHAT?!?" Maks demanded.

Lukyan chuckled.

"*Auga* got it into their third eye that he's some sort of Ononguli agent," Lukyan said. "Want the Horde to do something about that. What, I got no clue, but I expect a load of horse shit is about to be dumped on my back. I'm a big boy. You might be the one going to bring Uly home."

"Home?" Maks said. "Aren't you all getting ahead of yourselves? Nobody tells Uly what to do. Not if they don't want their horns sawed off."

"Yeah, I'm going to be between a cliff and a grass fire here," Lukyan agreed with a melancholy nod. "You play nice with everybody. Maybe go see the family and convince Clan Sobol to not get up on their high horse about things until the Lords of the Endless Plains have a chance to sort things out. I'd rather have Uly as an ally than an enemy. Plus, I have my own personal issues to deal with, now that I'm home."

"That why you stayed way over there for so long?" Maks asked.

He'd gotten tidbits and hints, but never the whole story.

"My brother can be an ass," Lukyan said. "Eldest Prince of the Clan thing went to his head, and all that shit. Plus—and this will come out when you hear people start talking—Nadiya fell in love with me, even though she was promised to my brother Bohdan. Political marriage sort of thing. Treaties between clans, and all that crap. Dunno if they have kids. Haven't kept up on the news from home, because a Conductor on his own deck is nigh a god, and Bohdan didn't have the authority to do anything but taunt me."

"But that changes, now that you're home?" Maks asked.

"Lots of things will change," Lukyan said. "If they order you to become my enemy, do what they say. Am I clear?"

"Lukyan, I would never—"

"You'll do what the Lords of the Endless Plains order, Maks," Lukyan overrode him with steel in his voice. "Period. You take care of yourself and your crew. I tried to give you folks who wouldn't necessarily be sucked into this mess, because I knew what was likely coming. Worse comes to worst, I'll haul ass and dump it in their laps."

"Where would you go?" Maks asked. "Back to Fifteen?"

"Anywhere that Bohdan can't find me," Lukyan growled. "Maybe Fifteen. Maybe Twenty-Two. Hell, I might load up and go see what things are like in Seventeen. Imagine bringing home a whole crew of Humans for Uly to add to his roster."

Maks shuddered. He understood that Uly was a special case, even among Humans, but he had also seen the level of casual violence among folks like Emil Beranger and Gennady Travers.

A whole crew of Humans?

Ick.

"Yeah," Lukyan said, obviously reading Maks's horns. "They might piss me off that badly, Maks. But you should be safe. Do NOT hesitate to blame me for everything and throw me under their hooves to save your own ass. I'll be fine at my end."

Maks paused and took a calming breath. He was a Sobol. That name meant things around here.

How bad was it going to get?

"What's the next step?" Maks asked.

"Krilic," Lukyan replied. "Closest major world, where we can lay in supplies and do a little maintenance work while we wait."

"Wait for?" Maks asked.

"Gross is going to send *Wardog Charlie* to Rayzian to notify the Lords of the Endless Plains about us. And ask them to send someone out to escort us home."

"Oh, shit."

"You got it, Maks," Lukyan nodded. "Stay cool."

Then he cut the line and Maks blew out a big breath.

He'd known that Uly was likely to upset some things around here. Throw in personal politics and shit and things were gonna get ugly.

How ugly?

Maks wasn't necessarily looking forward to finding out.

FIFTEEN

Uly hadn't planned to be at Taeli *Station* this long, but he had to admit that having a little extra time to hang out had already paid rewards, including a pair of smugglers from the far end of some chain stumbling in and surrendering instead of getting blown up.

More folks carrying the good word of Uly's crusade back towards Sector Eighteen. And beyond.

But today, he had Conductor Tkachuk in a conference room, where he, Uly, Dan, Ethir, and Rabiu were arguing technical arcana.

The Mazhin had all pretty much shrugged and gone about their business, though *Ahmadi* was still in system as well.

Life outside the station was almost back to normal.

"They'd arrest me the moment I arrive," Illya Tkachuk growled at Rabiu. Again. "How many times do I have to remind you that there are warrants out for me and my ship at Z'Gosza."

Uly nodded. They'd circled the point a number of times, and that seemed to be the one where Tkachuk wouldn't budge.

Then Ethir got that special gleam in his eyes. The one that told you he'd been sandbagging you, just waiting for this opportunity.

"So change flags," Ethir said.

Everything screeched to a halt. Ethir grinned.

"What?" Illya managed, after shaking his head once.

"You arrive at Z'Gosza flying Uly's flag," Ethir smiled. "We represent a new political entity, complete with a small yet growing navy. Uly hires you to haul a message to the Trade Factors, so you are officially working for him. You deliver the message. They turn around and deliver to you a representative, most likely a Senior Director, so we'll need to take some time getting the interior of your ship cleaned and pretty for those silly fish. You haul the aforementioned dork to the Ononguli Sphere under the protection of the Corsac Fox, establishing a long chain connecting those two nations. Uly, what did you call it? I've forgotten the term."

"A Silk Road," Uly said. "Exotic goods traveling from one end to the other, usually as a result of merchants hauling one or two links and selling things on, then going back for more. Occasionally, folks traveling the entire route, to see what was there."

"There you go," Ethir laughed. "Fish boys talking to goat boys."

Uly considered it. The scale. And the outcomes. Piracy would be something of a problem, but what if he started issuing travel credentials for ships making that run? Promises to protect them, while hammering pirates into the mud when he caught them?

What was that, but the next step up from what he was doing now?

"*Ironhorn* isn't a warship," Illya pointed out. "Sure, we're armed, but that's good for threatening freighters. Not taking on pirates."

"What about *Ahmadi*?" Dan suddenly asked, whipsawing Uly's head around.

"Uhm?" Uly said, or something equally eloquent.

Dan's smile lifted all the weight off his shoulders.

"The Mazhin ship is a little better armed than *Ironhorn*," Dan pointed out. "What if those two ships traveled in argosy together both directions?"

"Would Abbasi go for it?" Uly asked.

"The Mazhin are traveling merchants, more or less," Dan leaned in. "They go from point to point seeing the sights. Don't know why they wouldn't, if you managed to sucker them into accepting a commission. I got the impression that they weren't on a regular rotation of worlds. Might even enjoy traveling to Ononguli Space. That also lets them spread the word to their own folk."

Uly leaned back and considered it. He knew that his Mazhin folks were having a pleasant holiday meeting with distant cousins, as Haydar had explained it.

At the same time, both he and Nasrin had emphasized the *distant* part. The *not wanting to pack up and join an all-Mazhin crew* part, in spite of how much closer to home that might get them.

Except that Mazhin didn't do planets. They built ships and traveled. Saw the worlds. Did things.

Didn't stay on a surface for long. Some of his folks, if he understood the references, could count on their tentacles the number of days they'd lived on a planetary surface.

"We can ask," Uly said, turning to Illya. "And you can say no, Conductor. It was an idea that lets you slip away from your current activities without harming the interests of the folks who used to employ you. And it gets you back to your space, assuming you're interested. I can ask Speaker Abbasi. Should I?"

He watched the Ononguli conductor cycle through a variety of thoughts, a symphony of body language that Uly had actually gotten extremely good at translating across species lines, though he understood that most people couldn't.

"If he'll go for it, then I'm in," Illya finally said. "Got no better offers right now, and this actually sounds kinda fun. Crazy, but fun."

Uly nodded.

From the outside, it probably looked to folks like he was following some grand scheme, with dozens or hundreds of parts being carefully moved by a chess master.

In reality, he had a general plan and good people. Plus the willingness to adapt when a smart idea cropped up from unlikely circumstances.

Beyond gobsmacked, as the vocabulary had expanded to include more recently.

Now, he just had to make it work.

Uly turned to Dan.

"Let's go find Abbasi and see."

<h1 style="text-align:center">SIXTEEN</h1>

Haydar didn't usually consider himself old and jaded, but he supposed that he'd seen and done far more than these *children* had ever imagined. Even if Jamsheed Abbasi was physically older by at least a decade.

It was the light-centuries, not the years.

Innocence. That was what these folks conveyed, time and again. Nasrin had even noted it at one point, while away from the outsiders and talking in-clan. They'd gone out and traded. Sight-seeing and surveying. Done easy things.

None of them had ever been slaves. Or really delved that deep into the piracy side of things, so they might have been in trouble, had they come through this region two years ago.

Before Uly started cleaning it up.

Haydar supposed that it was a mark of good things that these innocents might not have to ever learn about the darker side of the galaxy.

Still, Abbasi was a pleasant-enough fellow. And they had a variety of Mazhin spices and—better by far—plants in pots that they were in the process of trading for other things.

Vahid was already planning new dishes. Or that legendary *Taste of*

My Childhood meal that they couldn't really make with ingredients from Khet worlds.

Even the Human things were starting to run out. Haydar had considered raiding a Human settlement somewhere, just to steal their chickens. That, and find cocoa trees for Dan.

"Ramezani, I still do not understand," Abbasi said, finishing one story and drinking some Khet tea. "Why do you not wish to join us? Why continue to travel with aliens?"

Haydar considered the man's words. He meant well.

It was the light-centuries, not the years.

"Your gumbo is brown," he finally said, drawing on one of Vahid's most cutting insults, though he knew it would fly right over Abbasi's tentacles.

Most of the room fell to silence. His folks snorted and grinned. The outsiders were lost.

Vahid spoke up from the far end of the table.

Spoke up. That was the measure of distance between the two sides, when Haydar used Human terms to convey the scents, the semaphore, and yes, the actual words.

"Gumbo is a Human dish," Vahid said, giving them a sense of the warm redness. The spices melanging gracefully. The textures on the tongue as you ate. "Many interesting things put into a pot in a particular order, then left to boil down slowly as things come together."

"And brown?" Abbasi asked.

That one was confused, but Haydar watched understanding begin to dawn on a few faces.

"Gumbo with few ingredients," Vahid said. "Beef stew, without anything but salt and pepper. Nutritious. Filling. Lacking excitement."

"You say we are boring?" a younger Mazhin spoke up from a corner. A touch indignant, too.

Gholam, if Haydar remembered. There had been many folks over such meetings. This one was for more important folks, so this Gholam must be impressive to the crew of *Ahmadi.*

"I suggest that we have had much more excitement, relative to you," Haydar replied diplomatically. "My clan has seen and done much that other ships hardly ever encounter. If anything, I might expect some of your youngsters to wish to travel with us for a time. We are not a proper family, let alone a clan, but we have many friends who are not Mazhin."

"Eight males and two females is hardly even a family," Abbasi interjected. "We have five hundred crew on *Ahmadi*."

"Precisely my point," Haydar acknowledged. "Perhaps twenty or fifty might choose to travel with the Corsac Fox for a time?"

"Or join him as family?" Gholam asked, even as several others whispered, murmured, or even tittered.

"You would join a family of all species," Nasrin interrupted, before Haydar could convey anything. "Uly *Speaks* for all of us as a Grand Convocation."

"What will the Elders say?" Abbasi asked, horrified from the way he held his tentacles.

But Jamsheed Abbasi was a safe Speaker. On a safe ship. And his gumbo was a beef stew as those punks in *Danumash* might have made it. Boil everything to death, then consume sourly.

No joy in gustatory escapades.

"The Hall of Souls is filled with a bunch of fussy old women," Roshan Anyari spoke up. "They will never understand Uly. But they might be smart enough to let him lead the Convocation for a time."

Roshan was Haydar's general competition for genius inventor with Uly's crew, because he hardly ever spoke, and hardly ever left his lab.

Introspective, in a species known for introspection.

Haydar watched the newcomers gabble and argue as they examined that concept. Noisily.

The Convocation was a matriarchal, clan-based republic, if you pressed him into a corner and made him define it. The Hall of Souls. The Hall of Voices. The Speaker For The Convocation itself, usually female, but occasionally males had ascended to the role. Though generally speaking on behalf of a female clan leader.

Yes, Haydar could see Uly in that role.

"Why does the Wild Rose not lead your own clan?" Abbasi asked, trying to deflect things before he lost control of his own ship and clan.

Nasrin's laugh cut them all to the quick. Haydar simply leaned back and watched, savoring what he knew was coming.

"We elected this old fart first," she said, nodding to Haydar, who nodded back. There had been blackmail as well, but the strangers didn't need to know that. "Then Uly came along."

"I do not understand how a Human could possibly *Speak* for Mazhin," Abbasi said.

Nasrin's smile was cruelty made flesh.

"Then perhaps you can ask him yourself," she replied. "He and Dan Sheridan will be here momentarily."

Haydar chuckled to himself as the room dissolved into utter chaos.

Then a chime at the hatch announced a visitor.

SEVENTEEN

Nasrin kept her eyes locked on Jamsheed Abbasi, but signaled to the older woman closest to the main hatch. This gathering filled a dining hall on the station. Forty strangers. All ten of Uly's crew, with even Omid being dragged here, in spite of her complaints about how the Ononguli she left behind would do the laundry all wrong without her supervising.

Laundry, like cooking, was one of the highest arts to a species with as many senses as a Mazhin. Humans were practically blind across almost all spectra.

Except maybe Uly.

The woman by the hatch rose and opened it. Uly and Dan, as she had picked up from the life support blowers. No others with them, so nothing critical, as both were quite relaxed.

Uly almost tasted triumphant in ways Nasrin found hard to describe.

Something good must have happened. Or be poised on balance, perhaps.

"My apologies for intruding," Uly announced, entering and coming to rest at a polite distance, where everyone was staring at him. "A subject came up that required consultation. Considering the general balance of participants, I thought that perhaps we could discuss a few things now, when I had been prepared to schedule something when I could assemble something similar to this group. May I?"

Nasrin rose and gestured him and Dan close. Technically, she was host today, as the Mazhin expected a female hand guiding things, in spite of Haydar and Uly.

And most of these sheltered fools would have probably expected Dan to be in charge.

Sheridan Chastain would make an inspiring Speaker.

Still not as good as Uly.

Nasrin moved to Uly's other side, bracketing him with Dan in a way that the Mazhin in the room would understand. Already, a few sets of tentacles began to recoil in uncertainty as they saw.

Nasrin smiled.

"Speaker Abbasi," Uly began with a nod. "I have, as you know, been consulting with Conductor Tkachuk about hiring his vessel to carry diplomats from Z'Gosza to the Ononguli Sphere, that they might establish formal trade and communications networks, even across this vast a distance."

Nasrin watched Uly pause, gauging the room with only eyes, yet seemingly tracking everyone's scent almost as well as she was.

Jamsheed nodded warily, like he could smell the trap coming.

It wouldn't be that bad.

She kept her smile in place and her tentacles calm and inviting.

"While Conductor Tkachuk expresses interest, he also has reservations, largely based on the combat capabilities of *Ironhorn*," Uly said. "It was suggested that perhaps I might be able to hire *Ahmadi* as well, were you interested, to accompany *Ironhorn* to Z'Gosza with a message, then to the Ononguli regions with cargo you know will be welcome and valuable on arrival, based on expertise here. Two armed ships should be in better shape to stand off any pirates you encounter, as I will send along indications that you are under my protection, should anyone bother you."

"Your protection, Conductor Fortier?" Abbasi asked, confused.

Nasrin managed to keep her face and tentacles calm. Haydar looked like he'd licked a battery, but he was behind Abbasi.

"My promise that anyone threatening your ships will be hunted down and destroyed," Uly said calmly. "And their command officers executed. If they cannot behave, they will be ended."

The polite, almost genial way he spoke masked the depth of what Uly was really offering, so Nasrin tried to create that as a scent she could push out to the others.

Quickly, the room flinched. That was the only term she could think of, as she never seen an entire room filled with Mazhin all spook so hard, all at once.

But Uly was serious. The Corsac Fox would hunt you to the ends of the galaxy and beyond. Maybe even a Human hell wouldn't be enough to protect you from Uly's rage.

The Mazhin around here didn't understand Humans. Nasrin tried to explain it to them as Uly politely waited, understanding that there were a variety of conversations happening around him in complete silence.

He even smiled back at her.

Nasrin couldn't help but blush, because Uly's look told her that he knew.

Even blind across so many senses, *Uly knew*.

Abbasi recovered about as fast as all the strangers. None of her people reacted, but they had spent all enough time around Uly to understand. They waited patiently for the others to catch up.

"What will the Ononguli say when we arrive?" the Speaker finally asked.

"They will likely welcome you more than most merchants," Nasrin interjected quickly.

You. Not us. I wouldn't travel with you people.

Your gumbo is brown.

"Why?" Abbasi pressed on.

"Mazhin don't like planets," Uly smiled. "You are not looking for a chance to settle down and perhaps colonize some world in their Sphere. Mazhin merchants bringing rare goods from distant lands, as well as stories and diplomats, might be their dream meeting."

Nasrin nodded. He was correct, based on what she'd learned, both from the ship's Ononguli crew as well as the folks on *Compass Rose* and *Scavenger Angel* that had preceded.

Most welcome.

And that message would get out to other Mazhin ships, given enough time.

Uly, creating new trade networks on the far side of Ononguli space that might never benefit him at all.

Save that it strengthened all those species and worlds opposed to the *Auga*, and their dread goal of slowly conquering and *organizing* the entire galaxy.

Nasrin loathed the thought of *Auga* bureaucracy destroying all art save that which those eventual overlords considered acceptable.

"I will have to see a proposal," Abbasi offered weakly.

Uly nodded. Bowed even.

"I will put something together for your review," he said. "Until then."

And he and Dan left, leaving all the Mazhin a bit stunned. And concerned. Maybe uncertain.

Nasrin wasn't fooled. Abbasi was already sold, just based on a quick poll of his senior crew and clan elders present that Nasrin could smell.

They'd be down to haggling the price.

Nasrin couldn't wait for Ethir and Piruz to get involved.

EIGHTEEN

Suka Kuri, Exemplar of the Arts, studied her two students as they danced.

She was Moss School, but Exemplars were beyond such *mere technicalities*. They expressed all things Emro. Learned things from all sectors of the universe, conveying them back to the others to learn.

Moss and Sabre Schools were simply ways of thinking for youngsters to adapt to, not rigid practicalities concerned about perfectly reproducing patterns millennia old. Life changed. Cultures changed.

Students must adapt. They must first learn how to learn, that it can then become a lifetime spent in pursuit of knowledge, with the hope that wisdom stumbled into your path occasionally as well.

Which was why most hardly even rose as far as Adept, falling short somewhere. Perhaps finding a spot they called *Good Enough*. Or surrendering into the inevitable failures one encountered along the way. Life happened.

Something.

Suka knew a Sabre School elder, an Exemplar like herself, who rose each morning from his bed and studied the face in the mirror, promising that nobody would outwork him today.

As he had for many decades.

She could see his echo in both Yanouk and Anari before her.

It brought her joy.

Most teachers never had a student capable of transcending Adept. Suka Kuri had two.

Technically three, but she did not include Dan Sheridan in that count. Not today. Dan wasn't ready to admit some things to herself, let alone the rest of the galaxy.

And Uly...

Suka Kuri wasn't sure any language she spoke had the vocabulary to describe Uly's potential, if he lived long enough.

Or what kind of school it might be that he represented. Or created from whole cloth.

Dan was Sabre School. An excellent teacher for both Yanouk and Anari, having expanded both women's minds to include Human combat forms unlike anything Sabre had ever encountered.

But then, even Sabre did not generally rise to the level of intentional violence that these Humans lived at every day.

Uly was Uly.

On the floor, while Suka watched, both women completed the longest form they knew. Dance and combat were obverse sides of a single coin. There were only so many ways to move an upright biped.

It all became choreography at some point.

Every punch was a grapple. Every grapple was a throw. Every throw was a punch.

Both women came to rest in perfect harmony. Perfect synchronicity.

Suka noted that both were perspiring, but the form was long and involved, facing each side of a hex equally, both offensively and defensively.

Strike, kick, block, tangle, throw. Repeat and rearrange.

"Come," she commanded the two, gesturing to the floor before her.

Suka had long since given up trying to kneel on hard decks, and had gotten the Ononguli engineers to build her a comfortable metal chair the right height and sturdy enough for her mass.

Yanouk and Anari knelt before her on the right and left.

She chose Anari first, having picked out a bright-eyed youngster several years ago, before even Yanouk had understood how special she was.

And those fool *Auga* had been utterly convinced that Anari Supasei was too intelligent to be Sabre School, so they had forced her into Moss, and then made her be an engineer.

Fools.

That was like painting watercolors with a squirt gun. It could be done. It would not be art, most of the time.

"What is the purpose of Sabre?" Suka asked Anari simply.

"To learn the arts of movement," Anari replied crisply.

One of the first things any Adept taught any Seeker.

"What is the goal of the student?" she continued.

"To learn," Anari nodded.

Suka nodded back.

Not to learn any one thing. Or even all things.

To learn.

The exceptional students learned how to learn things quickly, that they could learn many things. The best learned how to teach those new things to other students they met, that all useful things became conveyed to the entirety of the Schools across the vastness of space.

She turned to Yanouk, once a budding painter in Hiko's mode, though he liked to joke that he had three left feet when it came to dance. His eye for shading and color flow might raise him to Exemplar, one of these days.

That was why she had taken the young man as apprentice. Even today, he painted. And taught others how to see with his eyes, though Suka knew that he would impinge but little on the greater galactic happenings that she had gotten wrapped up into.

His art was observational. That was acceptable. Preferable, even, because that meant that the tiny elements of culture would not be forgotten in the process of shaking and shaping civilizations.

Hiko's paintings would live as long as the paints could be preserved.

Generations would know him personally.

It was good.

But she had Yanouk before her.

Another Moss Student, once. And so much more.

Suka smiled, thinking of how Dan and Nasrin had helped expand Yanouk's mind far beyond anything Suka Kuri would have taught her.

"What is the purpose of Moss?" Suka asked.

"To learn the arts of beauty," Yanouk replied, echoing and harmonizing Anari, because Moss and Sabre were the same thing, expressed in different ways.

There was beauty in movement, and movement in beauty. All were one thing.

"I have watched you dance," Suka pronounced simply, including both in her gaze.

Both women stood a little straighter. That was a formal phrase, not a casual observation. The start of a ritual.

Many Students failed to progress. Life intruded. Interests changed. Dreams were cut short.

Something.

"You move with grace and precision, both of you," Suka continued, drawing them into her weave with her words. "And you have learned something that even most Seekers do not find until much later."

Both wanted to ask. Wanted to speak. Wanted to learn.

Suka smiled at them.

"Moss and Sabre are artificial distinctions," Suka informed them. "Erected to help lesser students focus on a single thing, perhaps to the exclusion of others, as their studies progress. Hiko paints. He sculpts. Even composes music. He will not, however, master dance in any way impressive. He could be technical, but not artistic, and that is in no way an insult. He may be my peer, one of these days."

Both woman nodded, perhaps a bit wide-eyed. Being taken as a personal student of an Exemplar meant such potential was recognized, but even then, not always achieved.

"Both of you have learned much," Suka continued. "And Dan has greatly expanded your repertoire and potential. She, I would rank as a mid-level Adept against any Sabre School I met. And I have known many in my life."

Suka paused, savoring the moment. It happened so infrequently.

And she had two such students before her, both with amazing potential. She could see each driving the other to greater heights, because both were about learning, rather than competing with one another.

"Each of you will arise, and take the rank of Seeker," she pronounced with as much gravity as her old bones would allow.

Both faces fell to shock, in spite of the ritual, but they got to their feet without falling over.

Suka remembered her first promotion, oh so long ago. That recognition that she had firmly put her feet on a long, and impossibly distant goal.

To learn.

She rose as well, allowing the two young women to tower over her, Yanouk tall and slender, Anari tall and broadly muscular in ways that brought to mind the Human Solomon Wyndham, as he grew into his own height and mass, smaller but no less impressive relative to his kind.

He would never be a physical threat to either of these women, but even there, Suka could see the hand of Dan Chastain as his Adept, and him as a Student on the verge of turning into a Seeker.

She rose and stepped forward to hug both women at once, marveling that the fates had led her to meet one of the most interesting people she could have ever imagined in Uly.

And all his many friends, herself included.

NINETEEN

Lukyan had left Dmytro in charge of the *Rose* and crossed over to *Tanis Dragon* on one of Gross's shuttles. He was in the man's office, just the two of them, sipping some tea and grousing in general about the sorts of things that conductors did when they were alone with their own kind.

"I've read your executive summary," Gross said, shifting the conversation. "This Fortier sounds three and a half meters tall."

"He comes across that way," Lukyan nodded. "In person, tall and as skinny as a Mazhin. I think Dan outweighs him, and that species has the same sexual dimorphism we do. At about the same scale. But do not underestimate his mind. And his charisma."

"That's the part I don't get," Gross said. "How did he charm all of Sobol's old crew?"

"I don't think I could explain it easily," Lukyan shrugged. "Same with the Mazhin. And the Thogin. And the Emro. Hell, half the Humans with him were part of an enemy crew he and Dan captured originally. The one hauling all the Mazhin slaves from one world to another. And they are all behind him one hundred percent these days. Even those silly Khet at Z'Gosza have gone all in."

"So what happens when the Lords of the Endless Plains demand that he present himself here and answer for things?" Gross asked.

"I think they'd be better off asking politely," Lukyan shook his head. "Inviting him. Hell, making him one of us, though I'm not sure how."

"He's alien, Chayka," Gross snapped.

"His whole crew are aliens, Gross," Lukyan snapped back. "And yet, they are as tight as any crew I've ever sailed with. Ononguli. Khet. Thogin. Emro. Mazhin. Human. He hasn't, as far as I know, run into any Ugotha or Zuath that he liked enough to recruit, or he would have them as well."

"What about the *Auga*?"

"He honestly intends to drive them back and make them behave, Conductor," Lukyan said, shrugging at the how of it.

"And you seem convinced that he can," Gross pointed out.

"Yup," Lukyan nodded. "Humans are at least as militantly violent as the *Auga* on their craziest days. And not as beholden to the kinds of bureaucracy that have kept the overlords from making any serious inroads on the Sphere. His Khet advisor summed it up for me at one point by saying that *Uly gets shit done*. And I've seen it."

"Some sort of alien warlord?" Gross asked, pivoting again, eyes maybe a little wider.

"Maybe leading a fleet of everybody except the *Auga*," Lukyan nodded. "That's the thing I want the Lords of the Endless Plains to understand. Making him your enemy means he'll come after you when he's done with the *Auga*."

Lukyan liked that shudder that ran through Gross's frame. Senior Conductor. Well-known badass in the fleet. Anchoring this flank from the bridge of *Tanis Dragon*.

And Uly was more dangerous, kilo for kilo. Hell, *Corsac Fox* the ship might be able to take *Tanis Dragon*, maybe even with *Wardog Charlie* helping. And Uly had teenagers on his bridge. They were only going to get better as they got older.

Plus Uly.

"You said you, instead of us," Gross pointed out.

Lukyan had to stop and replay the sentence in his head, then nodded.

"I don't want to be his enemy," Lukyan replied. "I've seen what happens to those folks. I'd like us to recruit him. Maybe give him a bigger ship and find enough crew to make it really dangerous. Then let him go stomp on *Auga* toes for a while."

"They'll never go for it," Gross pronounced.

"That, Conductor, is the fear that keeps me awake at night."

TWENTY

Maks was settled in his command chair, aggressively shaping it to his butt, when a ship dropped out of warp nearby.

Wardog Charlie. Back from Rayzian.

Pretty damned quick, too.

"We're already getting hailed," Stepan announced.

At least Holub hadn't lit the override circuits and blasted everything. Maks could see asking Haydar Ramezani to program in a cut-out, like he'd done on *Corsac Fox*. Or at least let Maks dial down the volume some.

"I'll take it here," Maks said, bringing up the small screen on his right.

Holub looked hungry. Nothing new there. Mean. The kind of guy they would put in charge of *Wardog Charlie* and unleash on the galaxy, since he wasn't politically important enough to have one of the big ships.

Not yet, anyway. If war with the *Auga* was impending, that might change. Clans might be activating some of those ships currently in long-term storage then drafting crews.

Maybe even putting Maks in something more dangerous than *Scavenger Angel*, which honestly was most ships.

"Conductor Holub," Maks nodded respectfully.

"How soon can you depart?" Holub asked without any preamble.

"If we're running straight to someplace like Rayzian, I'm ten minutes from sailing," Maks said, silently thanking Lukyan for giving him a clock to work against. "If anywhere longer, we'd need to lay in some supplies here."

Holub nodded. Maybe those eyes showed a little surprise.

Expecting us to be sitting here with the Variable Pulse Spatial Generator torn apart for repairs when you arrived, weren't you?

Maks smiled politely and waited.

"It will take longer than ten minutes, but prepare," Holub said, then cut the line.

Rude, but the guy didn't have a rep as a polite conductor. Mad dog, most of the time. The sort of fellow you wanted on anti-piracy patrol. Uly would aim him at a place like Lacium, then sit back and pull the resulting pieces together with a broom and dust pan.

Maks turned to Stepan. Got a nod. Opened the shipwide.

"All hands, we are ten-plus minutes out from departure," he said. "Let me know immediately if you have something that will prevent us from leaving, and it better be good."

Lukyan had warned him. Told him how long they had.

And he'd nailed it to the half-day.

Things were moving fast.

Too fast?

What was waiting for them when they got to the capital?

Or who?

TWENTY-ONE

Lukyan had been taking a nap, but had left orders to wake him if anything happened, so the beep brought him to the surface quickly.

"What?" he said as he hit the button.

"*Wardog Charlie* just dropped out of warp," Slava replied.

He'd taken Dmytro's spot when Dmytro replaced Maks as Second-in-Command.

Lukyan rubbed his eyes and then ran a hand back over both horns and his hair, so it didn't look like he'd just woken up.

"Be right there," he said, rising and shrugging everything into place quickly.

Bridge wasn't far away. *Compass Rose* wasn't all that big a ship. Good long-sailor with firepower. Two decks. Thinned down with Maks's crew removed. Folks were stretched a little, but he'd be able to get more folks, now that he was in Ononguli space.

Though Uly had done remarkable things with mixing folks, the Horde would not. At least not without a damned good reason.

"Hail coming in," Slava said as he relinquished the command seat to Lukyan.

"Main screen," Lukyan said, settling.

Avhust Holub. *Wardog Charlie*'s Wardog himself.

"You are ordered to return to Rayzian immediately," Holub announced. "I've spoken with Sobol and he assures me *Scavenger Angel* is ready for flight. Are you?"

"What is our course, Holub?" Lukyan replied.

Physics was physics. If you knew the ship, you could predict its flight speed. Add in turnaround resupply, and however long it took the Lords of the Endless Plains to order Holub into motion again.

They were running a little slow, but he didn't know if that ship needed an overhaul, or the elders had dithered. He'd find out soon enough.

"Course has been transmitted, *Compass Rose*," Holub said. "I will be escorting you."

"Wouldn't have it any other way, *Wardog Charlie*," Lukyan said, catching the nod from Slava. "Departure in six minutes?"

"Six," Holub said, cutting the line.

Lukyan turned to Oskar.

"Talk to Maks or Stepan and confirm everything with them," he ordered. "We'll trail them like we did on the way here, and I presume *Wardog Charlie* will be on our asses the entire way, making sure these two wayward sheep don't stray."

Oskar and Slava both laughed, which was good. At the end of the day, both were merely his employees, if the Lords of the Endless Plains decided to be shits.

Or his brother got involved.

He'd deal with both in their time.

TWENTY-TWO

Uly had decided that momentous changes required new thinking, so he'd had *Ahmadi* and *Ironhorn* accompany him first to Lacium, being closer, then on to Z'Gosza.

System hadn't changed in the last year. Maybe more ships around, as regional yards were churning out more cargo carriers. And the local Governor had bought a few warships from Uly to create a small, local navy.

It was a start.

Not much, but enough to chase down pirates. Or chase them into operating in a different sector.

Uly couldn't save everybody, but if trade got safer around here, there would be more of it, however bizarrely capitalist it was to think that way. Ethir assured him that the Trade Factors would see it that way.

And other systems would get mad about dealing with pirates, so they might take his example and start their own armed space gendarme to do something about it.

Haydar had pointed out that piracy represented a failure of civilization, while smuggling was a failure of social policy. Uly would crush the former, and ignore the latter, except to point out that if folks wanted to smuggle, there had to be a reason.

Solve the need, and solve the problem. Or make their lives better enough that they didn't turn to destructive urges to deal with depression and nihilism.

"We're being hailed by the station," Haydar announced. "The usual queries about ships flying in argosy. I can almost taste the ship dealers salivating at the prospect of a sale."

Uly laughed. Haydar and Ethir understood capitalism. Had even explained it to him more than once.

Uly didn't think it would work, but he wasn't here to save the galaxy.

"Let them know that these are allied ships," he said. "Not for sale."

Uly turned to his Khet ambassador.

"Rabiu, you let Factor Bitrus and Factor Bukra know that we'd like their help with *Ironhorn*," Uly said. "State dinner sort of thing, since they get to treat me like a visiting governor. Ambassadors and contracts. And make sure that one particular lawyer is involved."

"Understood," Rabiu said, turning to his screens and starting to type furiously.

That one attorney had seen where Ethir's contract language was taking everyone, and had caught some interesting snares. Just the fellow to help Uly shape trade relations with the Ononguli Sphere, something that had never been done.

Who bothered across that many light-centuries, after all?

Uly leaned back and looked around his bridge.

His bridge.

Him.

Gobsmacked, maybe, but it was a thing that had to be done, and everyone had agreed that he was necessary to do it. Whatever that meant.

He caught Dan's eye and a rogue thought made him grin. Her eyebrow arched sharply in his direction.

Uly nearly laughed.

"Let's chat in my office," he said, rising.

Haydar, Sterling, and Drew could handle everything. Rabiu was already in motion, with Ethir and Piruz handy if they needed dangerous legalisms heaped on top of some poor sod.

Dan followed him and they faced each other across his desk.

No paperwork today, but Dan was getting better at defeating it. And forcing people below her in the food chain to take more responsibility for their own operations.

"You have a wicked grin," she noted, grinning back.

"Suka Kuri decided that I needed an all-female bodyguard," he began.

She nodded.

"We're at Z'Gosza, and I expect to have a few weeks while the Trade Factors roust themselves from whatever naps they had settled into. I'd like to do a bit more recruiting."

"Anything in particular?" she asked, leaning forward, eyes like a hawk now.

Every morning, he woke up happy that she was on his side.

"Symbolically, you need a Khet," he nodded. "And at least one of everybody else we might encounter. But only folks you trust with weapons. That's your responsibility. I'm going to see about hiring some folks to handle *Wren*. It's currently half-empty, with all that gear turned into ongoing credit that helps, but I don't like having to move my people over there to run it when I need Drew or someone in battle. And I think we maybe need to move it soon."

"To?" she asked.

Uly considered his words carefully.

"Lukyan and Maks should be home by now," he said. "If things go well, they'll be coming back here with messages. I'd like *Wren* to be here, rather than quietly shut down and functionally abandoned where we have it currently. Especially if the Ononguli react poorly to me owning one of their ships."

"What if they go the other direction?" she asked. "Invite you to visit them as a foreign leader?"

"Then we'd need *Wren* with us for resupply on a long run," he nodded. "We stole it as a mobile depot. We should take advantage of that. I've studied the ship, and a crew of about twenty should be sufficient, give or take."

"Hire the Khet?" she asked.

"Ethir, again, offers sneakiness," he laughed. "He suggested we hire a company to sail it for us, with all the necessary bonds in place against loss of the ship and cargo. Insurance I see, but he's planning to go beyond that and actually put someone legally on the hook to pay us back, if something happens to our stolen ship."

Her look was as puzzled as his had been, but Ethir Ewin had been quite certain it would work. And Haydar had agreed, once he looked over the proposal.

"We're becoming capitalists?" she asked.

He nodded.

"I need a shower," she said, grinning.

"I feel the same," Uly agreed. "But I'd like to see about turning the Corsac Fox, the man and not just the ship, into whatever it is that we think we'll need, as a foreign power recognized by both Z'Gosza and Lacium."

"And Taeli," she reminded him. "They may not be much, but they are functionally on that Silk Road to Ononguli space, so they might become hugely important in another generation."

"You think we'll be able to keep this up for that long?" he asked, suddenly seeing the scale of things they were putting in motion.

"You'll need a home port that we can utterly trust," she replied. "That might be Lacium, if the locals can hold on to power that long. Then, at some point, you might have to proclaim yourself Emperor or Party Secretary. Whatever government we end up with. And retire from starship command."

"That's going to be a while," he shook his head. "Unless someplace spontaneously announced I am their long-missing king or something. And don't you dare suggest that to anyone."

She laughed.

"Who?" she countered. "Me?"

"Yes, you," he grumbled good-naturedly. "I have enough issues now. Becoming some alien warlord would compound them, not relieve them."

"Might be necessary," she pointed out.

He fell silent. She did as well.

"Yeah, it might be," he finally agreed. "Tomorrow. Or overmorrow. I have other issues first."

"Agreed," she said. "Time to expand your harem."

He started to say something tart, and her grin defused him.

Then they both grew serious.

A look passed. Almost an electric spark between them.

A promise of other conversations to have at some point.

Overmorrow. Assuming things got easier.

If they ever did.

TWENTY-THREE

Lukyan hadn't been home in years.

Safer that way. For everybody. Him. Nadiya. Bohdan. Both clans. All relatives.

Took Uly to bring him here.

Force majeure, as it were.

Maks was with him. As far as these old farts had been concerned, he'd been First Officer on *Compass Rose* at the time, and thus culpable.

Plus, Uly'd sold him *Scavenger Angel*, then hired the kid to bring home personal gear.

Just off-center of the bullseye.

Because that would be Lukyan.

He'd dressed in his best outfit. The Horde wasn't at war, and all the ships out there were generally clan businesses or private enterprise, so nothing like a uniform. No lime, rose, white, and black about him.

Not like the folks in front of him.

He followed the escort/guard/goon squad down a set of shallow stairs into a pit sort of space designed to put even the tips of his horns below the elders up on their platform behind a table.

The Lords of the Endless Plains themselves.

He recognized a few from pictures, but hadn't ever been important enough to know any of these folks. Even Bohdan, *Eldest Prince of the Chayka Clan*, had been a minor player, since Chayka were a small group around here. At least for wealth and power.

And Lukyan had intentionally been gone for a while.

Fortunately, none of his kin were standing around the perimeter of the room, either. Just strangers.

Lukyan assumed interested parties, but he didn't seen anybody from Clan Kovalenko, not counting the one he'd known on the left end up there. Vitaly Kovalenko.

Hopefully, Nadiya was a distant-enough cousin that the fellow had no opinions.

And nobody from Sobol, either, which was good. Adrian wasn't home. Might not be coming home, depending on the *Auga*.

Lukyan and Maks came to rest, unarmed and surrounded by about eleven times their mass in goons.

But then, a lot of folks probably thought he'd changed sides, or something equally stupid on their part.

Instead of him trying to save the Ononguli Sphere from the *Auga*. And everybody else.

Because there's somebody even worse out there. You just haven't met that species yet.

Lukyan bowed his head the requisite amount when dealing with the elders. Maks did, too.

Silence fell.

Weird, being on a planet and not having blowers moving air around in the background all the time. Unnatural silence.

Worse, skylights overhead letting in light that wasn't broad-spectrum white.

Already, he missed being on a starship.

"Lukyan Chayka," the *Vatazhko* began from up there on the stage.

Anna Shevchenko, Chief of the Clans herself.

Never a good person to start with. But Uly'd warned him it was likely to happen that way.

He nodded to the woman, remaining silent.

"And Maks Sobol."

Beside him, Maks did the same.

"We have read the report you submitted," Shevchenko continued, her voice heavy in a way that weighed on his soul.

Unhappy to see him. To be called in to settle all these issues, because the Clans had let things get out of hand.

Except that Uly was a sovereign power. At least according to the Khet of Z'Gosza, and whoever else decided to play along.

Matters of State, which meant the Vatazhko herself had to be involved.

Lukyan and Maks were bit players thrust onto the stage. Hopefully, he'd be able to speak his few lines, then withdraw and spend the rest of the play in the chorus or off-stage.

Looking at the woman up on the platform, he didn't believe it for a second.

"Describe Conductor Fortier," she commanded.

Lukyan held the grimace inside.

He'd known this was coming. Uly challenged all their assumptions of racial superiority and isolation.

"Uly gets shit done," Lukyan said simply.

He'd still never heard a more succinct encapsulation of the Human.

"I note that he rejects being bound by our laws," she replied.

"Only part of his crew is Ononguli," Lukyan said. "The ones that broke out of an *Auga* prison with him and helped him steal *Iron Wasp*, subsequently renamed *Corsac Fox*, though many people use that term to describe Uly himself as well."

"Should he be punished for that?" she pressed.

Time to go for broke.

"He is not Ononguli," Lukyan reminded the room. "And the ship was in *Auga* custody because Adrian Sobol had gotten himself captured by the Empire. Unless you are prepared to treat him like he was Ononguli, you cannot expect him to recognize that you might have any hold over the man. His words to me when I asked, Vatazhko. I think he can become a powerful ally to the Horde if we do not alienate him."

"He is one person," she sneered. "A Human, whatever they are."

"And he has fashioned a crew of Humans from former enemies. Then from Mazhin. Emro. Thogin. Khet. And yes, Ononguli. They will follow him. By now, I'm certain others will as well, because he has the charisma to significantly affect this galaxy. People recognize that, and join his cause. I became involved because the Khet of Z'Gosza hired him to break a major smuggling and criminal port at Lacium. He did. Then he turned that place into an allied port that is going straight. Honest. Smugglers he ignores. Pirates he crushes. Slavers will probably get executed out of hand, but he has a significant number of former slaves among his senior people and they have strong opinions."

"What are you saying, Chayka?" she demanded, even as the other eight finally stirred.

"The galaxy has changed, Vatazhko," Lukyan replied. "Humans will alter many things. We're lucky that Uly came out first, because they are a violent, dangerous species and culture. Aggressive. Militant in ways that make the *Auga* look amateur. Uly wants to specifically break the power of the *Auga* so that they can't conquer everyone else. And is planning his campaigns exactly on that pattern."

Lukyan fell silent as the nine elders stirred and looked at each other. Around the edges of the room, the audience muttered and moved enough to generate noise.

The Vatazhko didn't need to do anything except look around for everyone to fall silent, but she was like that. Powerful. Charismatic in ways Lukyan recognized from spending so much time around Uly.

Those two would know each other on sight.

Her black irises and red eyeballs bored in on him now. Measured his soul, as his witch grandmother would have said, were she standing here with her biting, insightful commentary on things.

"Can he?" she asked in a quiet voice that still felt like a knife slipping between his ribs.

"With help," Lukyan replied. "With friends."

"Like you and Sobol?" she pressed, forcing the steel deeper.

Lukyan considered his options. His words.

His destiny.

"Yes," he nodded. "Like me. Maks?"

"Absolutely," Maks spoke up. "As Lukyan said at the beginning of it all at Lacium: I'd rather be on the winning side. That's Uly."

Lukyan had expected the room to explode in noise, so the utter silence that fell instead filled his soul with a dread he hadn't known since the last time he and Bohdan had almost come to blows.

At least when they hang us, we'll be on the winning side of whatever stupidity these folks intend to start, Creator of All have mercy on their dumbass souls.

She didn't let his soul go, but her eyes relented a little.

"And he will reject a summons from the Horde?" she asked.

"He will, Vatazhko," Lukyan said carefully, measuring out the rope in his mind.

"Then you will need to convince him to visit us instead, won't you?" she smiled.

Lukyan nodded.

Not a lot he could say at this point.

Not if he didn't want to be grounded forever. She had that power.

"As you command, Vatazhko," he replied.

Hopefully, Uly would understand.

Except that, knowing Uly, he'd already seen it coming.

TWENTY-FOUR

Maks was home. Currently having a few minutes to recover in the room he'd grown up in, because his parents had kept it as a guest room in the house.

Today, he felt like a guest.

Maks had been with Lukyan for a long time. Away from home, though they did send and receive mail with other ships. Folks could ship things along when they knew someone was headed that direction.

Adrian was the most famous of his various cousins and kin. And a lot of folks had thought that there was something not right in that boy.

Uly had described Adrian in a variety of ways and terms, but bully was the big one.

The word that got Uly really angry.

Everybody else was just happy Adrian was somewhere else.

Except that he'd managed to make the *Auga* angry. Or been involved enough that he was their victim right now, along with the entire Sphere.

A knock at the door and he rose from where he'd more or less plopped on the edge of the old bed to recover from meeting the elders.

The room felt like the one he'd grown up in, but he'd been gone for a decade and a half, and they'd repainted the walls and put a nicer quilt on the bed.

At least he hadn't been arrested and thrown in a cell. Lukyan and Uly had both mentioned that as a possibility, however unlikely.

Maks opened the door and Mom was standing there.

Lyra Sobol, originally of Clan Bondarenko.

Mom.

She held a tray with a tea pot and two mugs.

Maks stepped back and opened the door the rest of the way. Mom closed it with her hip and set the tray on the desk he'd ignored in the corner.

Too many years of homework, sitting at that thing.

Then she poured and handed him a mug.

She hadn't spoken.

Maks took it and sipped. She got herself some and pulled out the chair to sit.

Maks moved back to the bed, but on this side. Wasn't as comfortable as his command chair on *Scavenger Angel*, however soft it was.

But then, you can't ever really go home, can you?

"Conductor looks good on you," she finally said, grinning.

Maks blushed. Felt it all the way to the tips of his horns. Nobody but Mom could do that to him.

"Luck," he replied. "Lukyan automatically sided with Uly at Lacium because we thought it was Adrian and *Iron Wasp*. Uly didn't blow us up afterwards. Then he needed someone to haul gear and messages home."

"Because he didn't feel safe doing it himself," she nodded.

Maks nodded with her. The Lords of the Endless Plains were sometimes a gamble, because the Horde generally used chaos as a weapon to keep the *Auga* at bay.

"I've heard that the Clans are taking up a collection to pay a reward for what you did," she said.

Maks nodded. Not surprising. Personal junk was still personal.

"Are you keeping *Scavenger Angel*?" she asked.

Mom was the business brains. Dad liked to stay on the ground and work in an office.

Maks had always wanted to see space.

"Uly sold it to me for almost nothing, then paid me to bring things here," he replied. "It's a nice enough ship."

"If you were going to stay as a pirate," she interrupted. "Or a civilian hauling cargo."

"You disagree?" he asked carefully, mindful of the times his dumbass, teenaged self had gotten the sharp edge of her tongue.

Not that she'd been wrong, mind you.

"I heard what Chayka said," she nodded. "About Fortier. You realize that both of you automatically call him Uly, don't you?"

He stopped and thought about it.

"Yup," he agreed. "Everybody does. It's who he is."

"Interesting," she said. "I think that the Lords of the Endless Plains want to meet him in person. Take his gauge. See if he's going to cause the next war between the *Auga* and the Horde."

"Did the last one ever really stop?" Maks asked.

It had been before his time. Mom had been there, on a ship, but didn't like to talk about it. Met Dad later.

"It did not," she shrugged. "But the next one will arrive shortly. Your Uly has caused enough uproar with the *Auga*, from what people are reporting."

"All the more reason to make nice with the Human," Maks said. "He'll bring a lot of friends with him."

"Which is why you should sell *Scavenger Angel* now, while you and it are famous," Mom said sternly. "Put the money in a bank, or ask your Father for help investing it. He's quite good at handling money."

"Why?"

"Because that way, you will be immediately available, if the elders decide to activate the mothball fleet again and start building up for war with the *Auga*," she said. "And they can also send you with Chayka, when he returns to your Corsac Fox."

"Not my Corsac Fox, Mom," Maks corrected her. "The Corsac Fox. It's a name the *Auga* will fear. And the Horde will respect."

She nodded.

"I look forward to meeting him, then," she said, rising. "Dinner will be in about an hour, if you wanted to take a shower and change into something comfortable. Only family tonight, because I told Adrian's people that they could meet with you tomorrow at the earliest."

Maks nodded as she moved to the door and smiled at him.

She had his back.

Pity Lukyan couldn't say the same about his kin.

TWENTY-FIVE

Lukyan looked at the palace from the street end of the sidewalk.

Home. At least once upon a time.

Not his. Not anymore.

He drew a deep breath and squared his shoulders. Began his approach from where the ground car had deposited him outside the open front gate.

Someone was watching from inside, because the door opened when he was still only halfway there. Not a face he recognized, though male. Possibly a servant that his parents had hired since the last time Lukyan had been to this house, which had been more than a decade at this point.

At least it wasn't his brother.

Yet.

Or Nadiya, who would be expected to live in the palace with her second choice for husband.

Lukyan hadn't inquired about anything before arriving here.

He simply walked, stepping up twice to the level of the man standing there and forcing his face to calm neutrality.

"Conductor Chayka, welcome home," the fellow said, nodding politely.

Home? Sure. Let's go with that.

"If you would care to follow me, sir?" the servant asked.

Lukyan did. Ended up going down a side hallway to the library.

And not seeing anyone else.

Felt like a trap. An ambush.

Uly'd already gotten him in a better one.

Lukyan walked.

The servant opened the door and stepped to the side, gesturing him in.

Lukyan felt the door close behind him.

He'd always loved this space. Built-in shelves with centuries of old books, most of them off limits when he was a kid. Portraits of famous ancestors above that. Comfortable chairs, couches, and a table where several folks could sit and read, if they were of a mind.

And Bohdan Chayka, sitting in a chair at the far end, where there were only two. Near the main fireplace.

Man was dressed sober and serious. Dark browns like deeply stained old wood.

Not wearing the lime green of the Horde uniform, or anything near it. But their parents were getting old. Bohdan could be expected to be running most things, day-to-day.

Lukyan walked that direction. They were alone, for what it was worth.

Bohdan had a glass of something purple in his hand. Lukyan paused at the side table and poured himself a glass as well, then moved to confront his elder brother.

"Are you back?" Bohdan asked simply.

"No," Lukyan replied, moving on to the empty chair and sitting.

There was no fire in the fireplace between them. Only cold, dead embers.

"Are you ever coming back?" Bohdan continued, his voice less confrontational.

Like maybe they'd both had nearly two decades to think about it. Maybe find some level of regret for words spoken, way back then.

"I've not felt welcome," Lukyan offered. "Not really my house, as those things will be measured. Had to go out and find my own fortune, for what it got me."

"You are the talk of Rayzian," Bohdan noted.

"Uly is the talk of Rayzian," Lukyan corrected. "I'm just his messenger boy on this one."

"And yet, you will be entrusted with conveying one of the elders," Bohdan said.

Lukyan couldn't read his brother's face. Or his voice.

But they were strangers these days. Already, they'd spoken more words than any time since he'd left the first time.

Lukyan shrugged. Conductor of a low-grade pirate ship, operating in the middle of nowhere, and not all that much to show for it, except that he'd not had to come crawling back on his hands and knees, begging for a forgiveness that wasn't his fault in the first place.

"I am here, and then I will be gone," Lukyan replied. "The elder will be transported out. The Corsac Fox might bring him back."

"Would you come with him?" Bohdan asked.

Was that concern? From his brother?

The brother who had won, all those years ago?

Lukyan shrugged. He could offer his brother that much honesty.

Bohdan had everything, hadn't he? The house, the name, even the girl.

"You would be welcome," Bohdan said, quieter than before.

Almost friendly.

As if they could be friends.

Brothers, certainly. Unlikely they would ever be friends again.

Too many light-centuries between them.

"That will be up to other folks," Lukyan replied ambiguously.

He wouldn't have come home this time, save that Uly had asked. And sent the Horde a priceless gift mostly comprised of old junk and smelly sweatshirts.

"Are you staying on the planet?" Bohdan finally asked.

He didn't even mention here in this palace, perhaps recognizing that to be a bridge too far.

"I have not decided," Lukyan offered. "I could not be certain of my reception here at the Hall. *Compass Rose* is docked above us."

There. The threat to simply bow to his elder brother as convention demanded, and withdraw entirely from whatever game board the man had set up, here in the library where none of the rest of the family was present.

"You should stay," Bohdan said with a firm nod. "There is much we do not know of your adventures in space. It has been nearly a decade."

"It has," Lukyan agreed, thinking back to that slightly older punk who'd come home that last time.

Softer and calmer than the one who'd left a decade prior to that.

The same bitter recriminations and arguments had driven Lukyan out the second time.

He supposed they were both growing old. Maybe even growing up, but he wasn't willing to say that too loudly.

It was Tuesday, after all, and he still woke up every week nervous for what the fates would visit upon him.

Normally, one would inquire about the man's wife and family at this point, but that was Nadiya. Not a topic Lukyan wished to revisit. Possibly ever, as nothing good could come of it.

Nothing.

"How are our parents?" he asked instead, admitting his own cowardice in the comfort of his mind.

"Well," Bohdan nodded, probably understanding that there would be a gap in all conversations, going forward. "Aging, as one would expect, but still in good health overall. Complaining about the lack of grandchildren."

Oh? Lukyan kept his face perfectly calm.

Twenty years, and no children? Lukyan hadn't been home long enough to find out, and hadn't asked since.

Or really cared.

"I have none that I am aware of," Lukyan offered.

You never knew, considering some of the things he had done in the last twenty years. There might be a kid of his running around that nobody had ever mentioned to him.

Stranger things happened in this business.

"Perhaps it is time you settled down and raised a family?" Bohdan asked carefully, dancing around razor-sharp edges from the look in his eyes.

"War beckons," Lukyan replied. "I suspect that I will be too busy elsewhere to establish a proper household on Rayzian. Or anywhere else."

No, Bohdan, I am not here to steal your wife. Or even talk to her, if I can avoid it. Let bygones be bygones and bury those arguments under the accumulated detritus of irrelevance.

He took another sip and watched the Ononguli who would inherit this palace. And all that went with it.

"And you never intend to return?" Bohdan asked.

"This is not my place," Lukyan said, looking around as if for the last time ever. "It was my home, once, but I have been gone longer than I lived here, and it is not anymore. I am visiting because you are my kin. My family. I am not here to disrupt things any more than necessary, having gotten the invitation. I will dine with you all, then determine my next steps."

"You should stay," Bohdan replied sharply. "At least one night."

Lukyan shrugged. Dinner would be painful enough. Remaining under this roof might be asking too much. Especially if his brother and Nadiya had never had children.

He watched Bohdan have some conversation with himself, played out in the eyes.

Too many years as a pirate, learning to read people better than they understood themselves.

"Then we will need to make sure you feel welcome at dinner," Bohdan said, rising suddenly and walking towards the door.

Lukyan watched him go, uncertain what it all meant.

And old enough today to not really care, either. He'd spoken his piece. Had the most polite and quiet conversation he'd had with his own brother in many, many years.

Dinner might not be open warfare, after all.

Open, anyway.

Lukyan remained and drank his wine, wishing there was a fire lit to provide some companionship, as the room was suddenly too empty. Too cold.

Too much.

Then the door opened and Lukyan recognized the figure standing there.

"Hello, Nadiya."

TWENTY-SIX

Lukyan could see where she'd put on a little weight from the skinny teenager she'd been, once upon a forever ago. Grown into a woman's curves.

Any other woman, and he would appreciate them. Ogle them, even.

Not her. Not now. Not ever.

She hung at the door, indecisive, then closed it behind her and walked to the side bar. He watched her fix a glass of wine, then move to the chair her husband had vacated to sit.

They studied each other for a long minute.

It had been twenty years, and the only resemblance he had to that kid was entirely physical. Lukyan supposed that she would be the same way.

Complete strangers.

"You look well," he offered neutrally, leaving off the utterly exquisite beauty of her horns.

Or the way her hair was long and pulled sideways into a tail hung over her left shoulder. It was coming in gray now. His was as well.

Growing old. Maybe growing up.

"You, as well," she replied, voice uncertain.

How do you have a casual conversation with the first person you ever fell madly in love with, a lifetime later?

At least she'd never sent him any letters secretly. Nothing that might have convinced him that leaving had been a mistake.

He'd fought with his brother enough times.

"Are you staying long?" she asked.

Lukyan shrugged, wondering how much husband and wife had talked in those brief moments when they'd changed places in the hall.

He had no doubt that the room was being monitored. By whom was his only question.

"Dinner," Lukyan offered, the same deal he'd given her husband. "I cannot speak past that."

"You are welcome here," she said, ever so slightly choked up with emotions Lukyan would not allow himself to acknowledge.

"It is not my home," he countered, cutting her off perhaps a bit harsher than necessary, but sharp.

As he'd done then, when it had become necessary to end things.

Cut them short of what they might have become.

"Are you never returning to Rayzian?" she asked, which was probably the question at the top of all the rest for her.

Nadiya had always been beautiful. Like a fine wine, she had aged into a new form. Older, but still glorious.

"I only returned as an ambassador for the Corsac Fox," he said, again chopping. "Nothing more."

They could have had this conversation a decade ago. Or two.

Had there been less yelling involved then.

"And you will return to him?" she asked, understanding that whatever her hopes were, she wasn't going to get much.

If anything.

"I will," Lukyan agreed. "Then I will see what the Lords of the Endless Plains demand of me. And Uly. I am no longer a free agent, able to come and go as I please."

And I wouldn't have come here, even with an invitation, save to look around once, consider all the things that might have been, and depart.

But he didn't say that.

Couldn't. Not to Nadiya. Or Bohdan.

They had their own lives, however unhappily they had chosen to live them.

Lukyan was willing to admit a soul small enough to recognize how miserable those two had ended up. But hey, the two Clans had decided how things would work out, hadn't they?

Lukyan gave her a sad smile. Might-have-beens, but nothing more. Nothing left.

He'd had to come here today to recognize that he didn't love her. Not anymore.

Only the memory of her, from twenty-some years ago, when he'd been young, and dumb, and full of himself.

He finished his wine and rose to pour more, giving himself an excuse to move away from the woman.

"Tell me what news I've missed around the house," he requested as he poured, thinking about yesterdays lost and all the possibilities that might await, if he was no longer in love with his brother's wife.

TWENTY-SEVEN

Dan had allowed Uly to meet with the important Trade Factors of Z'Gosza, then offered them the extra reward of not having her team armed and lurking when they did that. Just the boys, as it were, though she supposed that Haydar, Ethir, and Piruz were probably more dangerous, as the conversations would be legal contracts and treaties between nations.

The Corsac Fox, leaving his mark on the galaxy.

She'd taken the women and gone down to the surface. They were all armed in public, to the dismay of some of the locals and the delight of others.

There was a distinct gender break on that list, as well. The Khet tended to be heavily male chauvinist in their culture. Women were homemakers and occasionally secretaries, but only rarely bosses. And even then, those were usually the offspring of rich, important men, so Dan assumed an aristocratic model more like *Danumash* there, where the children of the rich and powerful could get away with things that the rest of the population could not.

Down on the planet, Dan could meander around places like this market square and see things that Uly would miss from the heavens. And he was counting on her to do things.

And having a trio of Emro giant women along meant that everyone was watching them as they walked through another crowd of shops and stalls. Even Suka Kuri had accompanied them today.

It was a multi-colored team of armed, dangerous women. A new thing to Z'Goszan society.

They had eaten lunch on their first arrival, a few hours ago. Street food of fried fish wrapped in a flat bread with a pinkish sauce. Not all that messy. Spicy.

The spiciness was why Dan had come here. She didn't want dull people who ate flavorless meat.

She smiled and walked.

Behind her, the ladies alternatively smiled and glowered at others, depending on smiles and gender watching.

It was good.

"Dan, on your right side," Yanouk spoke up quietly. "Roughly seventy meters down, past the market center. Red sign."

Dan looked until she found it. Helped that she was taller than most male Khet, let alone female, so she could see over most everybody around her.

The sign, from here, looked like crossed swords. Just the sort of thing Dan had been looking for.

She knew it had to exist. Every culture had some subset that venerated close combat forms, however civilized they might see themselves. In fact, the more civilized the group, the more they tended to elevate such things to an art. Especially when it was no longer a daily necessity.

She made her way that direction. Glancing back, her group had accumulated a small tail of followers, though Uly's film crew was up on the station today.

Dan might have neglected to mention to Sani or Bello what she was up to, not wanting it to be part of Uly's legend.

Not yet, anyway.

Dojo. Or whatever the equivalent Khet term was.

Nice day, so the front door was open. Breezes and the requisite mister-gate kept it comfortable inside. Brightly lit. Not a lot of folks inside.

One Khet male on the training floor. Young middle age. A little squishy, but mostly built solid then expanded a bit. *Combat Buddha,* she had heard the shape called.

Currently, he'd been instructing a group of younger students. Not young, but raw. First or second year students in a civilian class.

Everything had screeched to a halt as the students had started to ignore the teacher and watch her, just inside the door but still back across that line on the floor dividing casual from serious.

The Khet instructor turned to see what was going on, goggled, then turned back to his students.

"Relax and sit," he ordered in an accented tone she was still getting used to around here, then walking towards Dan.

As expected, he paused at that line, turning to bow to a picture hung on a side wall. Elder or Founder. A thing that crossed many cultures. Respect for the teacher that has allowed you to learn.

"How may I help you?" he asked, coming to rest at a polite distance to look up at her. At most of them, as only Katya was his height.

Dan bowed as one teacher would when meeting another. Respect.

"I am Dan Chastain," she said.

"Indeed," he smiled. "The Corsac Fox's right hand."

She grinned. It helped that most of the planet had probably seen that initial documentary by now. And she supposed that she played a larger-than-life role in it.

As had all her women warriors with her today. Plus the wicked Elder responsible.

"We are recruiting," she said simply.

The man perked right up, then noted that the only males around were either outside on the sidewalk, or behind him on the training floor.

"Did you seek something in particular?" he asked, voice shifting into an extremely formal, precise tone.

Deadly serious.

She could see the Khet he became when violence was necessary, as opposed to the friendly teacher/elder instructing students.

"Warrior women," Dan said, flowing into his body language and tone like doing push hands with a stranger. "The Corsac Fox maintains a team of such women as his personal bodyguards."

The documentary had never once mentioned *harem*, though Z'Goszan history had something similar. Instead, the men making the film had shown her and the others storming an enemy-held station at gunpoint, including footage from helmet cameras with good narration to explain.

Like when Yanouk charged one of the last strongholds behind Painspheres rolling on a flat deck, while firing her squad exoblaster one-handed, then picking up the station commander in one hand by his jaw and holding him in the air.

Beautiful. And deadly.

The teacher paused. Then he nodded.

"I have a name," he said simply. "If you will give me a moment, I will contact her and have her come over."

Dan nodded and slipped to one side, taking a chair where proud parents might sit and watch their children in class. The others remained standing, with Suka Kuri closest.

"I'm afraid it would collapse under me," she chuckled when Dan gestured.

The teacher had moved to his comm and was speaking in a quiet tone. The students were restless, fidgeting and watching, afraid they were missing something.

The crowd outside was being updated with a running commentary from an older Khet woman who had moved to exactly outside the threshold, talking over her shoulder while hungry eyes tracked every movement.

Dan figured she would be on the evening news again, as soon as someone could send a crew. Or these folks got enough footage to send them something.

She smiled and remained calm. Still.

On stage, as one might expect. Uly was really good at it. She'd learned from watching him.

The instructor returned a few moments later.

"I have reached out to one of my senior students," he said. "She is more of a peer, though. She will be here in a few minutes to discuss things more fully with you."

Dan smiled up at him.

"I'm sorry we are interrupting your class," she said. "Perhaps your students might like to see some of our forms?"

His eyes lit up. Their eyes got even more huge than Khet normally were.

Dan nodded and rose, kicking off her shoes as the rest did the same.

Even Suka Kuri joined her in bowing to the picture before stepping onto the mat.

Canvas, of a sort. Packed sand underneath, where you could fall, but not hurt yourself as much, while still having a good grip for your toes.

The students had all fled madly to the mirrored walls around the outside, their instructor joining them.

At the front door, that one older Khet woman had boldly entered the dojo to hold a comm where the camera could capture everything.

Dan turned to Suka Kuri.

"Are you certain you wished to join us?" she asked formally.

Exemplar of the Arts. The woman was allowed by Emro society to do whatever the hell she wanted.

"I could have been Sabre," Suka Kuri grinned. "I chose Moss because it was much easier on the knees."

Dan shared her grin, then turned to Nasrin.

"Sunflower Fist long form?" she asked.

"I think that's a great place to start," Nasrin nodded.

They lined up in two rows, the three Emro women farthest from the door and the camera. The instructor moved all his students around to where they would see it best.

Nasrin nodded with all her tentacles, and began to flow.

TWENTY-EIGHT

Times always seemed to slow down for Dan when she was doing forms. Especially at the level that even Katya had reached these days.

Humans often used colored belts as a way of identifying a student's formal rank. In ancient times, the main designation had been between students who were invited into the inner courtyard to learn, versus those who only learned in public parks.

Katya wasn't the equivalent rank of the male Khet whose school they had overrun, but he was behind the rest of them. Helped that she had three Emro mixing Moss and Sabre schools, plus Nasrin, who had taken her own dance forms and come to understand that they were more than mere pretty movements.

Sunflower Fist. The long form on a hexagonal pattern. Human forms tended to be linear and square, touching the compass points. More advanced ones hit the corners of the boxes as well.

The Mazhin had a radically different perspective on things.

They went through the form twice. Slowly. Meditation in Motion, as such things were often seen. And filmed carefully by an audience fallen utterly silent.

Dan was sweating, but that was normal.

The instructor had already made arrangements with the old

woman for a copy of the video, and Dan had no doubts that he would be teaching himself Sunflower Fist shortly, then passing it on to his students.

And, being a capitalist society, she had no doubts that his classes would suddenly fill to overflowing.

Weird. But it would make him another ally later. Always useful.

A tiny Khet woman appeared at the door, nearly elbowing folks out of her way, as the group finished the last few motions, second time around.

Dan watched, but could do Sunflower Fist asleep these days.

Instead, she studied the newcomer. The instructor moved to the woman and bowed formally, so this was the one he had summoned.

Dan moved toward them as well, feeling the others fall in behind her, though all moved silently.

The only noise were the excited students, most of whom struck Dan as teenagers. Mixed gender. Kids whispering back and forth.

She smiled, then bowed and stepped off the floor.

"Commander Chastain, it is my pleasure to present to you Ciah Dambe," the man said. "One of my students, though she could open her own school, were she of a mind."

Dan studied the Khet woman.

Bright eyes and a tall headcrest, which helped offset the fact that the rest of her was maybe one hundred and fifty-five centimeters tall.

If that.

A darker blue to her skin and scales than most Khet, highlighted with more reds than oranges.

Ciah Dambe bowed. Dan matched it.

"How may I help?" Ciah asked, simply, calmly falling into something like parade rest, even as she was the smallest person here, looking up at everyone else.

The old woman was filming from about two meters away, her own mouth fallen open and catching flies, but Dan didn't turn and wink at the camera, as much as she wanted to.

"I am recruiting warriors," Dan told the Khet woman. "Specifically women, who will become part of the Corsac Fox's personal bodyguard with these other ladies."

Ciah looked up at each of them in turn. Careful appraisal.

"I am not capable of growing to that height," she said with a wry grin.

"Then perhaps you have speed?" Suka Kuri asked in a light tone.

"Perhaps," Ciah nodded to the elder. "Should I demonstrate my few and pitiful gifts?"

Dan caught the nod from the instructor.

Ciah turned to the man and bowed.

"I need a blade," she said. "I was at work, and simply left without explanation. I suppose that I will be on the news later, assuming they haven't fired me yet."

Dan didn't ask what the woman did. She was dressed in loose slacks and a blousy top that was nice, but seemed rugged. And a young woman was likely a minor cog in somebody's corporate machine.

Perhaps they would fire her, but if she was any good, a smart person would know better.

"Take mine," the man said, reaching toward a rack of training swords in black plastic and pulling one that he extended to her butt-first like a holy relic.

Then he turned to his students.

"All of you, line up just on the mat, facing in," he said, moving to the line, bowing, then forming his kids up to watch whatever Ciah had planned.

Dan followed him, as did all the women, leaving the old woman alone to witness, just beyond the line.

Ciah found a spot in the center of the floor, breathing slowly to oxygenate her gills and waiting for everything to fall to complete silence before she began.

The blade reminded Dan of a jian. A Chinese blade, long and slender, usually razor sharp on both ends for about twenty centimeters, then a heavy spine back to the crossguard.

A weapon for stabbing and extremely weak on slashing, when your foe wore no boarding armor. Part of the reason she preferred the Icemace.

Ciah began to move. The blade gave her reach, and the movements were designed to get her moving by an opponent with a slash or punch as she went. Blocks using the flat of the blade like the back of the hand, then circling into a chop or thrust.

Not a form Dan knew. Not a style of fighting she'd ever studied that much, mostly because her job had always been boarding actions, where you moved quickly in narrow corridors to overwhelm your opposition, bashing or shooting as you went while relying on exactly the kinds of armor that would resist such a sword pretty well.

But Ciah Dambe had a grace and speed to her motions. And a precise understanding of where everyone around her was, subtly shifting stances and thrusts to avoid poking anyone or stumbling over them as she moved.

As before, the old woman filmed it all. Dan figured that she would need to call her own documentary crew later, just so they could purchase a copy of the footage for whatever their next project was.

Ciah came to rest.

"That utterly sucked," she announced to the room, showing Dan exactly the scale the woman graded herself on, whereit had to be better, every single time.

Dan stepped up to the small woman and smiled.

"I've boarded enemy warships under fire, and not done as well," Dan said simply.

The instructor took this moment to step close as well.

"If you will pardon me for a moment?" he asked, waiting for Dan to nod before turning to his students. "Class is dismissed. I will see all of you next week, and hopefully, we will be able to work on learning Sunflower Fist. Now, stop giggling and git."

Everyone was laughing, cheering, and celebrating, but they left quickly.

Dan moved to the old woman, who surprised her by ejecting a chip from the side of her comm and smiling as she handed it to Dan.

"Someone would pay you well for that," Dan said.

"I have kept a copy," the woman smiled shrewdly.

Dan bowed to her and laughed, then watched her withdraw as well, closing the door behind her.

The instructor looked on expectantly.

"When is your next class?" Dan asked.

"That was it for today," he said. "What are your needs?"

Dan turned to Ciah.

"Early dinner?" Dan asked, turning to the only man in the room to include him, but he bowed.

"I will not be needed," he said, stepping back.

Dan turned to Ciah.

"Yes," the small woman said.

Dan smiled and nodded to the rest of her team, noting all the smiles there as well.

TWENTY-NINE

Dan had listened to Ciah tell her tale. The woman turned out to be barely an adult. Maybe the Human equivalent of nineteen, though Khet aged at a different rate.

She'd started extremely young.

"That's why I changed my name when I was legally an adult," Ciah concluded. "My mother always called me the troublesome warrior child. Ciah Dambe fit."

"Troublesome?" Suka Kuri asked, sitting directly across the table from Ciah and occasionally prodding her with questions as they'd eaten and talked.

"Hard-headed," Ciah nodded and shrugged all at once. "Stubborn. Unwilling to settle for a boyfriend and doing girly things in school. The dojo floor was my creative outlet."

"Have you ever fired a beam weapon?" Dan asked.

"No," Ciah replied. "But I think a crossbow is similar enough to Nasrin's omnibow, if I understand the physics correctly. I have used those. Obviously, much better with close weapons."

Dan nodded. Ciah's instructor had said she was his best student, female or male. Suka Kuri had indicated the young woman as a top level Seeker or perhaps an Adept, a rank the elder applied to Dan when pressed.

Dan wasn't Sabre School. She was a boarding trooper with a lot of open hand and melee weapon experience.

Maybe the same thing.

Dan considered all the things she'd heard and shared with Ciah over the last two hours and a nice meal.

"Would you be interested in professional warfare as a vocation?" Dan asked finally, after they'd danced around the topic enough without ever touching it.

Dan had seen enough about Ciah to approve. As had Suka Kuri, which was a higher bar to clear.

"Professional?" Ciah asked, a little surprised.

That was Ethir's favorite term?

Gobsmacked.

"All of us except Suka Kuri led combat teams when the Corsac Fox captured the station at Lacium," Dan reminded her. "Wherever Uly goes, we are his bodyguards."

"I've seen that part," Ciah said. "You think I could do that?"

"I have seen you move," Dan replied with a nod that the others matched. "A willingness to do violence to someone is the hardest part. The rest is study and practice, once you are willing to hurt someone."

"But I'm just a kid," Ciah said, almost pleading.

Suka Kuri's laugh cut her short.

"You are all children to this old woman," she grinned. "Nasrin is hardly older than you, relative to life span. Yanouk might actually be younger, comparatively. Dan and Katya are the elders here, such as it is. And Uly is an old soul hiding in a young body. That is what gives all of you the power to change things. Each of you are students of life as much as students of violence. You will fit in well with this group."

Ciah's eyes, already large in her head, got huge. Dan smiled. The others matched it.

"If you think I can do it," Ciah said quietly.

"I do," Dan replied. "Or we wouldn't be here talking."

She held out hand. Ciah took it.

"Welcome to the team," Dan said.

THIRTY

Uly was back on the ship.

Home, he supposed.

Another round of meetings over exquisite meals, where a Trade Factor got to show off his chef.

No wonder they were all squishy, considering how well and how much they ate.

He was in his office, mostly to hide from anyone who might decide to look for him in his quarters nearby.

Someone chirped the hatch anyway.

Uly sighed and opened it with the switch.

Ethir grinned and stepped in, pulling out a chair that fit him and climbing up to where he was eye level with everyone else.

"I won the coin toss," Ethir announced.

Uly fixed him with a disbelieving eye.

"There is news," Ethir continued. "Second Law of Thermodynamics precludes me from calling it *good* news, technically, but I think you'll like it."

When Ethir spoke like that, he was up to no good. The kind of wheeling and dealing that made Piruz the Horse Thief whistle in appreciation.

"Uh huh," Uly grunted at him, mostly as a prompt.

He was tired. He'd been *On* all day, and was looking forward to finally winding down and sleeping.

Hopefully, nobody would attack them this close to several armed stations.

"Part one, we've heard from the folks over on *Ahmadi*," Ethir nodded, still grinning. "Dunno what Haydar and Nasrin said to them, but we're looking at something like forty to fifty prospective recruits wanting to join us for a while. At least as far as back to Taeli, but he had the impression that we're getting the crazy artists off that crew, and leaving the old farts behind. Or something like that."

Uly nodded. The ten Mazhin he'd rescued had all been artists of some kind or another. Two Technicals, which was how *Danumash* had classified their scientists in Haydar and Roshan. Six Mechanicals, which meant machinists and engineers capable of building any device the two genius types invented.

And two Socials, which Uly automatically classified as Entertainer in his head, when *Danumash* had probably intended them as sex objects to keep the male Mazhin slaves happy.

At least no Humans from *Danumash* had ever lowered themselves to…

Uly didn't even know which verb might be appropriate. Fortunately, all those men were dead.

And the midshipmen and enlisted crew Uly had inherited had learned what topics to not even joke about.

"Okay," Uly said, mostly to keep Ethir in motion.

"Also, we have three bids for handling *Wren* that I'm willing to qualify for serious consideration," Ethir said, waving a hand before Uly could comment. "We'll handle the details. Mostly keeping you in the loop, because you'll end up signing contracts at some point. Fully licensed and bonded was a minimum for me, and I've got to go deep into their networks with Rabiu to see if any dead fish float up."

It was a weird term. Ethir had picked it up from Rabiu. A Khet thing, where they originally evolved from fish to amphibians to erect bipeds. But then, Humans had come from arboreal tree shrews at one point before coming down out of the canopy.

"I'm more interested in quality of work than pure profit," Uly reminded him.

"Oh, these are all profit-sharing deals," Ethir replied. "Gotta have fins in the game to know they are serious. You'll have a pot of cash for basic operations, with points on a quarterly bonus structure and secondary vesting schedules. I told them to think of the bid as an operating license for a station and let that guide their offers."

Uly felt his eyes cross, trying to parse that. Ethir laughed.

"Got those silly fish teasing at the bait," he assured Uly. "Once they get serious, I'll gaff them into the boat."

Uly nodded.

"And, best for last, Dan has news she wanted me to pass along," Ethir grinned again. "They found a Khet woman to recruit."

Uly nodded again. This might be the first thing Ethir had said that he was actually able to understand.

"And?" he asked.

"Local martial artist they identified down on the planet," Ethir said. "Young, from the looks of her, but Dan sent a video of the chick with a sword and she's seriously something scary to watch. Kinda cute, too."

Uly wondered about the guy he'd been three years ago. Back before he'd even really understood how many alien species there were out there, and how small Humanity's footprint was.

He'd never really had to stop and consider alien women as cute or not, but he did understand how parochial his old views had been.

He was working daily on getting better. At least he hoped so. He didn't anticipate ever needing to know any of them *that well*.

Good Lord willing and the creek don't rise.

Uly turned serious. Ethir leaned back, suddenly stone cold sober.

"I need a better catalog of all the species out there," Uly told him. "Suka Kuri is serious about recruiting that group. Dan's making it happen. I know about Thogin, Ugotha, and Zuath. I do not expect we'll ever have any *Auga*, but won't discount it, if it came to that."

"Yes," Ethir said.

"Who else is out there that might need to be recruited?" Uly asked.

Ethir blew out a heavy breath.

"Of the top of my head, add the Guezal, the Ancyn, and maybe the Yousses to that," he said. "The first two are fully conquered elements of the *Auga Empire*, but don't generally like that condition, unlike a lot of them. The latter are from way far away, but me and the cousins have encountered them a few times, exploring in from Imperial Sector Twenty-Five. Like I said, a ways from home. Kinda like the Mazhin that way. All rebels against Imperial Order, since that seems to be our starting point."

"It is," Uly agreed. "People who will want to help us push the *Auga* back into their box and make them behave."

"Can we really stop the *Auga*?" Ethir asked.

"Yes," Uly told him.

"What is it that gives you such utter certainty, Uly?" Ethir pressed.

"The two you mentioned," Uly said. "Guezal and Ancyn? They are rebels. I assume they got conquered by the *Auga* way back, and hate the overlords as much as I do. People like that will help."

"What about Humans?" Ethir asked. "Do we go back and recruit them to help with this war?"

"Eventually," Uly agreed. "Not today, but at some point. I need a lot of allies here first, though, because I suspect that Humans are using third- or fourth-hand technology that got stolen from somebody, then traded on later, before washing up on a distant shore in Sector Seventeen. People will be easy. I need fleets for them to take charge of."

"Will Humans be as bad as the *Auga*?" Ethir asked.

"Some will," Uly nodded. "Some will be on our side. That's why we will have a big operation here before expanding to include them."

"Because you want them broken to the polite way of operating, instead of adding more pirates," Ethir nodded. "Gotcha."

Uly grinned.

"Imagine one hundred million more like me and Dan," he said.

"There aren't two more like you two," Ethir disagreed. "However, I can see a bunch more like Drew Roscoe and Blair Mitchell. Yeah, we're better off building up everyone else first."

Uly nodded.

"You should sleep," Ethir said.

"I would, but somebody keeps waking me up with news," Uly grinned.

"Gotcha," Ethir said, climbing down from his tower. "I'll hang the Do Not Disturb sign on your door as I go."

"Thank you," Uly said. "And thank you for everything you and everyone have been doing to make my life easier."

"I got the easy job," Ethir laughed. "All I do is legally swindle folks that already want to give us money. You're doing the hard parts."

Uly supposed that he was.

Right now, he was tired.

And it wasn't going to get any easier, any time soon.

THIRTY-ONE

Lukyan had been summoned.

He'd stayed in the Chayka palace last night, door locked and a chair in front of it against anybody trying to sneak in while he'd slept.

For whatever...

Morning, and breakfast had been less social combat than he'd expected, but dinner had gone reasonably well. Mom and Dad were old. Worn down. Mostly retired and letting Bohdan handle everything.

Certain topics had remained off-limits. Which was good.

Then the messenger had arrived.

Time to dress in a nicer suit, though he'd given serious thought to how badly his reserve uniform would fit if he had to dig it out of a closet on the ship.

Probably worth seeing a competent tailor while he was on planet.

The invitation had not insisted on the lime. He wore a dark indigo highlighted with lavender instead.

Civilian, right up to the moment when that wasn't an option anymore.

Guards escorted him through the palace. Up and down quarter and half levels that felt utterly wrong to someone used to starship decks. Past closed doors and sections of the palace he wasn't comfortable in, because this was where power resided.

He could feel it in the stones themselves.

No way in hell Lukyan was going back to the chorus, though Maks might yet escape.

And *kzarbe* might fly.

The guards got him to a closed hatch. One identical to a hundred others he'd passed, all of them actually doors on hinges. Weird, but ground things.

He wasn't on a starship today, to his regret.

The goon knocked, opened the hatch, and looked in. Then she nodded at Lukyan and sent him through, closing it behind him.

The Vatazhko herself. In an office. Her office, from the looks of it. Nice landscape art on the two side walls. Plants in pots and other places. Fruit-bearing, because several were in various stages of ripening.

The light in here was bright white.

"Sit, Conductor," she instructed.

Lukyan did.

"I've read your file, Chayka," she continued. "So I was a little surprised that they found you at the family compound this morning, rather than in orbit."

Lukyan nodded. She wasn't the only one.

"Are things working out with your family, then?" she asked.

He considered something snarky. Or monosyllabic, but this was the Vatazhko asking.

The Chief of the Sphere itself.

"I spoke with my brother extensively," he said. "Then with his wife. Both conversations went well enough, since I am not really planning on moving back in, ever again. Today, I had intended to return to *Compass Rose* and await developments."

She nodded in turn.

"There have been rumors that Maks Sobol intends to sell *Scavenger Angel*," she said.

Lukyan perked up at that. Not that he was surprised, because he and Maks had talked about it.

But because she had to have an agent inside that compound, highly placed, to have heard something like that so quickly.

"Well-founded ship, for what it does," Lukyan offered. "Sailed well from Z'Gosza. Someone will be able to make a nice living hauling cargo around with it."

"Is he ready for combat command?" she asked.

The *Vatazhko of the Ononguli* asked. Serious business.

"We've been a small-scale predator and pirate on the fringes of Fifteen for long enough," he nodded. "Maks was my Second-in-Command for the last several years. I think he's ready. Uly was happy to sell him the ship under the known conditions. Everything worked out well."

He slammed his mouth shut at that, watching. Wondering. Waiting.

She merely nodded.

"Uly," she said, drawing the word out.

Lukyan nodded. Everyone called him Uly, rather than Conductor Fortier.

Or maybe Governor Fortier by now. Hard to say. It was Uly.

"I stayed up late last night, rereading all of your reports, Chayka," she continued. "He strikes me as dangerously competent."

Lukyan nodded. That was a lovely term to describe the Human. *Dangerously competent.*

A danger to the galaxy.

If you were on the wrong side of the battlefield from him. Or history.

"I'm sending *Compass Rose* to Fortier," she said simply, watching his face.

Left unsaid was who might be in command of the ship, if he screwed up this conversation. Interview?

Lukyan nodded. Waited. She was the supreme commander of the Sphere itself. Her word was functionally law, if she wanted it to be.

That included grounding dumbasses like him.

"I am also sending along one of the elders, with an invitation to Fortier to join us here," she continued.

"Include proposed treaty language," Lukyan said quickly.

Her brow furrowed in confusion.

"Z'Gosza treats him like a foreign power," Lukyan continued. "As does Lacium. A head of state, like yourself, with a much smaller economy or horde behind him. As yet."

"As yet?" she asked.

He nodded.

"If you treat him like Z'Gosza does, he'll be more amenable," he said. "Plus, he's got a really effective legal department."

"Consisting of two Mazhin and a Thogin?" she asked.

Lukyan grinned.

"Dangerous people," he said. "And a Khet business manager. You've obviously read what they did to the Trade Factors."

"A Chancery Court?" Madam Shevchenko asked.

"Stop pirates, take their ships," he agreed. "Get a court to legally award ownership to the Corsac Fox, for sale or use in his own fleets, if he feels the need. Or wants to sell *Scavenger Angel* to Maks cheap, in order to make a statement."

"A statement, Chayka?"

"All of Adrian's crew that got left behind," he agreed. "Their stuff is here on Rayzian now. Folks that stayed with Uly kept theirs. Uly is trying to make friendly gestures to the Horde."

"He's in one of our ships," she growled, changing the whole tenor of this interview in the wag of a horn. "With Ononguli in his crew."

"Part of his crew," Lukyan corrected her carefully. "He and I had this conversation before I left. He is not Ononguli, so he doesn't necessarily see himself bound by our rules."

"How do we make him Ononguli, then?" she asked.

Lukyan's mouth fell open.

He watched the woman like a mouse might suddenly see the owl on the branch overhead, hoping to remain invisible.

Then she pulled up her reader and flipped to a page. Put it on the desk between them and turned it around for him to see.

"You suggested in your report, perhaps irreverently, that a marriage into one of the clans might make him fully subject to Horde law," she said, tapping the paragraph in question.

Uly's rude response had been left out. Lukyan had merely been reporting all options.

All of them.

He closed his mouth before he caught any flies. Thought furiously.

"We'd have to offer him something grand and expensive," Lukyan finally said. "He'd be surrendering a lot of his freedom of movement and planning, if we did that. What does he get for it?"

"And not having the Horde as an enemy isn't enough?" she asked.

"The *Auga* are currently Uly's enemy," Lukyan pointed out carefully. "He intends to break them."

"You think he can?"

"Yes," Lukyan said. "And I really don't want to be next on his shit list after that. Or worse, first because he feels the need to break the Horde before going after the Empire."

Lukyan wondered if he'd just gotten himself grounded forever.

Might be worth it, if she listened to him.

Or didn't, and he got to say *I told you so.*

Forever.

Instead, she leaned back, watching him. Lukyan breathed shallowly through his nose, mouth remaining shut.

"I will update the elder on your thoughts," she finally said, about the point he figured he was going to be arrested.

"Who are you sending?" Lukyan asked.

He still didn't know if he'd be in command when that happened.

"Harald Perzi," she said.

Lukyan allowed himself a bit of relaxation. Not one of the fire-breathers who hated all aliens. There were a couple of those on the platform with this woman.

Not that they were wrong, because the Sphere maintained itself as Ononguli space.

At the same time, the *Auga* were coming. Lukyan understood that That Next War was going to be here in years instead of decades or generations.

Best start preparing now.

"You are Ononguli, Conductor Chayka," she said, like she was reminding him.

"Yes, Vatazhko," he replied automatically. "I'm trying to do best for the Horde, at a time when they might not understand some of the implications of decisions possibly made in ignorance."

"Like Uly?" she asked.

"Especially Uly," he nodded. "Once in a lifetime opportunity. Maybe once in a civilization. We need him on our side."

"Keep that in mind, when you see him," she said, smiling.

It took Lukyan a moment to process her smile.

Then he nodded.

He would be in command of *Compass Rose* when they got there.

As long as he didn't screw anything up.

Thank the Creator that it wasn't Tuesday today.

He'd have to make sure how he arrived on a Wednesday or something.

THIRTY-TWO

Maks awoke to find messages. Lots of them.

Lots more of them, he supposed, on top of all the thank you cards and such he'd gotten yesterday.

Looking closer, these were folks inquiring about buying *Scavenger Angel*.

Already?

He hadn't more than thought seriously about it with Mom and Dad over dinner.

And yet...

He showered, dressed, and joined them for breakfast.

He handed her his comm as he gnoshed on a fresh sweet pastry.

She merely nodded and went back to her tea.

"I know," Mom said. "I put the word out last night."

Maks started to ask just how many people she knew, but caught himself.

Obviously, she was more connected, to bigger players, than he'd realized. Or maybe the Bondarenko side of the family had more friends. At least as many as Sobol?

Her knowing smile spoke volumes. Dad just nodded and kept eating.

Maks wondered if he'd been set up.

No, that much was obvious. Why?

Yeah, better question.

"What don't I know?" he asked, waiting for that other shoe to drop.

"The Vatazhko is going to move fast," Mom replied with a nod. "Lukyan Chayka has been summoned to the palace this morning and she'll be discussing things with him."

Maks nodded.

Things seemed to be running deep in still waters. He was glad Mom was shielding him from a lot of it.

"Okay?" he said, prompting her.

Dad spoke up instead.

"I can help you review the offers," he said. "About half will be serious, while the other half merely want the prestige of owning the ship after you."

"After me?" Maks asked, confused.

"It will be an object of curiosity," Dad nodded. "Park it and offer tours. Or convert it into an exclusive, boutique hotel sort of thing. Lesser profit up front, but a much longer scale with the ship in good shape for profit on the long tail instead of suffering the usual wear and tear."

Maks blinked several times. Then remembered that he'd moved out as soon as he could, and spent most of the last fifteen years off-planet, only visiting these apparent strangers who had raised him.

He'd obviously missed a few things. Their grins gave them away.

"The first reports from Chayka came in and people started talking," Mom informed him. "We've had some time to plan."

Maks stopped and considered this new horizon arriving.

"Do we have a cousin I should look at selling it to?" he asked. "Keep the profits In-Clan, as it were, while earning some credit?"

Mom and Dad glanced at each other. Hers a touch sour, him triumphant. Then Mom pulled out a coin and handed it to Dad.

Dad's grin might have lit the dawn. Maks watched, more confused.

"You two bet on me?" he demanded, almost plaintively.

Worse, they both laughed.

"Not all pirates learn to take that long, careful view," Dad replied smugly. "The lifestyle tends towards the instant gratification mode of investing. If you really wanted, we could sell a majority stake in the ship to someone close, retaining a share of the profits."

Mom had said that Dad was good with money. Maks hadn't really appreciated how good, because he had all the other Sobol cousins to compare to.

And they all went off into space to become famous.

How many of them lived quiet lives and made nice residuals on the side? Worse, Dad almost sounded like that one Mazhin advising Uly. Piruz the Horse Thief.

Maks considered things.

"I'm going to be famous, aren't I?" he asked, face screwed a little sideways as new thoughts intruded like an armored boarding party.

"More famous," Mom said, grinning almost as wickedly as Dad. "You should probably rethink your next decade or longer."

The way she said it suggested that she had eligible women she wanted to introduce him to.

Lots of them.

But they both had his back. Dad would see the funds invested, and not blown on a bar or partying because the world might end tomorrow. Mom might be about to turn him into a respectable Ononguli.

Maks shuddered at the thought, but a lot of pirates fell out of the life before they reached their mid-thirties. Died. Retired. Injured too badly to continue.

Few were successful.

Fewer made it last.

He swallowed all his complaints and questions. Only one really mattered at this point.

"How long do I have on Rayzian?" he asked, going back and forth between the two of them.

"Assuming things go well at the palace this morning, long enough to resupply *Compass Rose*. Assuming you wanted to be aboard when Conductor Chayka was sent out."

Ten minutes ago, Maks would have agreed wholeheartedly. Packed and gone.

Now…?

Something in her eyes held him back.

"And if I didn't go with Lukyan?" he asked slowly, waiting for someone to crack his fingers with a ruler or something.

"Then there are a few folks I might want to introduce you to," Mom said, Dad nodding along sagely. "Folks who might help your career. Professionally as well as commercially."

Maks nodded and kept his mouth shut.

Things were going on around here, and he and Lukyan had missed it. Or stumbled into the wrong barn.

Mom and Dad had his back. Maybe he needed to stay here and make sure he had Lukyan's.

Especially if the rest of Clan Sobol might be a little pissy about Adrian remaining in an *Auga* prison, at a time when the *Auga* might be about to invade again.

"I think that would be a wise decision," Maks ventured.

Mom smiled.

Maks hoped that some of the ladies she intended to introduce him to were cute. And rich. Hopefully smart, because he'd spent some time around Dan Chastain and appreciated how she did things.

That woman reminded him of Mom. In good ways.

THIRTY-THREE

Lukyan had been escorted from the meeting with the Vatazhko, Anna Shevchenko, to another office, not all that far away. Moved in, sat down, offered tea.

They stared at each other from across Harald Perzi's desk.

Older fellow. Elder, as the title proclaimed, but not all of them were actually that old. The Vatazhko was hardly older than Lukyan, when you got down to it. Perzi had maybe a decade on her. Maybe fifteen years on Lukyan.

Old enough to be a respected figure.

"Anna filled you in on everything?" Perzi asked simply.

Lukyan nodded over his mug.

He had a hard time thinking of her as a person, rather than a title. And she was a person. Even an attractive one, when you got down to it, but so far out of his league, that he hadn't even thought those thoughts.

Safer, all the way around.

"I retired from the lifestyle some thirty years ago," Perzi continued. "About the time most of the big fleets were being mothballed after the last time the *Auga* got pissy. Didn't do much civilian work after that."

"Not a lot has changed, from what the oldtimers I knew told me when I was a buck," Lukyan replied, still finding his ground with this person who would be on his ship for however long.

Elder. One of the Lords of the Endless Plains themselves, though he'd just spent an hour with Perzi's boss. Way more dangerous woman.

Perzi nodded. Contemplated things as they sipped.

Lukyan appreciated being able to relax a shade. The Vatazhko had kept him balanced on a knife edge for too long this morning.

"How long do you need for resupply?" Perzi asked after a time. "Understanding that we're footing the bill, as long as it doesn't involve drydock."

Lukyan nodded.

"The Corsac Fox paid for us to undergo a full refurb on Z'Gosza before we set out," he said. "Mostly, I need supplies of consumables. Food, water, spare parts, metal for the machine shop. Normal wear and tear. Is *Scavenger Angel* going with us to haul some of our supplies this time?"

"I have not heard one way or the other," Perzi replied enigmatically, suggesting that he knew more than a mere conductor needed to know. "Let us plan as if we are flying solo."

Lukyan nodded, doing math and geometry in his head.

"In that case, we need about twelve hours to reshuffle everything around while docked to a station and drawing on their docking space," he said. "Then we can cram enough of everything aboard to make a single run to Z'Gosza without risking anything or needing to stop for resupply midway. There are a few places I'd like to check in along the way, mostly so we don't just pop out there into whatever is going on."

"That would be wise," Perzi replied. "The *Auga* are paying attention as well, so they might try to intercept us. Or at least put ships out into that path and hope to stumble across diplomats traveling like yourself."

"Are we really that important?" Lukyan asked. "I've largely been away for most of a decade. What's happening around here that has everyone alather?"

"The *Auga* sent an ambassador to complain about the Corsac Fox," Perzi laughed. "To Anna, mind you, personally. Told her that she had to do something about the Human, or they would. And, while holding on to Adrian Sobol and his top officers, even as they delivered all the rest of the crew. I've never seen an angry *Auga* before. It was rather illuminating."

Lukyan swallowed past a tongue suddenly too thick.

"Do they not realize that the Horde will basically shift to a war footing, one way or the other?" Lukyan asked.

"I'm sure they have that on a checklist somewhere," Perzi nodded, still grinning. "But the Emperor was apparently personally offended that the Human broke out of one of his jails, stole a warship, then went and stole a second ship out of a motor pool, before getting entirely away and disappearing. At the time, nobody knew who this Human, this Corsac Fox, was or where he'd gone, so you can imagine what happened when your reports arrived on *Wardog Charlie* subsequently."

Yeah, he could see that.

Crap.

"And we're going to make Uly an ally, right?" Lukyan asked.

"Those are my orders," Perzi replied, sobering. "I have a lot of latitude, but everything will be put to the council at some point, so Anna will have the final word."

Lukyan nodded. As it should be.

But he wasn't going back to the chorus anytime soon.

Lukyan decided to roll the dice. Again.

"In that case, I should probably get back to my ship and start the reload process," he said.

"Agreed," Perzi said. "We have a shuttle to orbit scheduled for about an hour from now. I figured you'd like to sit in a quiet place first, because everything will go crazy pretty quickly after that."

Suggesting that someone had a pretty good personality file on him. But then, the Vatazhko—*Anna*—had known which buttons to push to get him to move, so he supposed that every conductor had such a thing.

Against these sorts of situations.

Lukyan nodded.

"How soon did you want to leave?" he asked the elder.

"As soon as you are comfortable with the load-out," the man said.

Yeah, Lukyan was afraid he'd say that.

THIRTY-FOUR

Haydar was aft, welcoming the newcomers with Nasrin.

And explaining to them—again—that Uly was in charge, and not Dan.

Yes, a youngster, even among the Humans. No, Haydar was not fibbing. Nor was he EVER going to assume Speakership again of anything, so stop asking.

Kids these days.

Eventually, that got through. Enough.

Trade ship, so not a lot of warrior types, though a few willing to learn. More that understood engineering. A couple wjo Vahid was willing to take on as apprentices, mostly to see if they were any good as potential cooks.

Vahid's standards were higher than even Omid's when it came to professionalism.

However, their laundry was clean. And smelled lovely, regardless of what had been cooking for the most recent meal.

And no, Humans had absolutely no sense of smell, hardly any color sense, and were blind in the dark. You'll like them anyway.

Then Marlowe Michaels arrived and took everyone for a tour,

with the other three Human engineers: Cleve Toft, Leon Tyson, and Kit Simonson.

Sadek, Bahadur, and Taher would meet up with them aft, under the gaze of Azad. *The Wrench* who was the identical twin of Vahid the Spatula.

But the Mazhin folk needed to understand that the Humans and Ononguli were as much in charge as the Mazhin they might meet. And that there were more of them than Mazhin until today, so they needed to behave. Or he'd tell Uly to send them back to *Ahmadi* at the next rendezvous.

That seemed to be a fate worse than death, but more than one had commented today on how brown their gumbo had been, and none of them had ever realized why.

Omid turned to him and smiled that smile of hers that was so dangerous.

"Vahid is baking tarts for you and Nasrin for dinner," she said coyly. "Perhaps you two should go do some quality control sampling, before it gets served to Uly?"

Haydar grumbled at her, catching the grins and winks on both women, then assented.

Vahid. Best cook Haydar had ever known, even if he liked cooking Human dishes more than anything.

They still needed to start breeding chickens. Or finding a meat substitute.

Haydar had no hope of finding something like chocolate for Dan.

Not without sneaking into an Earth colony.

It might come to that.

"Shall we?" he asked Nasrin, watching Omid following all the new kids and leaving the room surprisingly vacant.

They'd also recruited a few dozen Khet for various tasks, to the point that, shy of actually having to do an armed boarding action, the ship could run. And Ethir had gotten the contract he wanted, so *Wren* would be loaded up and sailing in argosy with them to Lacium first, then Taeli.

Then...?

Haydar held out an elbow in the Human fashion. Nasrin snorted and took it, but she treated him like a doofus uncle most of the time, anyway.

Not that she was wrong, mind you.

"Are we doing the right thing?" he asked as they exited via a different hatch, headed forward.

"We are," she said. "Each of those folks will turn into the nucleus of a new way of looking at the galaxy. Uly's way. And he's right. More trade. Less piracy, regardless of how easy it can be, when a criminal can outrun the reach of the law."

"Nobody's tentacles are long enough," Haydar shrugged.

"Nobody's," she agreed. "But Uly is going to change a lot of minds, if he lives long enough. That will bear fruit long after we're gone."

Haydar nodded. Hopeful, but uncertain.

But then, he'd lost everything when that damned *Danumash Striker* had suddenly caught them broadside and wavebolted the ship into submission. All the others had similar stories, each gathered up from disparate sources and moved around, time and again, until they had ended up together on *King Hewitt II* on the most fateful day of his life.

So far.

Haydar rapped a knuckle against the bulkhead for luck as he walked. Nasrin did the same, listening to him mutter with scent and words as they walked.

Ahead, he could smell Vahid's kitchen. And tarts, with a bowl of frosting nearby, slowly merging down into a single splash of citrusy sweet.

And Uly finally had enough people to maybe change the galaxy.

Haydar chuckled at that.

Nobody would understand what was coming.

They would appreciate it later.

WARLORD

THIRTY-FIVE

Uly looked around his bridge. Drew in a proud breath at what he'd accomplished, noting Human, Mazhin, Thogin, Ononguli, and Khet faces looking back at him expectantly.

He finally had enough crew to have officers. To have departments and divisions, though he hadn't gotten too enthusiastic about it.

Marlowe Michaels was serving as Chief Engineer aft, apparently having *lost* a coin toss with Kolya for the job. Solomon Wyndham was twenty centimeters taller than when Uly had first met him. Still skinny, but growing sideways now and working on a wispy beard. Security was in good hands, especially with all of Dan's ladies handling related jobs and Nils Shevchenko stepping in as Solomon's assistant.

All of his Ononguli crew were fully integrated now. Yuriy Kovalchuk was learning how to pilot from Drew, with eyes and horns on becoming a Sailing Master, one of these days, while Sterling was training up several folks of different shapes to handle all the day-to-day tasks of a ship in service.

And Uly had all the guns crewed with expert veterans, the next time he had to sail into harm's way.

"Mr. Kovalchuk, what is the status of our force?" Uly asked, watching everyone nod.

"*Wren* is ready for transition, Conductor," Yuriy replied crisply. "Awaiting the order. Mr. Huff has already transmitted the flight path for *Ahmadi* and *Ironhorn*, and both of them signal green on the boards."

Uly nodded.

Two years ago, he'd been the lone officer assigned to a forlorn hope, boarding a badly damaged *King Hewitt II* as his own ship left, and hoping he could salvage something from the mess left behind.

Now, he wondered if he had transcended Conductor as a rank. *Batyr* had Captain (O-7) and Fleet Captain (O-8), but he might be the equivalent of one of the flag ranks: Echelon, Vanguard, Marshall, or even Fleet Marshall, depending.

He might need to invent something, because as far as he knew, the Ononguli didn't have anything for a commander of a squadron or a fleet. Nor did anyone else, save the *Auga*, most likely.

Nobody else took war seriously as a vocation. Pirates didn't count.

Uly looked around once. Drew and Sterling, ready at their positions. Everyone else watching.

"Mr. Kovalchuk, secure your station and take mine," Uly said, unbuckling and rising.

Yuriy blinked rapidly and froze. Uly gestured the man to his feet.

Eventually, Yuriy settled in Uly's Conductor's chair.

"You give the order, Mr. Kovalchuk," Uly said quietly.

More blinks.

Ononguli pirate who had originally volunteered to help Uly break out of jail, and had been qualified to sit bridge watches, mostly minding life support in those days.

Best time to get experience was when nobody was shooting at you.

And Uly needed everyone more experienced, for when he was ready to start bapping the *Auga* on the nose to get them to behave.

Yuriy turned to Rabiu.

"Mr. Khadijan, order the squadron into motion," Yuriy said nervously. "Mr. Roscoe, give them a ten count and follow."

Uly nodded, smiling at how Yuriy slumped a little.

"You'll do fine," Uly said. "In fact, you assume command for now and I'm going to go do paperwork."

Yuriy's eyes got big again, but he nodded. It helped that Drew and the others smiled back at him.

Training day. Uly believed in everyone learning new things, all the time. Yuriy wasn't ready to become an officer like Sterling or a qualified civilian like Drew, but he was getting there.

And if Uly took the rank of Vanguard, he would need many conductors, many ships, and many people who he had trained to help run a force, either as a communications officer or a conductor themselves.

He nodded for Dan to join him and exited. Rather than slip into his office just up the corridor, he started walking. Ambling, really. Headed aft and nodding to various crew members as they passed.

Eventually, he reached the wardroom, drawn by the smell of cookies. Or something close. Wasn't oat flour. That sugar didn't come from beets. The berries inside were close enough to raisins, at least for Uly's needs.

He snagged one and filled a coffee mug with something close enough to coffee. Dan had remained silent beside him, ending up across a trestle table.

"Trading up for troubles," he said as he took a bite.

"Not surprised," she grinned. "It's you. That's what you do. But we're in motion. Are we really going to Ononguli Space?"

"Haven't decided yet," he said. "Have the supplies. Have the crew. Lukyan will have gotten there by now, but nobody can predict how they'll react to his arrival, or what will happen after that."

"What troubles are you dealing with next?" Dan asked.

"Thinking about four ships in a squadron," Uly replied. "Obviously, the other three are not warships, though *Ironhorn* can fight some if they had to. Got to thinking about rank structures."

She nodded.

"Then now is probably as good a time as any to tell you," she grinned.

Uly paused, eyeing her carefully in spite of her smile.

"Omid has finally had a chance to come up with a uniform design she likes," Dan said. "She has most of them for the crew, but had to go back at the last minute and order more for the Mazhin that have joined us, since something cut for a Human or Khet will bag so badly on them. Was originally going to spring it on you when we got in motion, but had to delay. She's a little upset about that."

He started to ask why nobody had told him anything about all this, but remembered that he'd put Dan and Omid in charge of it.

One less thing for him to worry about.

They had.

He nodded.

It was all those little things that a crew had to do, every single day. Laundry. Food. Maintenance.

New uniforms.

"What did she decide on?" he asked.

It was Omid. It would be her decision, because she had assumed command of that section of crew operations, then defended it like an angry dragon.

Laundry, however, had never been as pleasant, fresh out of the shower when he'd served in the *Batyr* Navy.

"Medium blue," Dan said. "A jacket or tunic that buttons up the front, plus pants a little more baggy than we're used to. Black boots in a matte finish. Everything trimmed in scarlet and lime. Looks really nice, but she held off on telling everyone because she and a few others are furiously taking in things for all the new Mazhin, so everyone will be able to transition at once. Probably two days."

"And *Wren*?" he asked.

"Contractors," Dan replied, smiling. "They had a completely different uniform written into the contract. *Ahmadi* and *Ironhorn* are not officially your ships and crews, so they continue as they were."

He nodded.

"Do we continue to use our odd mix of *Batyr* and Ononguli ranks?" he asked her. "Conductor and Commander with Lieutenants after that?"

It was her turn to blink.

It felt good that he could still surprise the woman. She spent too much time ahead of him while he caught up to her.

"I think so," she confirmed. "Conductor is a rank the Ononguli know, as well as anyone who deals with them. We're breaking everyone into the way the *Institutional Republic of Batyr* does things, at least for the navy. If and when we recruit more Humans, they will slot right in, and nobody else really has a rank structure to begin with."

"My same thoughts," he agreed. "And right now, I am a conductor, but at some point, I will move up to something else, presumably."

"Governor?" she asked.

"We'd need a planet that I rule," he replied. "One that elects me to run their government. Lacium doesn't really count until they've had long enough to decide what they want. Right now, I'm just the dread warlord that keeps everyone in line. That's not a basis for a stable government."

Dan nodded.

"Warlord always works," she noted.

Uly rolled his eyes at her and let her laugh.

It was a silly concept. Him? Warlord?

And yet...

Even Fleet Marshall was a military rank. The top one, but beholden in turn to the civilian authorities—mostly the Party—in all things.

As it should be.

He'd signed a contract with Z'Gosza, and later Lacium, recognizing Uly as the head of a foreign, sovereign power.

"You okay?" Dan asked.

"Thinking about *Warlord*," he replied. "At the end of the day, anything else is simply a fancy euphemism."

She nodded.

"Not the guy I wanted to grow up to be," Uly chuckled.

"You'll be good at it, though," she noted.

"Only because of the team of people supporting me," he reminded her.

Uly finished his cookie and picked up his mug.

"Where are we going next?" Dan asked, joining him.

"Aft," he smiled. "I'd like to see my new uniform. Maybe start wearing it before everyone else, so they can see what's coming."

"The Corsac Fox will lead," she replied, only half-joking.

He drew a breath and agreed with her.

Where was he leading them next?

THIRTY-SIX

Lukyan had decided that he'd had enough of *Wardog Charlie* and the attitude problems of Conductor Holub. Conductor Gross and *Tanis Dragon* had been nice enough, but Lukyan didn't need to check in with those folks for his outbound flight, so he'd purposefully told Dmytro to find a different path out of the Sphere.

One not really marked on any maps. The quiet sort, where pirate raiders looking to cause trouble might slip around the side, instead of walking in the front door.

Elder Perzi had commented once, then simply smiled as they crossed the light-years. Probably all those old memories coming back to the guy.

Nobody knew when the *Auga* were going to get around to doing anything.

Or what they would do, when that day finally arrived.

By now, the Empire ought to know that Uly had gone to the far ends of Sector Fifteen, but they didn't have shit for forward bases in that direction.

Would they start building something? Dumb idea, as it might take years.

At the same time, if the Horde was gearing up for the next war, the *Auga Empire* might be able steal one hell of a sneaky march on everyone by instead starting to build roads and forts into Fifteen.

Thinking these thoughts, Lukyan had asked Elder Perzi to join him today.

It was the reverse of the last meeting back on Rayzian. Lukyan behind the desk. Elder over there.

Both thinking serious thoughts.

Lukyan had finished his explanation, and was waiting for Perzi to comment.

"Rude, that's what I think it is," Perzi finally said, then broke into a grin. "I can't find any holes in your logic, save that the *Auga Empire* has never really gone in for sneaky like that before. Usually, they waddle up with a big hammer and try to bash you on the horns with it. If that fails, they go back for a bigger hammer."

"I only mentioned it because Uly does everything in a sideways kind of style," Lukyan replied. "The Horde is probably starting to activate ships. What happens if the Empire doesn't end up coming after us? If instead they start hitting targets farther out in Fifteen instead of bothering us?"

Perzi grimaced.

"Nothing," he said. "Those regions are primarily inhabited by Zuath and Khet. Lesser numbers of Emro and Thogin worlds, and most of those are already Imperial. Plus the *Auga* themselves along the inner edge of Fifteen where Uly hit them before. Vynchen and Cyne and Zhoralong. The Horde will be mobilized, but will not bother reacting if the Empire goes sideways."

"And that's where I think we might have a problem," Lukyan said carefully, reminding himself that he was speaking to one of the *Lords of the Endless Plains*, right here in his office.

"Oh?" Perzi asked.

"They want to go after Uly," Lukyan continued. "And take more and more worlds from Sector Fifteen, since they really only control maybe a third of it on a good day. What if nobody stops them?"

"There are no Ononguli worlds over there," Perzi noted dryly. "Why should we care?"

Lukyan had made sure not to have this conversation on a Tuesday. Bad *ju-ju*.

"At what point will the *Auga Empire* maybe successfully conquer everybody else?" Lukyan asked. "Surround the Sphere and be in a position to start conquering the Horde from all sides."

"Never happen," Perzi growled.

"The Empire is nothing, if not patient," Lukyan reminded his boss. "They've spent several thousand years growing and consolidating. We've pushed them back as much as we could, but even then we lose a few worlds in every war. How long until they push us out, or conquer Rayzian?"

Perzi growled at him, but Lukyan held his ground.

"This is what Uly's trying to do," Lukyan reminded the elder. "Stop them now. Gather up everybody, everywhere, and push the Empire back until they behave."

"He's a barbarian from the ass-end of Sector Seventeen," Perzi snapped.

"And we're barbarians from the ass-end of Sector Twenty-One," Lukyan snapped back. "If the Empire takes all of Fifteen, how soon until they start pushing into Sector Twenty? Until their patrols start bashing horns with our Spinward flank and maybe trying to bite off chunks?"

"We'll stop them," Perzi said firmly.

"We'll need allies," Lukyan retorted. "That's those same people that you intend to ignore and abandon to the Empire today. What do we do when there are none left?"

Perzi started to say something hot and angry. The Ononguli were good at that. Kinda defined them as a people and a culture.

Lukyan was half-aghast at challenging the old fart on the topic, wondering what had gotten into him.

But he knew.

The *Corsac Fox*. The ship, more than the man, if you could separate the two.

An Ononguli ship, with a crew of half a dozen species, when no Ononguli conductor worth his salt would allow that.

Hell, sailors who ended up serving on somebody else's mixed crew ships were usually looked down on. The assumption that they couldn't cut it with the Horde.

Lukyan had been rethinking all that, too.

"Uly better be as interesting and impressive in person," Perzi finally said, settling some and sipping his tea. "He sure has changed you into a different person from the one I'd been expecting."

Lukyan nodded.

He saw the same thing, looking in the mirror each morning.

"Man's trying to save the galaxy," Lukyan replied. "Least we can do is help."

THIRTY-SEVEN

Maks had let his new crew know, before Lukyan and *Compass Rose* left, but only a few had chosen to return to the wilderness.

Most had stayed on *Scavenger Angel*, helping clean.

He'd gathered them up this morning in the aft cargo hold, where the ship had previously been packed to the horns with stuff.

Empty now. Cleaned within a centimeter of its life.

Almost new.

Expectant faces stared back at him.

"Good news," he grinned. "Got a potential buyer coming by later today to inspect the ship. Wanted to let you folks know my plans."

"You grounding us, Maks?" Oleksandr asked from the back to laughter.

"Technically, yes," Maks replied, causing everyone to sober. "However, my plan is to set up some profit-sharing from the sale."

Dead silence. Uly had sold him the ship outright. Lukyan had forwarded the crew. They were back on Rayzian, where they could get new gigs by lunch if they really wanted.

"My plan, after talking to some really smart people, is to sell a majority share of the vessel and distribute proceeds," Maks told them.

"You have two options from there. One, you take cash up front and be done. Two, and this is what I'm doing, you can retain a small percentage in a new entity that will own a minority stake in *Scavenger Angel*."

"What happens to the ship?" Stepan asked.

"I gather that the new owner intends to turn it into a hotel," Maks said. "Fancy cash to spend a night or weekend, pretending to live something of the pirate lifestyle on a fairly famous ship. We won't make much money initially, but my advisors expect the ship to continue to generate significant returns for at least three years, with a tapering off closer to five years out, depending on political and social events outside our control."

"Such as?" someone yelled.

"Such as a full mobilization requiring the ship be put back into service," Maks nodded. "Unlikely, since it is mostly a cargo carrier that shouldn't get anywhere near a shooting war. If that happens, *Scavenger Angel* is probably back to cargo hauling and we're still making a portion of whatever profits come in. Alternatively, if no war, maybe something big happens and more people remember us for longer."

"Like Uly arriving?" Oleksandr asked.

"Something like that, yes," Maks agreed. "Any option we pick brings risk. If you want money up front, you can let me know privately and I'll cash you out from the proceeds. If you want to stay in this as investors, that's the default unless you tell me otherwise in the next few days."

"Who's investing?" Stepan asked.

He was the sharp one. There'd been a reason Maks had make him 2IC.

"A Bondarenko cousin on my mom's side," Maks replied. "Not one I know all that well, but highly recommended by my parents, so I'm willing to give them the benefit of the doubt. This inspection is as much meet-and-greet as technical, so everybody pay attention, but stay on your best behavior. Unless you want to go back to hauling cargo for a living. My goal is that we're clean and ready, then I'm kicking all of you out to go have lunch on me and stay out of my horns this afternoon."

Lots of laughter at that. Ononguli rarely went into the business for such mundane things, but it happened. Mostly, they liked to be pirates. And got pretty good at it.

Maks was finding that he'd rather be rich than famous.

THIRTY-EIGHT

Maks checked the time. Close enough.

He rousted himself, checked the mirror to make sure he was presentable, and headed aft to meet his cousin.

Not anyone he knew directly, but Clan Bondarenko was bigger than Sobol by pure numbers. Nowhere near as infamous.

Had to wait near the rear hatch for only a few minutes, as Mikhail was exactly on time. Always a good sign.

Maks opened the hatch when it rang, admitting two figures in cloaks with the hoods up, then closing it behind them.

Weird look, but things happened. Maybe they didn't want business competitors knowing what they were up to. It had been Dad's idea, apparently, and word had worked its way slowly around the clans to the right guy to put up some cash.

First figure was male as he tossed his hood back. Tall. Skinny. Long face. Paler skin than most, to the point he almost reminded Maks of one of Uly's Human engineers, Koyla Roux, who had pink skin, red hair, and something called freckles. Little spots that weren't anything more than pigmentation.

"Mikhail?" Maks confirmed.

"Yes," Mikhail Bondarenko nodded. "Distant cousin, as those things are measured."

Maks had wondered. Wasn't a name he'd recognized. Or a face.

Still, money to make him hopefully wealthier than merely selling a semi-famous pirate Cutter would.

Maks turned to the other figure. Like Mikhail, hooded enough to hide from casual watchers on the dock.

Then she flipped the hood back off her horns and Maks nearly swallowed his tongue.

He made a sound kinda like, "gack," but nothing useful came out. Felt his eyes try to bug out of his head.

What the hell was the Vatazhko doing on his deck?

Her grin was triumphant. And compelling.

"Ma'am?" he finally managed on his third try.

Mikhail, at least, commiserated.

"One of my primary investors," Mikhail said with a wry grin. "Anna Shevchenko, Maks Sobol. I understand you've met, but not socially."

That was putting it mildly.

Maks's mind stammered more than his mouth.

"Hello, Maks," she said with a nod. "Let's keep this our secret, for now?"

Maks nodded. More or less.

Then his brain caught up. Rebooted. Something. He turned back into a conductor on his own deck.

"We're mostly shut down and operating on station power," he said. "Why don't we start forward on the bridge, then work our way back here?"

"Excellent, Maks," Anna Shevchenko nodded. "You lead."

He did.

THIRTY-NINE

Maks was exhausted.

He hadn't been prepared for how much that woman knew about starships. Or how detailed her questions and inspections could get.

Lucky for him, Uly had gotten it all cleaned out at Z'Gosza, because it had meant that his current crew could keep it clean for her. When she was crawling down into accessways.

They'd left the cloaks in the cargo bays, so more than once he'd ended up staring at her bottom from about twenty centimeters away, following her down into the guts of *Scavenger Angel* on hands and knees.

For a bureaucrat, she looked to be in better shape than him. And that took some doing.

Smarter, too. Like, dangerous smart. Uly smart, which was the level above Dan, in Maks's vocabulary.

They were in the kitchen. Tea machine was working. Three of them slightly dirty but nowhere near as bad as it could have been before Z'Gosza.

Maks looked at Mikhail. He'd hardly said ten words in the last two hours.

Mikhail grinned.

"I'm just the front here," he apologized. "Pretty face. Small percentage on my side, plus operations contract and profit-sharing. Ask her."

Maks blinked and turned to the Vatazhko. The Chief. THE Lord of the Endless Plains, if you wanted to get extremely technical.

And she had.

Anna Shevchenko had a pretty smile. And pretty mischievous, too.

"I have good spies," she offered. "Your mother contacted one of them about this venture, and I saw a great way to make a lot of money. Someone was going to. Might as well be me."

"Ma'am?" Maks asked, still possibly drowning here.

Lukyan had muttered more than once about swimming in the deep end of the lake with the scary monsters.

Didn't get much scarier, did it?

"*Scavenger Angel* has a fantastic pedigree, Maks," she smiled. "The various families of *Iron Wasp*'s crew will all know it. And turning it into a fancy hotel means that they can save up and make it a destination vacation. Especially if the Vatazhko herself takes to renting the whole ship from time to time to have diplomatic retreats. The right people will know about the ownership, and we already do things like that by spreading things around. I won't be Vatazhko forever, but I can set this ship, you, and your cousin up to also make money. Think of it as a reward from the state. I know that you've already gotten paid by Fortier to haul the cargo. And a reward from the families. Now, you will be in business formally. With me."

"So I gather," Maks replied, thinking about some of the conversations he'd had with Uly and Dan. And that whole team of experts in business. "What are the implications?"

"War with the *Auga Empire* seems to be a question of when, not if," she said, nodding to Mikhail. "He'll run this venture, he and a few others I'm familiar with. Quietly, with a lot of profit."

Maks nodded. The Sobol side were big, loud, brash pirates, but what had that gotten Adrian?

A small box on an *Auga* prison world. Probably doing manual labor.

"And me?" Maks asked carefully.

"Lukyan Chayka is going out to meet the Corsac Fox," she said. "Convince Fortier to come visit us, since we cannot compel him."

Maks nodded. The Embassy.

"You, Maks Sobol, will help my government understand what Fortier means for the future of the galaxy," she said in a voice that brooked no opposition. "And help us prepare for what's coming."

Maks nodded again.

Lukyan had written it all down and sent it ahead, but it hadn't felt like folks had been listening.

Turned out they had. They just hadn't said anything.

Maks was going to have to turn into something of a spy, wasn't he?

FORTY

Last time through Taeli, Uly had met Illya Tkachuk and Jamsheed Abbasi. *Ironhorn* and *Ahmadi*.

Station was under new management these days. They sent out a big welcome message as soon as his lightspeed wave reached them. All four ships sailed down close and settled.

Uly was having a meeting of local conductors, captains, traders, and interested whoevers in one of the bigger spaces on the station. No new Ononguli present, but the news was that they had largely started migrating back to their home Sector in anticipation of the coming war.

Mostly Khet and Zuath folks today, with a new Emro and Thogin he'd spoken with.

A Zuath captain had cornered him. Or something. Not aggressive. Aggrieved?

Dan and Yanouk had both stepped close enough that the woman had immediately calmed her tones.

"What about Ixtin?" she demanded in a sharp voice.

Rude, but strangers.

"I'm sorry," Uly replied. "I didn't catch your name, mistress?"

That caused her to flinch back. Probably expecting some stranger yelling back.

You catch more flies with honey than vinegar.

"Captain Purnima Begum," she replied, quieter. "The cargo lighter *Zh'Adom.*"

Not a ship he knew, but there were thirty or so in harbor right now, most of them tiny things hauling local cargo to the hub at Taeli and then off on spokes to other worlds.

"Where is Ixtin?" Uly followed up, still polite and friendly in his body language.

Zuath body language was hard to discern. In person, they reminded him of the ancient cockatrices of legend. Chicken-like head with a short beak and a red crest. Feathers in a variety of colors even wider ranging then Humans. Mostly white with some brown in her case. Hexapod, with legs, arms, and stubby wings that might help one glide a bit when falling. And reverse-hinged legs like a chicken.

Eyes on the sides of the head seemed to be the best gauge of emotion.

She blinked. Calmed some more. Dan and Yanouk did as well.

"Upstream and inward," she said.

It took him a moment to translate that. Spinward and Anti-Spinward as the galaxy turned occasionally got referred to as upstream and downstream, assuming a point of view "over" the galaxy and looking down. Inward meant towards the bar core of the galaxy itself.

"On one of the trade routes from here back towards *Auga* Space, yes?" Uly asked. "I've spent more time on the far edge of Sector Fifteen recently."

"That's right," she said. "The *Auga* suddenly moved an occupation force in there a few months ago and have started building a new station. Way outside their former lines."

He and Dan shared a glance.

This did not sound good. The Empire normally spent decades planning and executing new expansions. The *Auga* shouldn't be building new forces this direction, last he'd heard.

Unless they'd decided to chase the Corsac Fox to the far ends of space. Then it made a great deal more sense.

"I'd be interested in looking at your records, Captain Begum," Uly said. "Perhaps we might arrange for you to come aboard *Corsac Fox* tomorrow and brief us?"

Not the response she was expecting, but Uly had no idea what that might have been. From the look in her eyes, she didn't know, either.

"Yes, okay," she muttered.

"Excellent," he said. "If you could give us an hour or two warning before arrival, we'll arrange something special."

Like Vahid, fixing her lunch, while she could see the full crew. In their spiffy new uniforms.

Blue, scarlet, and mint. It did cut a dashing figure. And seemed to fit well with every skin tone he'd accumulated so far in his crew.

Begum nodded and wandered off. Dan slipped close.

"Should I start digging?" she asked.

"Quietly and mostly for information," he agreed. "I'll bother Haydar and Ethir and get them to asking around as well."

She nodded.

Uly found Ethir first, talking to Jamsheed Abbasi from *Ahmadi*.

"Sir?" the little man chirped.

"Ixtin," Uly said. "Planetary system closer to the Empire, I gather. What do you know?"

"Not a lot," Ethir replied after a beat. "Never got arrested anyplace with a name like that. Jamsheed? This is your region of space."

Uly turned to the Mazhin captain. Abbasi's tentacles began to meander, a sign he was in deep thought.

"Small system," he finally mused aloud. "Not much larger than Taeli. Central trade port, with a small colony on the planet below, mostly harvesting grains for regional export. Well off the primary trade routes, but *Ahmadi* never kept to the tourist roads for things. Haven't been through there in a decade, though."

"I doubt much would have changed, then," Ethir added. "Places like that tend to run on autopilot until something breaks. Why?"

"One of the other captains demanded to know what I intended to do about an *Auga* incursion or invasion at Ixtin," Uly replied. "She's coming aboard tomorrow to chat. I'd appreciate if you could find out more about the system itself so we're better prepared."

"Would you do something about it?" Abbasi asked, shocked.

Of course, he would be heading on to the Ononguli Sphere with *Ironhorn*, so they would simply need to make sure they sailed a different direction. Again, once they knew which ones were safe.

If any.

Was the *Auga Empire* suddenly lurching into motion? And what did it mean to the rest of the galaxy if they were?

Everything that everyone had told him to date spoke of a bureaucratic, deliberate place that made Z'Gosza seem wild and exciting by comparison. This was out of character for them.

How did he take advantage of it?

"I will investigate," Uly said, replying to Captain Abbasi. "From there, we will determine what, if anything, needs doing. Obviously, you and *Ironhorn* should exercise care, if you are known to be in my company and one of my allies."

"Indeed, Corsac Fox," Abbasi nodded. "Let me seek answers."

He left while Uly and Ethir watched him go.

"The *Auga* are punks," Ethir offered. "Big and bad, but punks."

"Bullies," Uly agreed. "If, however, I have caused them to start trying to take the rest of Sector Fifteen, then it is beholden upon me to perhaps do something about that."

"Time to go blow shit up?" Ethir asked brightly.

But then, he'd spent a lot of time in *Auga* jails for various petty offenses. Ethir did not have a high opinion of the Empire.

"We'll see," Uly offered. "I won't know much until tomorrow."

"Gotcha," Ethir said. "Lemme go frisk people for information."

And Uly was alone.

Well, not alone. Surrounded by a number of friends and many friendly strangers.

It was still his decision to make.

FORTY-ONE

Dan met Captain Begum at the airlock, but didn't bring all the ladies with her. No intimidation needed, as Captain Begum was by herself and this was a friendly call in station.

The Zuath woman was still getting used to Humans, though.

"Where are your people from, again?" she asked as they walked.

"Upstream and well rimward," Dan replied, intentionally leaving it vague because the last thing *Danumash* or *Batyr* needed was an *Auga* warfleet suddenly appearing at their borders.

Human tech, as near as Dan had been able to tell, was a couple of generations behind the rest of the galaxy, offset by Human inventiveness in coming up with new ways to kill each other.

Scale would matter, though. The *Auga* had thousands and thousands of worlds to draw on. Their fleet, if they needed one, could bring along more Devastator-class monsters than *Batyr* had ships of any size combined.

Humans would become another *Auga* client species, though Dan figured that they might have a couple centuries of indigestion trying to get Humans to behave and conform to Imperial standards.

That might even be fun to watch.

Humans tended to make Ononguli look mellow and relaxed.

She got Begum to the forward conference room where Uly was waiting. Suka Kuri had taken it upon herself to serve as tea master today, not mentioning who she was.

Or what.

Merely an elderly Emro woman with a tea service.

Haydar, Ethir, Drew Roscoe, and Rabiu were advising Uly. Dan took her spot on the end, with her ladies around the outer edge of the room.

Not to threaten.

To learn.

Suka Kuri was holding class today, as every day.

Tea got served. Captain Begum was served second to last, ahead of only Uly, putting her in the place of honor. She gulped and sipped.

It was really good tea. And they'd found something close enough in flavor, texture—even antibiotic tendencies—to replace Human honey. Similarly, a tree-nut infusion similar to cow's milk.

Perfection, as only Suka Kuri could deliver.

Uly gestured to Drew.

"My Sailing Master," he said simply. "He can ask the highly technical navigation questions I would need."

Begum pulled a flat wallet from the inner pocket of her jacket and slid it over to Drew, who opened it and pulled out a couple pages of flatrendering.

Everyone else sipped.

"Eight days normal sail for *Zh'Adom*?" Drew asked after a few moments. "Direct from here?"

"Roughly that, yes," Begum replied, surprised.

Drew nodded and turned to Uly.

"Four for us if you wanted to push."

Dan suppressed a grin. Of course, Sterling and his people would scan every vessel in harbor and understand their physical capabilities.

Then Drew would be able to judge each one for speed and reliability.

As they had.

Drew slid the packet to Uly.

Uly spent a moment reading it, then handed it to Ethir first. It slowly made its way around the table as Uly spoke.

"I'd appreciate if you didn't head there and tell everyone we were snooping about," Uly told the Zuath woman. "As you requested, I think we could easily take this detour and investigate Ixtin. I'm not sure what we might do to stop a formal invasion, but if this is merely an incursion—an occupation without a full fleet presence—then we might be able to assist."

"Just like that?" Begum asked, more surprised.

"The *Auga* are bullies," Uly said, turning stern. "I don't like bullies. People, of all shapes, sizes, and species, should be free to decide for themselves where happiness is found. The *Auga* and their Empire tend not to do that. My goal is to teach them some manners."

"You are one ship," Begum said.

From where Dan was watching her, the woman was rethinking that original outburst in Uly's direction yesterday.

However, the damage was done.

Uly was involved.

The Corsac Fox would do something.

"Today," Uly agreed. "Later, more ships. More people. Others who wish to live free lives."

Dan nodded. She simply watched Uly spin his spell about the Zuath woman. Draw her in. Make her believe.

"One station, currently under construction?" Uly continued.

"That's right," she managed, almost enthralled now.

"What sort of construction equipment?" he asked.

"One enormous cargo vessel," she said. "Larger than your *Wren* by about double scale. All the hull components were aboard, and they have been slowly assembling the outer shell first, with decks next after that."

Uly turned to Ethir.

"Usual pattern for them, yes," Ethir replied. "Shell, then they'll build in from there. Power will come along about midway, so it's just a derelict starship with no engines for the longest time. Gotta wire things up, then you add generators."

Uly nodded. Dan watched his eyes turn abstract and find a spot on the horizon.

"How big is the construction crew?" he asked.

Begum shrugged. Uly looked around.

More shrugs.

"Then we need to determine that number," he said. "I'd rather just blow up the station without having to kill civilians hired for a job. If possible."

If possible. Dan understood his distinction.

War would change things, but right now, the Corsac Fox was a pirate in the eyes of many. Especially those of the *Auga Empire*.

He needed better public relations, closer to Sector One.

"Trojan Horse?" she asked.

All eyes turned toward her. Haydar's tentacles flexed hard once, then got perfectly still. But he'd read Human history and literature to better understand his previous captors.

"Talk to me," Uly said.

"*Corsac Fox* is a known vessel," Dan replied. "*Iron Wasp*, once upon a time. *Wren* might not be. Probably isn't, but we shouldn't make that assumption too hard. Sneak into the system aboard something else we hire, slip in and storm the station when nobody is looking, then turn around and capture the construction crew? Safe way to get everyone out before we blow it up. Or whatever we end up doing."

"Almost makes me want to go looking for another *Auga* maintenance yard," Drew chimed in. "Ethir, how likely is it that such stations are perfectly standard, modularized, and deliverable from a single ship as pre-cut parts?"

Dan grinned as the little Thogin's eyes got shifty.

Way shifty.

"Not taking that bet," Ethir replied.

Everyone laughed except Begum, but she wouldn't understand. Zuath were merchants. Not pirates.

"Later problem," Uly pronounced. "Let's chat with folks around here about renting a ship and scouting the place."

"What about *Zh'Adom*?" Begum asked.

Dan liked the way the woman flinched when a whole pack of sharks turned to look at her.

Hungry faces.

"If the *Auga* take over, I have to move my entire operation somewhere else," Begum said firmly. "Doubt they'd go for the things we haul around."

Uly nodded.

"I'll need to do some research on our needs and the size of any force we might send," he told her. "Let's have a working lunch and talk about tonnage requirements."

Dan nodded and rose as he did. It would be her operation, so she caught the eyes of her team.

And Suka Kuri, though the woman was not allowed to strap on armor and help them.

Even if she was an Exemplar of the Arts.

Time to get sneaky.

FORTY-TWO

Uly listened as Dan and Drew both peppered Captain Begum with questions.

Ixtin Station wasn't any bigger than Taeli. It almost sounded like maybe folks were buying prefabricated components in many instances, then assembling them on site.

The only major difference seemed to be adding in more decks or extending the docking terminal arms, both of which could be done in place later, if the system ended up growing.

The *Auga Empire*, it seemed, had decided to add a watchtower to the Ixtin system. A forward observation post, presumably to let them send patrols deeper into the territory that Uly was in the process of...

Claiming? Cleansing?

What was this Warlord Corsac Fox doing with the outer portions of Imperial Sector Fifteen?

He'd started out intending to get paid to smash pirates. And had made a great deal of money doing it, while making sailing safer for everyone.

However, this was war coming. The *Auga Empire* making a precipitous and random move.

The *Auga*, who planned things over generations.

Had he gotten that far under their skins?

Useful to know.

Certainly, nobody had ever broken out of an *Auga* jail. They'd have been doing things differently, had anyone even managed it. Then to steal both *Iron Wasp* and *Wren*? Two more new events in their consciousness.

What did that third eye see, when they thought of the Corsac Fox?

Captain Begum answered questions sharply. Drew and Haydar had taken her information, requested more, and gotten additional dumps from *Zh'Adom* that seemed to satisfy them.

Things had gotten arcane.

"Honestly?" Ethir spoke up, drawing all eyes his way. "I think you are better off renting a certain volume of space here at Taeli, Captain Begum. Offloading all of your cargo and whatever food you don't need, then letting us fill it in until you come back to claim it."

Begum fell silent. As did the rest.

"Not like anything is going to happen to it here, after all," Ethir continued. "Since we'll be leaving the *Fox* local while we slink off like burglars."

Uly grinned. He'd gotten some of those stories, where four Thogin cousins operated like a tight team. An octopus, almost, slipping in someplace and stealing things.

The times they'd spent in jail were usually vagrancy or possession of stolen goods, because they'd gotten good enough to rarely get caught in the act.

Captain Begum turned to Uly. He smiled.

"Ethir's right," he agreed. "We can rent your vessel. Maybe hire your crew, but we can also leave them here where they'd be safe until we return. I've got enough people to manage a cargo lighter for two weeks."

Those side eyes blinked. She turned her head side-to-side to look at him. Left, then right.

"I'd like to go," she said. "And I think my crew would as well. Not like there are that many of us."

"Excellent," Uly nodded. "We can bunk in the cargo bay then."

"No," Dan said firmly. "I will bunk in the cargo bay with my team. You will be here on *Corsac Fox*."

Uly scowled at the woman. She was, as always, immune.

"I will, however, allow you to accompany me as an escort to Ixtin," she grinned.

Uly relaxed some.

It was her operation. She did those things, while he commanded starships.

Uly nodded sourly.

Warlords didn't lead boarding actions.

"Acceptable," he said. "Like we did Lacium, then, but trailing off and surprising them after you've had a chance to erupt from hiding?"

"I think so," she said. "We'll need to walk *Zh'Adom* to be sure. Then determine life support capabilities."

He watched her reach out to indicate her team. The ladies who would be leading the rest.

The Corsac Fox would accompany them. And get all the blame later, which was fine. Uly was learning how to separate off that other person like a cloak he could hang on a peg, just inside the hatch, when he returned to his quarters.

Uly versus the Corsac Fox.

"Understood," Uly acknowledged. "*Wren* will stay here. *Ahmadi* and *Ironhorn* will set off on their journey. We'll rendezvous back at this location later. I leave it in your hands."

And he meant it.

Warlords didn't lead boarding actions.

He only got to watch her do it. And worry about her. About all of them, but Dan in particular.

What would he do without her?

FORTY-THREE

Dan was on the bridge of *Zh'Adom* as the ship made final approach to Ixtin. In the three weeks since the ship had left port for Taeli, construction had continued apace. It looked like the outer shell would be complete in another two months, give or take. From there, decks and conduits, then thousands of kilometers of wiring. More kilometers of ducting for life support systems.

A great deal of finish work. At least a year until it was anywhere close to operational.

Faster than the *Auga* normally worked. Painfully slow to her instincts.

And the *Auga Empire* had only stationed a handful of Ultra-Bombers or Probes in the system to protect the construction.

Granted, Ixtin *Station* itself was armed, but Taeli had been, as well. And Lacium. These were civilian outposts in the middle of nowhere.

Corsac Fox was more dangerous. Uly simply didn't want to risk damaging the vessel that was the source of his power. Not yet.

Eventually, Warlord Fortier would have fleets. Then one heavy Interceptor would be less critical to their destiny.

Today was not that day.

Dan turned to Purnima. Captain Begum.

"Thoughts?" she asked.

Purnima had spent far more time around here.

"Coming together, but not there yet," the woman agreed. "And we'll just sail blithely up and capture the station?"

"They'll never see it coming," Dan pointed out.

Purnima nodded. This was just nerves. They'd been over the plan many times.

Utterly sneaky.

Uly and the *Corsac Fox* hadn't even sailed with them on this mission, in case someone were to see them at a stopover and say something that might alert the local authorities.

Or the *Auga*.

Everything perfectly normal.

"Captain," the pilot called, a Zuath male named Farid Kumar. "We've got docking instructions from the station. Any change?"

"Negative," Purnima replied. "Casual. As you go. We've been gone for a while and are looking forward to drinking and partying on station."

He laughed. Dan chuckled.

Only two other crew members were aft tending engines.

The rest were her people. Not as many as at Lacium, but more than enough to capture the bridge here, if they did it right.

Or cause a tremendous amount of damage while calling for the *Corsac Fox* to rescue them.

Dan had no intention of letting it get that bad.

Purnima took a deep breath, sighed it out, turned to Dan.

"Good luck," she said simply.

Dan nodded. Shook her hand, which had taken a little for the woman to get used to.

Headed aft.

Time for violence.

FORTY-FOUR

Nasrin had been with Dan the longest of all the women around them. Something of a second-in-command, though both Yanouk and Anari were starting to surpass her for skill. Would do so, one of these days soon. When they got older.

Nasrin was an artist, after all. Yanouk had been, initially, but Suka Kuri had modified her training curriculum for the young woman.

At the same time, Nasrin was much closer in age to Yanouk than she was to Dan or the two Emro women. Or Ciah.

Still, Nasrin was Second-in-Command today. Someone else would have it tomorrow. Nasrin wasn't sure if she'd ever go back to just being a singer or something simple, but she didn't have to decide today, either.

Today, they were geared up in the cargo bay. Boarding armor for everyone. Helmets that could seal, but that was automatic. Armed.

And Dan had brought along fifty friends. Six teams of eight people, led by Dan's women commanders.

The six of them automatically checked each other, then turned to their groups. Ciah was the second youngest in terms of age, just older than Yanouk, and had the least experience with doing crazy things, so she would be with Dan.

Nasrin was leading, because her tentacles gave her a significant sensory advantage.

Katya would hold the rear as a reserve that could be called on as necessary.

If things went desperately wrong.

Dan caught her eye. Nasrin nodded, then indicated that her men should move to the airlock. Most of the teams were Khet and Ononguli, with a few Mazhin from *Ahmadi* originally that had some training and had volunteered.

Those were armed with stun weapons only for now. Later, Dan would certify them for something heavier.

All of the teams had stun weapons. The six of them in command positions had deadlier firepower available, as did a dozen others that had been there at Lacium.

Slung across backs for now.

Nasrin loaded a Painsphere onto her omnibow and smiled.

"Everyone out of sight," she called over her shoulder. "Estimated time to customs?"

"Three minutes," Dan replied. "They called and were bored, so they'd moved to the dock. As soon as we are locked in and ready, Purnima will send a signal and open the hatch."

Nasrin nodded, smelling the scent of excitement around her, tinged with nervousness and a bit of fear.

Normal, when doing something like this. She left her faceplate open so she could track things while she waited.

"Cargo deck, stand by," Purnima called from forward.

Nasrin nodded and slipped back. Most of the lights were off, so the cargo bay itself was cast in deep shadows.

Hard to hide that many people.

The airlock hatch beeped loudly and began to open.

Light spilled in from the station, cut by two shadows standing slack.

"Hello?" a male voice called as they started walking forward.

Into the shadows.

Nasrin was on the left. Dan appeared on the right. The two customs officers stepped into view.

Nasrin pointed her omnibow at the men and smiled. Dan pushed the button to close the hatch behind them. The lights came up.

"What's going on?" the first man asked.

Both Zuath. Fancy uniforms that didn't mean anything to Nasrin. Gray. Badly laundered.

"You are my prisoners," Nasrin announced. "Would you like to behave, or do I need to beat you unconscious as a lesson first?"

Four arms and two pairs of stubby wings went into the air.

"In," Nasrin nodded.

Her team appeared and took stun pistols and gear from the men, then tied them with their hands behind their backs and put gags in their mouths.

Nasrin knelt in front of them.

"The Corsac Fox is coming," she said simply. "He's going to capture your station, destroy that *Auga* platform, then leave. You will be released unharmed when we're done with you. Nod if you understand me."

They did.

Nasrin smiled and stood up, looking around at her team.

"We have our maps," she reminded them. "And surprise. We'll walk somewhat strung out, like a group of tourists, until we have to run, then I'll expect you to keep up with me."

That got a harsh laugh, but the Ononguli who'd been with them when they first stole *Iron Wasp* had told all the newcomers about that mission. And the need to be ready to run the length of the ship without stopping.

Nasrin moved to the hatch and nodded at Dan.

"I'm ready."

FORTY-FIVE

Nasrin keyed the hatch then stepped out and onto the station.

Her omnibow was a long stick, seen from any distance. The Painsphere was smaller than some fruits. She held it low at her side, while her team all had stun pistols in hand.

She moved quicker than perhaps normal. A fast walk wanting to verge over into a jog if she'd just let it.

Behind her, Dan and Ciah would be slipping out soon, but Nasrin needed the biggest head start.

They were docked in a cargo area, off from where civilian yachts would be. Folks with money who wanted pretty surroundings. This was gray and stinky. Oil-stained and gouged with wear and tear.

Yuck. But she'd smelled worse.

She approached the first hatch with the omnibow low but ready to fire. She nodded to one of the men and he held a set of ID cards up to the lock.

Station Customs. It opened immediately.

Somewhere, a clock had started ticking. Would the bridge notice that their customs folks hadn't checked in? Were currently already done with the ship, more than half an hour earlier than they should have?

Were moving towards them?

Time was short. Critical.

Next hallway was also empty. They were in something of a back alley, if a station could have such a thing. Not the pretty places where rich tourists might walk, a promenade with bright colors and various food stalls.

More gray.

More spaces in need of a serious steam cleaning. Good thing Uly wasn't planning on keeping it when they were done.

Next hatch surrendered just as quickly.

The walls were white now. More soothing, she supposed. Bureaucrats, instead of dockers?

Something.

Behind her, Nasrin's team had stayed bunched up and close. They'd left hatches unlocked for Dan and the others, but Dan was counting on her to strike like her tentacles had teeth on the ends.

Snakes, which was so weird a creature description that she'd had to look them up in Uly's records. And seen the woman that she reminded them all of.

Nasrin couldn't turn people to stone, though that did sound like fun.

A figure turned a corner in front of them, at the next intersection.

Zuath. Male. He staggered to a halt, beak fallen open and eyes wide.

Nasrin snapped a shot that detonated a Painsphere almost exactly at his feet.

She always expected them to explode. To whump loudly and drive people back in a gust of wind and maybe flames.

The truth was something of a letdown, at least until this Zuath collapsed with a scream cut to a gurgle before he could get any oomph behind it.

Nasrin reloaded.

"All directions at the intersection," she ordered. "We're close and that might have set off an alarm somewhere."

She was locked into the distance, her omnibow having the best range on this team. At least among the stun weapons in hands.

Two men pivoted left. Three pivoted right, the way the Zuath had emerged from.

Nothing.

Good sign or bad?

"Map," she said simply.

"Right, down one more long corridor, then on the left side," one of the men called, holding a printout in hand.

Her job had been to take point. The tip of the spear, as Dan had called it.

Closest warrior to the enemy, even if she was an artist.

Painspheres could be art, if used correctly.

"Move," Nasrin ordered.

Because there were three men on that flank, she ended up behind them.

"Faster," she ordered a few moments later. "We're close."

Everyone began to jog. Then run.

Someone opened a hatch and started to emerge, ahead of them.

Her shot was just as automatic as the other two that hit the Khet woman stepping into the corridor.

Nasrin's was the only one that exploded.

The woman went down.

Alarms began to sound.

FORTY-SIX

Anari had been born Sabre School. Then forced to be Moss for a few years of stupidity, because the *Auga* were morons.

Now, she was Sabre again.

Yanouk was good, but still had moments where she had to stop and think about her action.

At the same time, she was basically a teenager who had only become an adult recently.

Anari had at least gone through technical school and served the *Auga Empire* for a time.

Until Uly and Suka Kuri had rescued her.

She had point today.

Her little sister's team—because how else could she think of Yanouk, who was a few years younger?—was back a notch, leaving a gap between them that let one flow in to support the other.

Presumably, Anari would run into trouble and Yanouk could step up. Or slide sideways and hammer someone from a flank with surprise.

Lacium, all over again.

Anari grinned.

Alarms began to wail.

"We've been made," she yelled over the noise, glancing back enough to see that Yanouk had the same thought.

Nice to train with someone so closely that they could read your mind.

Anari started to run.

Emro legs gave her an unfair advantage. Uly had once joked that her legs were as long as he was tall, which wasn't true.

Wasn't all that wrong, either.

The Khet and Ononguli with her fell behind. Yanouk caught up.

Emro legs.

Two of them against a whole station?

Bring it.

Anari had an Exostunner carbine that fit her like a pistol. Yanouk had gone with her favorite squad-sized version. Still stun, because Uly wanted everyone okay after this.

They got to a hatch that was sealed.

Anari liked to bitch to herself about those years of Moss School, but they also let her do things that Sabre couldn't.

She dropped to her knees and pulled a screwdriver from a pouch, jamming it into the casing of the control board and snapping the facing off. Maybe in pieces, she wasn't checking.

Inside, a board. Logic circuits. Wires. Basic stuff.

Auga Standard. Literally.

She traced a gold line quickly, then scrapped off a chunk of solder and popped off a chip with her lever.

Anari tapped the button relay and the hatch slid open.

Auga Standard. It had downsides, when you ran into some sneaky Moss School engineer with a gun.

Yanouk was through the hatch as soon as it opened. Already firing, from the sound.

The rest of their teams were just now catching up. They went through without breaking stride.

Anari rose and followed, last now, but that would likely change.

Flight bay.

Damn it, they'd been too late.

Ground crew were scampering for cover, but most of them were down.

Two of the three Ultra-Bombers and one of the three Probes were already launching down their tubes, though Yanouk had apparently nailed one flight crew in the open and others were pinned down.

Anari grabbed the two closest troopers.

"With me," she said, turning to the right and starting down that long wall at a dead run.

Behind her, the two did a credible job of keeping up, but she was firing as she went and they had their heads down.

Yanouk had gone straight into the flight bay. Anari was taking her flank.

Stun weapons let her fire randomly at movement, so Anari would be swapping out battery packs soon. There was a reason she had six on her.

The men with her were doing the same.

There.

Anari shifted her line and ran right at a long storage box that was about a meter and a half tall. Perfect cover for a pair of Khet hunched down behind it that had managed to stay awake this long.

Both took turns firing stunners at Yanouk and her people, but that meant that they didn't see Anari coming.

Until she was almost on top of them.

Sabre School.

Dance, with weapons.

Still dance. Much deadlier.

Anari leapt in the air without breaking stride.

Long Emro legs. Lots of adrenaline.

She planted one foot on top of the shipping crate, even as the two Khet looked up, their fish mouths falling open in surprise.

Anari pushed off her jump and got even higher.

Useful, because one of the Khet brought up his pistol to fire at her, but expected her to stay low.

Not to plant one foot on the side of a Probe, thrust up and back, and turn a back flip over their heads.

Firing straight down at them.

Gods, she'd always wanted to do that.

Her two helpers stood there with jaws so far open it probably hurt.

Anari laughed.

Around them, all the fire had tapered off to nothing. The alarms stopped as well.

Hopefully, that meant Nasrin and Dan had taken the bridge.

"Anari?" Yanouk called.

"Clear here," Anari yelled back. "You?"

"Three got away," Yanouk yelled. "Letting Dan know."

Anari nodded.

It had been a gamble, but things were like that in war.

Still, they'd captured three of six local defense ships.

Hopefully, it would be enough.

FORTY-SEVEN

Dan listened to Yanouk's report, nodding.

It had been a gamble. Hadn't paid off.

At the same time, she was in control of the station's bridge, because Nasrin had caught the locals enough off guard.

Dan turned to the Zuath woman currently sitting perfectly still in front of a control screen, watching the two troopers pointing weapons at her. Exostunners, but the bore on those was larger than the 'ripper, so more frightening if you didn't know what they were.

This woman didn't.

"Step one, bring all the electroshield arrays on, full power," Dan said sternly, a teacher with an unruly student awaiting punishment.

The woman moved with great care and precision, opening up a cover and then flipping the switch underneath.

Her screen turned red around the edges, warning everyone that the shields were live.

"Step two, put a local display in the main projection, centered on the station itself," Dan continued.

The bridge didn't have that many workstations, or that much crew. Nasrin was watching over the generators and life support, with public orders to use excessive—read *lethal*—force protecting them and herself.

"Show me the edge of the warp bubble the station generates," Dan ordered.

Every station had a Variable Pulse Spatial Generator, but only small ones. Designed to keep ships from being able to get too close in warp and maybe slam into the station itself.

Instead, the bubble kicked any ship out.

Or, in this case, kept them from entering the warp to escape her.

Dan checked the time.

They'd gotten ahead of schedule. This was the one time that wasn't to her advantage, as Uly and *Corsac Fox* were still out there in the darkness, getting ready to come down and help.

"Order them to surrender," Dan told the Zuath woman.

Behind her, a yelp of indignation got cut short. Sounded like an open-handed slap.

Dan turned to the interruption.

Station commander, currently off in a corner, handcuffed and under Ciah's scowling gaze.

She'd smacked the man.

Dan nodded for him to speak as Ciah stepped to one side.

"They are *Auga* vessels," he said, exasperated. "They will not listen to orders from the station."

"We're at war with the Empire," Dan told the Zuath. "Currently, our hope had been to destroy the new watchtower being built, to drive them back to where they belong. I'd prefer not turning your system and your station into a war zone. It won't stop me."

"This station can't threaten them," he explained.

"The Corsac Fox is coming," she growled. "He can. He can annihilate all of this if he has to. We're trying to avoid that."

The man blinked. Then he turned to his assistant.

"Tell them," he said.

Dan nodded.

"*Auga* patrol forces, this is *Ixtin Station*," the Zuath woman said in a voice that almost sounded calm and collected. "You are ordered to return to station and surrender, or you will be destroyed."

Two Ultra-Bombers. One Probe/Cutter.

Not really a threat, considering the station itself.

One of the Ultra-Bombers responded by rotating on its axis and loosing a wavebolt at them.

"Incoming fire!" the Zuath woman screamed.

Rather than try explaining it to her. Dan slammed a fist down on the control panel in the right spot.

The alarms started up again.

Dan blinked in surprise herself when the Zuath woman got lifted out of her station bodily. An Ononguli male took her spot.

Vitali Havrylyuk. One of Dan's people. He'd been with her when they stomped into engineering on *Iron Wasp*, in the way-back.

"All gun stations, stand by for defensive wavebolt fire," he said crisply into a microphone. "Give me two into the incoming wavebolt. Neutron Omnipulsar teams, engage as you bear."

Dan leaned back and nodded. The Zuath woman wasn't emotionally equipped for what was coming. Hopefully, Vitali was. Sounded like it, and that was what mattered.

On the screen, Dan saw a pair of purple dots detach from the station and move to intercept the wavebolt threatening.

"This Battery One," a new voice came over the intercom. "We at war with the three-eyes? Permission to engage?"

Vitali looked up at her.

Dan considered her options.

This was her operation. Commander Sheridan Chastain.

Uly's right hand.

Today, that meant mailed fist.

Rather than relay, Dan leaned down and keyed the control circuits herself.

"All batteries, engage three hostile targets on your boards," she said. "These are the only hostile vessels until I say otherwise. And be prepared for the *Corsac Fox* to move in to assist when it arrives shortly."

Hopefully, he was watching. The three weren't a threat, but they might decide to run. And then they'd get away.

The *Auga Empire* would learn soon enough, but she wanted them to find out after Uly had left behind the smoking ruins of that station, rather than forcing him to destroy it today, while there might be people aboard.

Dan blew out a breath and listened to the station's gunners cheer on the comm as they opened fire.

It was about to get extremely messy around here.

FORTY-EIGHT

"All hands to action stations," Uly relayed over the speakers to every room. Every crew member. Everyone. "Drew, take us in. Sterling, stand to your guns."

Both men nodded.

Corsac Fox had come in quiet. Most systems broadcasting any signal had been turned way down, meaning that someone had to be pretty much on top of them in order to see the ship.

Everything lit up now.

"I've got a runner!" Sterling called. "Drew, move me to where the Pulse Generator can hamstring that Probe. He looks like he's leaving."

"Not on my watch," Drew growled.

Uly sat and observed. NOT doing something right now was the hardest part, but he had good people. As conductor, his job was to let them work.

On his screen, Uly saw the horizon shift. *Corsac Fox* had a lot of gyroscopes. More than a ship this size really needed, but it was an overarmed Interceptor. Almost a very light Striker, at the end of the day. Especially for firepower.

"Battery One, put a 6dm into the Probe, plasma fist and not lance," Sterling ordered. "We want his attention and his surrender, if possible. Stand by to hit him with a lance for the second shot if he doesn't behave."

"Fist then lance," Battery One replied in an almost bored voice. "Firing one. Standing by on two."

Uly watched the bolt.

A simple plasma ball, wrapped up in a magnetic field and powering its movement with that energy. The larger the bolt, the farther it could travel. And the harder it hit.

Two settings. The first bolt raced down and would be a hard right cross to the jaw. The second, if necessary, would be a shiv to the heart.

"Probe engaging our bolt with one, repeat one, Neutron Omnipulsar," Yuriy called over the general noise. "We will get a hit, unless he fires a defensive bolt. Doesn't look like he was prepared. Or maybe not loaded."

Uly looked over, and Yuriy nodded sharply.

Maybe it really was a Probe, and not the more common Cutter. Armaments were generally the distinction. Probes were traditionally long-range scouts or survey vessels. Cutters sacrificed some of that sensor power for firepower.

Maybe they hadn't?

At this range, the ship was merely a bright spot, were Uly to look at it with the naked eye. Instead, his scanners were locked on it and he watched the bolt slam into the Probe's electroshield array with a tremendous flash of light that filled the sky for a moment.

Had that explosion been more than plasma, or had it hit hull, the vessel might have rocked hard. Possibly gone into a roll.

King Hewitt II had taken a lance shot on bare metal because they hadn't been awake enough to get their shields up in time.

Decapitation strike, in that case.

"I'm getting a surrender on channel five," Sterling called. "The Probe has had enough."

"Tell them to stand down," Uly said. "Any maneuver at this point draws fire. There will be no mercy if they tempt me."

Sterling gulped and nodded. Uly had to stop and remember that the man was still only seventeen years old. Roughly the same age as

Yanouk. Solomon Wyndham was the only person younger on the vessel.

And Uly had to be the hardass now. That would get through to people later. If you surrendered, you were treated well. If you went back on that, you'd be destroyed.

Behave, or face the consequences.

"Ultra-Bomber One is dead," Drew announced, drawing Uly's attention to the other part of the battle.

Two Ultra-Bombers against a station. Not a fair fight, even with surprise. Worse, they'd gone bow in and attacked, instead of running like the Probe had done.

"Hammer and anvil, Drew," Uly ordered. "Cut them off. Sterling, engage number two, but be prepared to kill your bolt if they decide to survive this."

"Understood, sir," Sterling replied.

Again, *Corsac Fox* slid around hard, heading off on a new vector that would close the door and trap the last enemy ship.

That one might try running at this point. Drive straight at the station, then pull up at the last minute and try to head out the back.

Except that the station was firing on him, as well.

Two 6dm bolts emerged. The Ultra-Bomber had one Neutron Omnipulsar, and not any small bolts.

Plus one bolt from *Corsac Fox*.

It almost looked like a hammer smashing a grape as the Ultra-Bomber died. The effect was similar.

"Anybody else feeling frisky?" Drew asked the room.

"Negative on scans," Yuriy replied. "I'm getting surrenders on all channels at present."

"Hail the station," Uly replied. "This is Dan's operation. She'll handle them. Someone ask Vahid to send up some more coffee?"

Uly leaned back.

Maybe he could relax.

FORTY-NINE

Dan finally let herself smile.

Most species didn't do violence. Hell, Humans were only really violent when backed into a corner.

You had to train sailors to be boarding troopers. To embrace that aggression and use it as a tool.

Even Sabre School was for scholars, and not necessarily killers. Though they did that well.

She'd seen Anari's stunt on the tape. Dan figured she would have broken her own neck if she tried something similar.

Vitali had things in hand. The local gun teams were locked down, because she didn't want someone deciding to take a shot at the *Fox*.

Dan studied local space in the projection.

One Probe, meekly returning to base, when the alternative had been to be destroyed like the two Ultra-Bombers that had tried to do… something.

Not like they had the firepower to threaten this station, but maybe they had the dedication.

Something.

It had gotten them killed, but this was a war, and those things happened.

The rest of the station seemed to be quietly waiting for the other shoe to drop. Civilians. Merchants. Just folk.

Having their day interrupted by a pirate raid that was actually something much worse.

At least in their eyes.

"Contact the cargo ship with all that steel," Dan ordered Vitali. "Find out what their current status is."

"Looking at station notes, Commander," he replied. "They are mostly shut down, and the crews are on that station working. Enough folks to keep the ship itself running, but not much more."

"Excellent," she said. "Look deeper and see if we can steal it. Ask Sterling and his folks to scan it as well. Be a shame if they lost the transport at the same time they lost the watchtower."

"On it, sir," Vitali replied.

Dan turned to the station commander, still sitting quietly in the corner when she walked over.

"You tell everyone that terrible pirates showed up and held a gun to your head," Dan told him. "Not far from the truth, at least as far as the *Auga Empire* cares. We'll spike your guns temporarily when we leave, so you can get back to normal business in a few days, like nothing happened. Am I understood?"

"Yes, mistress," he murmured.

Dan marked that down as a win.

Blow the half-completed station. Steal the container ship that had brought it. Maybe steal the one Ultra-Bomber and three Probes while they were at it, just to show that much more profit on this mission, as well as damaging the Empire.

The war had begun.

Dan paused and looked around the room. Her people, plus a few locals who'd been held during the battle.

"The war has begun, people," she repeated in an outside voice. "The Corsac Fox is going to free the galaxy from the threat of the *Auga Empire* conquering everything and everybody. Remember that later, when things start to get ugly. Your choices are freedom, or the yoke of the *Auga*. The Corsac Fox is trying to make sure you get to choose."

Her people nodded. The others were aghast. Surprised. Nervous. Fearful.

Dan turned to the Zuath woman who had been seated where Vitali was now.

"I need your help to get all the workers safely off the new station currently under construction," Dan said in a voice loud enough that everyone would hear. "And they can't go back to that big freighter, because we're stealing it when we leave. Are they better off on the station temporarily, or down on the surface?"

The woman hemmed and hawed. Looked at her boss, but Dan barked at her.

"I'm responsible for them, not him," she said. "And not you. We could simply open fire and kill them all right now. That's the outcome I'm trying to avoid, if you'll help me."

That got through.

"On the surface, I think," she replied. "Nearly one thousand workers. They'd overwhelm us up here, and we'd have to bring up food. Plus, they might get mad and try to do something stupid."

"Then let's start arranging shuttles to haul them to the ground, shall we?" Dan asked.

The woman nodded. Dan gestured for Vitali to stand up and ushered the woman into the seat instead.

Nobody had been killed yet on the station. Only the two Ultra-Bomber crews were casualties at this point.

The *Auga* might not appreciate that, but others would.

Dan intended to make sure of that.

FIFTY

Drew supposed that, had things turned out differently, he might have ended up flying a ship like this.

Imperial *Auga* Cargo Vessel 00356142895. AKA *Workshop*, at least for now.

If he'd finished his training under Hylda. Gone on and gotten his proper *Danumash* Sailing Master certificate.

Then gotten hired to pilot a beast bigger than anything he'd ever seen. Even *Wren* paled in comparison, but the *Workshop* was basically a small troop transport with stupidly enormous cargo bays attached. Plates some twenty meters wide by four hundred long, with enough headspace that the curve of the plates themselves could fit inside.

You shut down gravity and left it off for most of the ship. The remaining crew had been sixteen folks who Dan had taken onto the station with the same shuttle run that had delivered Drew to fly and a dozen engineers to get everything turned back on.

Or at least enough turned on to steal the beast.

Back home, *Wren* was big cargo bays, half of which had been emptied out for now. *Workshop* could hold large villages back there.

But he sure as hell didn't want to go back to *Danumash*.

Uly needed him. Hell, the galaxy needed him.

Heady stuff.

A comm line chirped.

"*Workshop*, this is Roscoe," Drew said, looking around his empty bridge.

Only needed one person to fly it, really. The others were for monitoring things. And there was a pretty command chair where one useless Ugotha female had sat when she commanded.

Drew was where he belonged, in the pilot's seat.

"This is Dan," the Commander replied. "We're ready to launch from here."

Drew reached over and hit the big purple button on his dash.

"Bay doors are opening now," he replied. "Mind your ceilings on landing."

She laughed. *Workshop* had more headroom than the flight bays on the station.

One by one, three Probes and an Ultra-Bomber eased out of their launch tubes and lined up.

Drew brought them in one at a time, aftmost bay being the emptiest one.

Corsac Fox launched a shuttle at the same time, but it parked off his stern and watched.

Eventually, it landed as well, and Drew watched each of the four ships disgorge a pilot and an engineer, who boarded that shuttle and departed with it.

Drew eased the bay shut again and triple-checked that everything was secure.

He was flying a small planet today. At least it felt that way.

Similar turn radius. And about the same acceleration.

"*Corsac Fox*, this is *Workshop*," Drew finally announced. "We are ready for flight."

Zh'Adom was already gone, having disappeared in all the chaos, while everyone had been watching Dan and Uly work.

Confusion.

Drew didn't figure that ship would return to Ixtin for a long time. Maybe never. Folks around here might not be as understanding in the short term.

"*Workshop*, this is *Corsac Fox*," Sterling replied. "Begin acceleration on your current heading and transition to warp bubble as soon as you can."

"Moving now," Drew said. "See you at the first rendezvous."

Only rendezvous. Back at Taeli.

This beast would take nearly three weeks to make that sail, when *Zh'Adom* had done it casually in eight days, and Drew had piloted the *Fox* to doing it in just under four.

But the war, as Commander Chastain had said, had truly begun.

FIFTY-ONE

Uly looked around at his cast of characters. His officers, if this were a formal navy, but only Sterling technically qualified there. Uly wasn't sure if Drew would, but Drew Roscoe had been a civilian at the beginning and hadn't changed. Plus he was back on *Workshop*, sneaking quietly home via a route Drew had worked out to hide from everyone.

Dan had stepped up from formerly being an enlisted sailor. Haydar had allowed himself to be blackmailed into acting like an officer when needed. Rabiu was an ambassador. Piruz and Ethir qualified as Uly's legal department. Or something.

Suka Kuri had made tea, then joined him at the table, as had all of Dan's combat group. Nasrin, Yanouk, Anari, Katya, Ciah.

Hell of a team.

"Ixtin is neutralized," Uly reminded them. "The new watchtower station was destroyed. We stole *Workshop*, as well as the four surviving guardian vessels the *Auga Empire* had stationed there to protect the system. I like Dan's phrase. *The War Has Begun*. Where do we take it from here?"

Folks turned to look at each other. Nobody except maybe Suka Kuri had walked in expecting a proper Council of War, but that was what it was. She'd made tea with all her formal seriousness today.

Uly had just declared war on the most powerful political and military entity in the known part of the galaxy.

Now, he had to make it work.

Ethir got a look on his face midway between mischievous and malevolent. It fit him, as he was generally laid back, but could get mean when he had to. Uly saw the same things in the mirror these days.

"Let's assume the *Auga* are being their normal selves, okay?" Ethir began, looking around for nods from folks. "That this was a one-off, heat-of-the-moment sort of thing, where some regional bigshot decided to shift a new station from wherever it had been supposed to be installed, and instead dropped it at Ixtin, where it put them in a position to move a big fleet forward to hassle us, farther out on the edges of Sector Fifteen. With me so far?"

Uly nodded. The others did as well.

"What happens when that explodes spectacularly in their third eye?" Ethir grinned.

"The *Auga* governor in question gets removed from office in utter disgrace," Suka Kuri spoke. "Their entire administration probably gets fired or demoted with them. A replacement is sent, but it will belong to a rival faction, rather than anyone friendly with the fool who cost them so much time and materials for absolutely no gain."

Uly liked that idea.

"It will be worse than a Trade Factor going down," Rabiu noted. "Everything this governor has done in office will be questioned. Possibly undone, but at a minimum, reviewed in audit level detail."

"How long will that take?" Uly asked the room, reminding everyone that the Humans were still technically barbarians from the far side of Sector Seventeen.

Unused to how the *Auga Empire* did things.

"Knowing the Empire, at least a year," Haydar interjected. "Possibly two to three, but only if the *Corsac Fox* more or less vanishes from their scanners and allows the bureaucracy to settle back into the mode of grinding wheat to make flour."

"Do we go low profile?" Dan asked the room. "Does that turn the

Empire inward while we build elsewhere, if we don't poke them with any long sticks for a while?"

"It might," Ethir replied. "Hard to say, because we don't have any spies on the inside, telling us how big the social and political explosion is going to be. Things like this get handled quietly. Folks transferred or taking a sudden retirement, while outsiders are brought in to replace them. Dunno if it would be whole departments, or if they'd merely swap out department leaders at first, then move on and replace staffs once they had a hold on things. But yeah, a year is a likely minimum starting point."

"What can we do with a year?" Uly asked. "We've got five new ships to sell, four of which will be easy enough to handle. *Workshop* will need to go to some Trade Factor back at Z'Gosza for disposal, I expect, where it will give him a huge leg up on transporting massive amounts of cargo. Perhaps enough to alter trade routes to accommodate, because something like that hauls things between major planets."

"How soon do we expect to hear back from the Ononguli?" Rabiu asked. "I know we're sending them more ambassadors and trade, but I'm not entirely sure how long it takes to get wherever and then return."

"Hard to say," Haydar replied. "They should have gotten there some time ago. As to how long it would take the Horde to gather themselves up and respond...?"

He shrugged, shoulders and tentacles combined to create something of a seismic effect.

"First things first, we get back to Taeli," Uly reminded them. "We'll have time there, considering how long it will take Drew to catch up, so maybe there will be news. *Ahmadi* and *Ironhorn* are headed inward, so they might also run into someone coming this direction and can update them. What I don't know is if I take two months getting *Workshop* back to Z'Gosza, or find someone to sail it for me. We cannot be two places at once, without splitting this crew down too much. I'm already missing Drew here on the *Fox*, but that's part of the mission. If I'm going to the Ononguli Sphere, I need him with us."

"Then we need to head to Lacium," Rabiu said seriously.

All eyes turned to the Khet.

"They'll buy the four, no problem," he noted. "Three cargo Probes that can be adapted as Cutters easy enough or just turned into specialist cargo ships. One Ultra-Bomber they'll probably keep for themselves. Then you hire or order someone to transport *Workshop* on to Z'Gosza for the court to adjudicate and then someone to sell."

"I don't have an agent on Z'Gosza credentialed to handle that task," Uly said, eyes locking with the Khet.

Rabiu would be the perfect person for the task, but Uly knew the fishman would rather be with him than returning home. The adventure bug had bit him.

"We'll hire someone at Lacium," he replied. "I have a few names in mind. Alternatively, we have Lacium's Chancery Court dispose of *Workshop* for us instead of Z'Gosza, to remind the Trade Factors back home that you have options. Then whoever we hire at Lacium sends a note to Factor Bitrus and Factor Bukra, announcing the sale and inviting bids. They'll have to travel to Lacium to handle it, meaning that they'll bring a lot of trade goods and ships out, binding themselves into better trade with the ex-pirates and helping better anchor your expected home base while you are gone."

"Can we trust them?" Ethir spoke the words before Uly could.

"Contracts with the right businesskhet will be ironclad," Rabiu turned to Ethir. "We'll need to nail down some agency contracts and adapt them, but I can tell you where the soft spots in the language are currently. Uly needs competent folks handling his operations while he's gone. His own Trade Factors, if you will, since he'll be the Governor over everyone. This is a good time and place to set everyone else into the pattern most profitable to us."

Uly nodded. He wasn't about profit, but the Khet of Z'Gosza had raised it to a religion. And Rabiu was right that he needed to start building up something that might turn into a governmental network, one of these days.

Warlords needed those things.

"You three sort it out," he said, including Piruz in the dangerous business triad. "Taeli will become an outer edge of the region I operate in. I hesitate to say my national boundaries, but keep that thought in the back of your mind, though it never goes down on paper. We'll put a mental border at Taeli for now, and the *Corsac Fox* will operate outwards towards the farther edges of Fifteen from there. Questions?"

There weren't any. Or rather, none with expectant answers. Uly understood that concept. He lived it, most days.

"Then we'll run hard all the way to Lacium from here, instead of stopping at Taeli," he decided. "Rabiu, find your people and get them initiated. Then find me a crew that can sail *Workshop* back from Taeli and get them up to speed. We'll have several days to get back, considering how slow even Drew can move. I'd like to make the swap at Taeli, and have Rabiu's new Corsac Fox agents handle things from there. This will be their chance to show me that they deserve a long-term contract and a place in my trade organization, so remind them that they can be fired just as quickly if they displease me. From there, we can start after our own ambassadors and visit the Ononguli Sphere and see what they think."

Folks nodded and rose. He'd laid out the pattern. These people were going to make it happen for him.

It was a heady kind of power, and he frequently paused to remember how much of it was built on sand instead of granite. He could change the galaxy, but he didn't have much margin of error for mistakes.

Therefore, he couldn't make any.

FIFTY-TWO

Lukyan had gotten into the habit of meeting with Harald for coffee or tea or something daily, just after lunch. Social as much as anything, but no agenda. Just talk.

The Elder had caught him up on all the gossip he'd largely missed over the last...generation? Wow.

Lukyan had talked to Harald about how piracy and trade had evolved, so far from the edges of the Ononguli Sphere that talking about the Horde was frequently a euphemism for *forever away*.

Coffee today. Dark and heavy. With some things added to more or less supplement the midday meal.

Harald was comfortable in the guest chair. Lukyan was stretched out behind his desk.

"You do realize that Anna's not going to buy any of it, right?" Harald asked.

Lukyan shrugged. They'd chewed on this bone enough times.

"Uly is Uly," Lukyan replied. "He'll do what he intends to do, unless and until someone manages to stop him. I'm trying to not be on the losing side of things."

"But the entire damned Empire?" Harald pressed. "With as many worlds and people as we have, with as many ships as we can call up from mothballs when they get out of hand, all we've ever done is hold the line. And even then, every time there has been a major war, we've lost a world or more. Hardly ever population, because the Ononguli on those worlds generally pack up and leave, but the real estate permanently changes hands."

"And Uly broke out of the same prison that was holding Adrian Sobol—the great and mighty pirate badass Adrian Sobol, mind you—and got away," Lukyan smiled. "Then he stole Adrian's ship with the assistance of some of Adrian's crew, none of whom wanted to go home with me and Maks. Then he stole another ship from the *Auga*. Man's leading a charmed life, and you know the old saying."

"*I'd rather be lucky than good*," Harald quoted. "Is Uly going to get us into another war?"

"Haven't we been at war with the *Auga Empire* for six or seven centuries now, Harald?" Lukyan shot back.

The mark of weeks traveling, Harald Perzi had changed from a stiff elder into just a dude. Helped that he'd had a chance to talk to the others on the crew about Uly and Dan, so it wasn't just Lukyan's perspective.

Harald grumbled.

"That's why Anna won't like it, I think," the elder finally said, his horns coming forward for emphasis. "This is the next war. Fine and dandy, but you make it sound like Uly and his Humans are demigods sent down to walk among us."

"He has charisma," Lukyan replied defensively. "And the Humans come from a much more violent culture than ours or even the *Auga*. Wouldn't it be nice to shove them back for once? Reclaim some of the places that used to be part of the Sphere?"

"He's not one of us," Harald snapped.

"That sounds like a problem for you and Anna, then," Lukyan snapped back, kinda surprised at himself for referring to the Vatazhko herself like that.

But he was just the messenger here. The ship hauling the personal representative of the Vatazhko and the Lords of the Endless Plains out to meet Uly. And Dan. And everyone else.

It was the *everyone else* part that made Lukyan smile.

EVERYONE else, when it had just been the Horde in the past. What could they do if the Horde had friends? Lots of friends.

Stop-the-Auga friends.

Harald grumbled some more. Subsided. Sipped his coffee.

"How soon until we get to Taeli?" he asked. "That's our next stop, right?"

"Is," Lukyan agreed. "Don't really need supplies, but that system is close to the region of space that Uly operates in. If nothing else, they might have reports that either put him most recently at Lacium or Z'Gosza, so we can plot our path more directly. That way you don't have to stand around looking tough and scaring the poor Khet that they have one of the Lords of the Endless Plains themselves in-system."

Harald laughed. Lukyan grinned.

Harald Perzi was an elder. Into his seventh decade, give or take. Skin losing that sharp red luster. Hair coming in white. Horns starting to yellow with age. Lean and predatory in build.

"Anna's the one they need to worry about," Harald said.

"No," Lukyan corrected him. "Uly is the one they need to worry about. Then Anna. Then, I suppose, you."

"Or you," Harald said. "You're here for the long term."

"I'm wherever Uly or the Vatazhko tell me to go," Lukyan replied.

"And if they give you different orders?" Harald asked pointedly.

Lukyan took a sip of his coffee and thought deep and dark thoughts.

"I'm hoping it doesn't come to that," Lukyan replied. "But when it happens, I suppose I'll have to pick sides, won't I?"

Harald let that one go, but his eyes told Lukyan that the elder expected *Compass Rose* to side with the Corsac Fox.

Lukyan needed to find a way to keep from facing that split.

FIFTY-THREE

Maks had started out this silliness as the now-minority owner of the venture that owned the semi-famous *Scavenger Angel*.

Today, he was sitting across the desk from the Vatazhko herself, sipping her tea and acting like this was a normal thing.

"And nobody knows more than *the far edges and some tiny, back corner of Sector Seventeen*?" she asked. Again.

"Affirmative," Maks replied.

Didn't help that the entire *Auga Empire* functionally sat between Sector Twenty-One and Sector Seventeen. The Empire, in the early days, had mapped the entire visible galaxy from their homeworld of Ajorn. Then set out and conquered all of Imperial Sector One.

Before moving patiently, deliberately outward from there.

"Do we know what Adrian was doing when he captured them?" she pressed.

Maks had to stop and think about that. Dan had talked about it, hadn't she?

"They'd captured that first cargo ship," he said slowly, digging out the details.

"They one with the Mazhin prisoners, correct?" she asked.

"Slaves, but yes," Maks corrected.

Uly and Dan had both had extremely tart opinions on slavers. *Hang them in low gravity or push them out an airlock without a suit* kinds of opinions.

"As I recall, they were sailing away from Human space as they knew it," Maks continued. "Looking for some small Human colonies, or folks used to dealing with Human ships. Adrian pounced on them and took them without any fight. Then *Iron Wasp* was headed back home, circling wide and running along the line between Nine and Fifteen when he was taken in turn. That took them to Vynchen. After he escaped, Uly hit Zhoralong, then moved to the outer bounds of Fifteen. Eventually, he and his expanded crew ended up at Z'Gosza, then Lacium, where *Compass Rose* came in."

The Vatazhko nodded. They'd gone over this before a number of times, but Maks couldn't figure out where she was taking things.

His job was to answer her questions. Period. Technically, he was a conductor, rather than a first mate, but she was the Lord of the Endless Plains. The Boss.

"If we had more time, I'd be tempted to set you up with an ultra-long-range Probe and send you looking for Human Space, Maks," she finally said, smiling as Maks felt his eyes try to pop out. "The problem is that you'd likely hit that other group of Humans first."

"The *Combined Crowns of Danumash*," Maks nodded. "Uly's enemies, though they don't know that. And only in the sense that he belonged to the other Human group called *Batyr*."

A rap at the hatch, then it opened and one of Anna's aides slipped in long enough to hand her a printout and leave, never once speaking.

The Vatazhko read it. Then read it a second time. Then she smiled.

It was not a smile that brought Maks joy.

"You'll need to return to your parent's and pack immediately," she announced.

"Ma'am?" Maks asked carefully.

"You'll be traveling with me," she said. "The Corsac Fox has sent another embassy. Or rather, the Ononguli vessel *Ironhorn*, in argosy with a Mazhin merchant ship."

"Illya Tkachuk?" he asked, surprised.

"You know him?" she asked.

"Smaller ship," Maks nodded. "Worked a different section of space than we did, but we ran into them occasionally. Usually, they were the ones hauling mail back and forth from farther out. That next link in the chain that connects Z'Gosza and the Sphere. Oh, shit."

"What?" the Vatazhko demanded.

"Chains," Maks said, suddenly seeing some of the pieces that had been obscure before. "Uly's coming."

"You're certain?" she asked.

"*Ironhorn* tended to operate closer to Taeli and inwards," Maks nodded. "That tells me that Uly is expanding, and specifically in this direction."

"Taeli?" she asked

It was his turn to nod.

The Vatazhko handed him the note and Maks read it.

Yup. Uly was coming.

Now what?

FIFTY-FOUR

Maks had changed into his lime green uniform, though it had no rank insignia anywhere. Technically, he was allowed to wear the solid circle in rose gold on either his collar or shoulder, but he'd never put them on this uniform when he'd taken off the open circle that he'd been allowed as a ship's officer. Hadn't had any reason to on *Scavenger Angel*.

And he was only along today as an advisor to the Vatazhko.

She also wore the lime uniform, trimmed in white, rose, and black. Her collar had the rayed sun of Rayzian, done in silver.

Vatazhko. The Lord of the Endless Plains.

Uly's equivalent, but Maks didn't even think that too loudly around the woman, let alone mutter it.

The ship was *Storm Crow*. If the Horde had a flagship, this would be it. Fast Devastator. Heavily armed, but not quite as big and mean as some of them. It was, however configured for the Vatazhko to travel anywhere quickly and in style, with enough space for all her assistants and folks, plus extra kitchen and laundry crew to handle this mob.

Vahid and Omid had taught Maks a great deal about how the support functionality of a starship could be made better, if the person in charge of cooking and cleaning took it serious enough.

One of the reasons *Scavenger Angel* had been so clean when they got back to sell it, in spite of the bitching of his crew at the time.

A couple of Mazhin hardasses.

"What are you smiling about?" Anna asked as she suddenly stepped close.

Maks had been towards the back of the group in boarding an hour ago. They'd finished the standard welcome from Conductor Klyment Gavrilyuk, Anna's personal chauffeur, though Maks didn't say *that* either.

Maks would have waved her off and let it go, but this was the Vatazhko, and a number of folks had turned to watch them. Most didn't know him as anything more than some punk who had been spending a lot of time around her, after a decade beyond the fringe.

Anna Shevchenko's look would not be waved off. He motioned her close instead. Close enough to breathe on, but also enough that most folks would miss what he said.

It helped that she was almost as tall as he was. Kind of like dancing, but she was almost his Mom's age.

"Thinking about *Corsac Fox*, the ship," he muttered, waiting for her to nod. "Uly has a cook who is amazing. And the Mazhin woman who runs the laundry has an iron fist about it. At the time, I didn't get it, but the Mazhin have incredibly broad senses, so food and clothing would be things that they notice sharper than anyone else."

"And?" she nodded, eyeballing him.

"And those two treat their departments with more seriousness and professionalism than most of your conductors would handle a raid to cut out an *Auga* warship from drydock," he said simply.

She studied him for a second, then a little light bulb appeared.

"I see," she breathed. "Yes, this is why I needed you around, Maks."

She smiled, and turned back to the mob watching them. The Horde, in many ways, as she'd brought Ezgi Vasylyshyn and Bakhtiar Teke, two other Lords of the Endless Plains, with her.

Teke was a fire-breather like Pasternak, who'd stayed home. Hated anyone not Ononguli because they weren't savage enough. Tough enough. *Something* enough to be dangerous.

Maks smiled when confronted and agreed with those fools.

Dan would tie any of them in complicated knots if they pissed her off. Then you had the two Emro women. Maybe three. Maks wasn't sure he wanted to tangle with any Exemplar of the Arts, regardless of her being Moss School. Or elderly.

You didn't get to be that old without learning a few tricks.

Instead, Anna took charge and issued orders to everyone. Sailors started leading them to where they would bunk on the trip out and presumably back. Maks, in uniform without rank tabs, caused a lot of folks to prey-eye him. Worse, none of Anna's people felt like explaining it to *Storm Crow*'s crew, which elevated him into rare air.

Clan lord, or something equally silly. But hey, all they had to do was ask.

Maks's revelation nearly tripped him over his own feet, but he managed to only stumble and not spike his horns into a bulkhead. Someone caught his arm, then smiled at him when he recovered.

None of these Ononguli would ask him. They'd all of them—every single damned one—go on being tougher than everyone else. Stubborner. *Somethinger.*

After all, they had horns and a reinforced skull. Once upon a forever ago, they'd literally knocked heads to impress the girls. Still did, at least metaphorically.

And didn't have to.

Uly demanded that your professionalism rise to pure excellence. But he also stopped and asked questions. Listened to random advice, even from the lowliest wiper in the engine room.

Because he didn't assume he knew everything already.

Could *anybody* in the Horde really say that?

Maks paused and caught the eye of the person who'd helped him not face-plant.

Pretty woman. He'd seen her around the fringes of the group, but couldn't remember her from before. Young adult, maybe five or so years his junior. Well dressed.

"Thank you," he said simply, watching her eyes get a little big.

How rare was it that an Ononguli male said that? Too busy being too tough?

Maks smiled at her. She smiled back.

"Maks Sobol," he introduced himself, still being pleasant and friendly.

Plus, exceptionally pretty girl. Woman. The sort he might have to get to know better, especially if they were all trapped on *Storm Crow* for a few days.

"Chervonya Borisov," she replied, finally letting go of his arm. "Thought you were going to fall."

"Almost did," he agreed. "Had an idea so utterly ludicrous that it did that to me. Need to tell the Vatazhko later. It will help her with the Corsac Fox."

"Oh, should you chase Anna down?" she said. "Should I help? She's my aunt."

And Maks took a HUGE mental step backwards, though he didn't move physically.

The Vatazhko's niece? Sure, pretty. Probably just as smart, if she was going on this mission.

Trebly dangerous, in that case.

"It can wait," he told her, not wanting to get himself into something he didn't understand. "Nothing that matters even before we get to where we're going."

"If you say so," Chervonya replied. "Wouldn't be that hard."

"No, but the explanation might take some time," he sidestepped things. "Thank you for your help, though."

Again, her eyes got a little confused. Not used to the sorts of politeness that he'd picked up mostly from hanging around Uly and Dan? And everyone.

He nodded deeply and gestured for the woman to precede him, mostly so he had time to recover mentally and think.

And maybe ogle her bottom a little as he went.

FIFTY-FIVE

"Sterling, identify that vessel," Uly ordered, indicating a new icon on his boards as they emerged at Taeli.

Returned to Taeli, really.

Sterling had guns and sensors today. Bello Temitope was flying under Sterling's command. And Drew's training. A Khet sailor that they'd hired when they added gunners and more crew, and the man was coming along nicely, sitting bridge watches in the same manner than Yuriy had.

"Conductor, ship identifies as *Compass Rose*," Sterling said with a broad smile. "Secondary note indicates that they are carrying an ambassador."

"Anybody else interesting in-system?" Uly asked.

"Negative," Sterling replied. "Have a note from the station that *Zh'Adom* was here, checked in, and left, so folks are aware of what happened at Ixtin."

Uly nodded.

"Bello, sail us down close enough to the station that I can talk to *Compass Rose* without much lag," Uly ordered. "Yuriy, let them know we'll be close enough to talk in real time in an hour or so, since I'm in no hurry."

Bello had looked a little nervous, but was handling himself well. Sterling, for all his youth, was treating everyone like another midshipman, same as he'd been two years ago.

Officer-trainee who needed to learn skills and polish, with Sterling as the eldest brother, for all that Bello might be twice his age.

A new way of thinking. And Yuriy was coming along nicely to the point that he might deserve a lieutenancy soon.

Uly would need that, when he started building out his forces.

Warlord. Him, though it boggled the mind.

He needed women and men he could trust. Who had been there with him in the hard times and knew how he thought.

Uly turned to Dan and caught her eye.

"Coffee?" he asked.

She nodded and rose as he did. Dan Chastain might be his Second-in-Command, Commander to his Conductor, but she didn't command starships. Didn't need to, while he could train up folks who would fly them for her.

Did that mean he'd have to put her on another ship, one of these days? Or simply step back and promote her to conductor of this vessel, secure that she'd watched him do things and that her crew had been trained up right?

They got to his office and settled with mugs of hot brew.

"What evil plans are you hatching now?" she asked.

So, he explained things. Thoughts. Misgivings. Dreams.

Dan listened, focused on him and sipping.

"It might be even worse than that," she said with smile when he finished.

"Oh?"

"I'm already something similar to your Chief of Staff, Uly," Dan pointed out. "If you step back, I should probably do the same, because at that point everything turns political."

"Party Secretary while I'm President?" Uly asked.

"Maybe not," Dan shrugged. "The First Secretary is usually in command, and the President is just a figurehead. Do you plan a Secretariat, like *Batyr* has?"

Uly leaned back and considered it. Z'Gosza had their Trade

Factors, forever in competition with one another under the benevolent gaze of their governor. It was also a place where the laws were as ironclad as a religion built on business could make them.

The *Combined Crowns of Danumash*, conversely, was guided and controlled by an inherited aristocracy based on the Seven Kingdoms that had come together originally. Rule by blood and marriage, with wealth something of an afterthought, because the powerful controlled the wealthy, and married them in regularly for money.

Batyr—the *Institutional Republic of Batyr*—had the Party. A meritocracy of will and capabilities that didn't really care about your birth, though Uly knew he'd been considered by many to be a Princeling on account of his father's most recent rank as an Assistant Deputy Secretary, one rank below the Secretariat itself.

It had gotten him transferred from *Vanguard Lesauvage* when that ship had gone into drydock for at least a year for repairs, though his time on *Marshall Castillon*—all three weeks of it—had not been pleasant.

Captain Savatier had probably assumed Uly was a spy for the Party, and had assigned him the worst duties, while making sure Uly's peers treated him like an outcast.

Sent him on a forlorn hope, presumably to die or be captured by *Danumash* when they came back for *King Hewitt II*.

Instead...

"Honestly?" he asked.

Dan nodded, poised.

"Right now, I think we've been reduced to me as some primitive warlord as our entire means of government. I should assign my Chief of Staff to come up with something better. Something more long-term that has the stability to not immediately collapse when I'm gone. Most of them do, from my historical studies. The only ones that last very long are built on strong and stable bureaucracies, for good or ill."

"Temper the energetic and blunt the stupid?" Dan asked, reminding him just how smart the woman really was, for all she liked to claim she was a mere sailor's daughter from the wrong side of the starport.

How many more like her hadn't been discovered by the Party,

mostly because of the color of her skin? Afro-Siberian. Beautiful, at least in Uly's eyes, but he understood that her coloration had probably been an impediment along the way.

She had no limits today.

"Something," Uly agreed. "The Party back home will outlive any single member, even a First Secretary. *Danumash* is too busy measuring lines of inheritance and privilege to really bear down on *Batyr*. The Corsac Fox needs something more than Ulysses Fortier."

"How much more?" she asked, causing him to perk up and study the woman.

"Empire?" he hazarded, mostly to see how she responded.

Her calm nod almost made him panic, but her smile assured him.

"You have something in mind already?" Uly asked.

"No," Dan shook her head. "But I've given this some thought as well. And I'll take it on as your Chief of Staff. I have some ideas. And will ask some people. You keep handling the military side of things. I've got the political."

Uly managed not to gasp, but he should have known she'd at least have kept up with his thinking. If not surpassed it.

He reached across the desk. She took his hand and they shared a smile.

Uly knew he could do anything with her help. Hopefully, she felt the same way.

FIFTY-SIX

Lukyan had moved himself and Harald back to his office, rather than have a big conversation in the non-privacy of the bridge.

Not that it mattered much. Most of his people had met Uly, not counting some of the new recruits he tended to assume were spies sent by the Vatazhko or someone.

Lukyan didn't really have secrets, and his loyal people badly outnumbered the yahoos, if it came to that.

Fortunately—and luckily—it was not a Tuesday.

So, he'd set up a camera and screen where both of them could sit side-by-side and talk to Uly. Potty break. Fresh tea. The kitchen had even baked something flaky and fruit-filled, once they learned that Harald had something of a sweet tooth.

As casual as Lukyan could arrange, at the moment when the Horde had made their first official contact with the Corsac Fox, may the Creator of All have mercy on everybody's souls.

The screen came live.

Uly hadn't aged, *per se,* but seemed to have grown into his face, though it was still weird that he didn't have horns. Lukyan unconsciously saw him as another Ononguli, and knew that was part of the reason he had part of Adrian's crew. They did, too.

"Corsac Fox, allow me to introduce Elder Harald Perzi," Lukyan began, noting that Dan was sitting next to Uly. Probably that forward conference room where they'd hashed out so much before *Compass Rose* had left. "Harald is the personal representative of the Vatazhko, and himself one of the Lords of the Endless Plains. Elder Perzi, Uly Fortier. The Corsac Fox. Seated next to him is Dan Chastain, his Commander and First Officer."

"It is my pleasure, sir," Uly spoke first. "Thank you for traveling this great distance. I shall try to be worthy of your time."

Lukyan felt the tiny jolt of surprise that passed through Harald. Silly git had listened to everything Lukyan had told him and Anna, and still expected Uly to be a punk?

"Thank you for meeting with me, Corsac Fox," Harald replied without much lag. "As Conductor Chayka noted, I am the representative of the Vatazhko. Her emissary, come to investigate such reports as we have had about your efforts to end piracy on the fringes of the *Auga Empire*."

"Trade benefits everyone, Elder Perzi," Uly said. "I gather that my most recent trade ambassadors to Ononguli Space traveled by a different path?"

Harald looked over. Lukyan shrugged and leaned forward again.

"We didn't encounter them, Uly," he said simply.

"We met *Ironhorn* here at Taeli, some time ago," Uly said. "They agreed to carry a Z'Goszan trade embassy to Rayzian for me, connecting the local Khet with the distant Ononguli. Additionally, they travel with a Mazhin merchant vessel loaded up with goods that should sell quite profitably at the far end."

"A Mazhin vessel?" Harald asked, surprised.

"Indeed, Elder," Uly nodded. "It was my expectation that they would be the sorts of merchants that might thrive in the Sphere, since they don't really wish to establish any permanent presence on a planet, but will instead travel about, bringing goods in demand."

Lukyan had to bite his lip to not grin. Mazhin might be the only folks welcome, for that very reason. Trust Uly to understand that better than any other outsiders.

"What kinds of goods?" Harald asked.

Lukyan listened to Uly reel off a list of things. All high value and probably commanding a premium on Rayzian.

Obviously, someone had told Uly the kinds of things that Ononguli merchants might want to buy from Khet.

Lukyan grinned.

Harald glanced over. Lukyan nodded, admitting at least some level of culpability that any outsider might be able to sell things to the Horde for a profit.

Uly had infected him, too.

"So, Corsac Fox," Harald said at one point. One of those breaks in the conversation that happen. "What are your plans for that ship and crew?"

Lukyan found himself holding his breath. Uly had let him have the sharp edge of his tongue, when Lukyan had raised that point before.

"The crew are all volunteers, Elder Perzi," Uly said simply. "They have had numerous opportunities to join other vessels. Even to return to Horde Space aboard *Compass Rose* and *Scavenger Angel*. As to the ship, I stole it from the *Auga Empire* directly. And had it adjudicated as my personal property by a Chancery Court located on Z'Gosza. I understand that the Lords of the Endless Plains, including yourself, are unused to such a situation occurring, and would be quite interested in hearing your proposals for how such a situation might be resolved delicately."

Then he leaned back. Lukyan nearly laughed, watching Harald's horns waver a bit in confusion.

Nobody was ever prepared for Uly.

"What are your other plans, Uly?" Lukyan slipped into the conversation now. Before Harald drowned. "We have heard some level of gossip about Ixtin, but came via a different route this time. What did you do?"

Because you should assume that some other fool had underestimated Uly, to their detriment.

Being on the losing side...

"News reached us of a new watchtower being built at Ixtin," Uly nodded. "The *Auga Empire*, presumably getting ready to send a major fleet incursion deep into Khet space around Z'Gosza and Lacium. We took the station, captured the defensive forces, stole the cargo vessel with most of the station itself still aboard in pieces, then the blew up the remaining shell being constructed."

Lukyan nodded. Harald sounded like he was swallowing his tongue.

Lukyan looked over, but didn't speak. Harald's eyes were huge.

Told you so...

But he didn't say that. Not to one of the Lords of the Endless Plains. Not if he wanted to stay in command of *Compass Rose*.

Long, pregnant pause. The best kind, when you were only a little mouse, watching safely from the corner. Lukyan kept the smile inside.

"How?" Harald finally managed, looking as much at Lukyan as Uly and Dan.

"They were unprepared for me," Dan spoke up, smiling in a way that only a fool would consider innocent. "The War has begun."

"The War..."

"I boarded the station with my combat team," Dan nodded. "Captured it. Then Uly and the ship arrived and bottled up everyone else for me. Remarkably few casualties resulted, which was our intention, as we could have simply annihilated everything there, were we of a mind."

More choking sounds.

Harald would learn. Hopefully, the good lessons and not the bad ones.

Losing side ones.

"Uly—and Dan—I'm bringing an ambassador, obviously," Lukyan interrupted. "Can we prevail upon you for a formal dinner? The kind where you give Vahid a day's warning and instructions to get crazy?"

Both of them smiled. Lukyan had been seduced by good food, among other things. Dinner with friends, instead of arguing across a conference table.

The Corsac Fox way.

"I think that would be a lovely idea," Uly replied. "We're expecting Drew and his prize ship in about thirty hours. Why don't we do the dinner in forty or so. That gives you time to come aboard and we can have some preliminary rounds of talks, then we'll get around to serious business. Would you find that acceptable, Elder Perzi?"

Lukyan looked over and hoped Harald had his horns screwed back in straight by now. The elder nodded.

"I look forward to it, Corsac Fox," he managed.

"We'll be in touch," Lukyan said, then cut the line and blew out a quiet breath.

Harald gnoshed on some turnover and scowled at Lukyan. Lukyan waited for the boom to fall.

He'd warned them. More than once.

And it would only get more interesting from here.

"Anna has no idea, does she?" Harald finally muttered.

"You didn't," Lukyan carefully pointed out. "Uly is special, Harald. He gets shit done. I challenge you to say that about many people."

"Anna," he nodded. "Not sure past that. And this is much bigger than she expects, isn't it?"

"*The War has begun*," Lukyan quoted. "Don't underestimate Dan either. She took Lacium Station by boarding it under hostile fire. You think the *Auga* are prepared? They might have raw numbers, but you and I both know how long it will be for them to get off their asses and actually decide to commit sufficient forces. What can we do to them with surprise? Real surprise, like the Corsac Fox and the Horde joining forces to stomp on some *Auga* punks?"

"He's not one of us," Harald offered weakly.

"So bloody what?" Lukyan snarled at his boss. "Fix that. Make him one of us somehow. Some way. Hell, if it was up to me, I'd put him in charge of all Ononguli forces for a year or three, just to see how badly we could maul the *Auga Empire* before they managed to get their shit together and stop us. Assuming that they could."

Harald started to snarl something back, but caught himself. Smiled. Took those last two bites of turnover and chewed instead of speaking. Lukyan drank coffee.

"Going to be an adventure," Harald finally said obliquely.

"Welcome to my life," Lukyan replied. Or maybe it was a Tuesday, after all.

FIFTY-SEVEN

Anna Shevchenko studied Chervonya as her niece talked.

"And he didn't want to chase me down and say something?" Anna asked when Chervonya finished. "Whatever it was?"

"No," she said, then smiled. "I think I rattled him a bit much when he realized who I was."

Anna laughed. Chervonya did that to most people. It was only worse when they realized who her aunt was.

"What are your impressions of Maks?" Anna asked.

"He almost felt alien," Chervonya replied. "Though I'm not sure how to quantify that."

Anna pulled out a datacard and handed it to her niece.

"This is a copy of everything we've pulled together regarding the Corsac Fox, based on Chayka's reports and details I've picked up from Sobol," Anna said. "There are sections on both of those conductors. Feel free to include your observations of Maks. He is different, but I wasn't sure if it was just me noticing."

"Alien," Chervonya nodded. "Is this Corsac Fox that impressive a person? What is a Human, anyway?"

"It's all in there," Anna said. "Physically, about our size, minus the horns and with tiny, round ears. Pink or brown skin, instead of red. White eyeballs and irises that don't shine at night. Much broader range of size and coloration than most Ononguli. New species that has emerged from the far side of *Auga* Space and seem to be making a name for themselves."

"Do we assume a normal Ononguli male, compare them to Maks Sobol, then assume Maks falls somewhere in the middle of the spectrum, with Humans at the far end?" Chervonya asked.

"That is one theory I have been testing," Anna replied. "You read up on the older personnel files we have on both Sobol and Chayka, then compare both to where the men are today. I presume a good portion of that change is the Corsac Fox."

Chervonya nodded.

"I presume you see this Corsac Fox as an ally, somehow, in spite of being alien?" Chervonya asked.

"I do," Anna agreed. "I sent Harald Perzi out to take the man's measure and report back. Lukyan Chayka has a quote in his materials that causes me great concern."

"What's that?"

"*Uly gets shit done*," Anna replied. "Quote, unquote. I want you to study Maks Sobol closer and see what you can learn about the man. He's been away from the Sphere for most of a decade at this point, functionally. How alien is he? And does that compromise him as an advisor? To date, he's been useful, but I need to know how far to trust him."

"How close should I get?" Chervonya asked, eyes glittering with what felt like mischief.

"That's your call," Anna said with a smile. "Don't burn him, because he's been useful so far, and don't ostracize him or frighten him, either. None of the people I brought with me on this mission really understand his purpose, to say nothing of the crew."

"You have him because you can use the man to measure the Corsac Fox's shadow as he casts it over Sector Fifteen," Chervonya noted.

Anna agreed.

"I'm on it," Chervonya said, then departed.

Anna smiled.

Maks had his secrets. Anna didn't need to know all of them, but then, she had contacted Maks's mother quietly and asked a few things that nobody else was aware of.

She'd see what her niece might dig up.

FIFTY-EIGHT

Dan had found Suka Kuri and set up a coffee date. Nothing formal, and she hadn't let the woman make them tea, because she wanted Suka Kuri focused on other topics.

Dan had access to an Exemplar of the Arts, after all. A vast and deep collection of wisdom and learning. She might as well take advantage of that.

"Your smile says that you are up to no good," Suka Kuri pointed out, grinning.

Dan matched it.

"Had a conversation with Uly, when *Compass Rose* first appeared," Dan replied.

Had it only been yesterday? Felt like months. Maybe years.

But then, everyone was adjusting to the new galaxy on the verge of being born.

Whatever shape it was going to take.

"And?" Suka Kuri pressed.

"Uly and I formalized a few thoughts," Dan said. "I'm moving to become more of his Chief of Staff, going forward, which is honestly what I've been doing up until now. I can issue orders while in command of the bridge and the ship, but those only work because I had sharp people interpreting what I say and doing it correctly for me. Never trained for anything like starship command."

"I would trust your instincts in battle," Suka Kuri nodded. "Not that much different from the dojo floor, when you get down to it. Slower, with more time to make mistakes and recover from them, but quite similar to the push hands drills that you practice."

Dan nodded. That was a quite cogent way to view it. And it helped calm her.

Dancing with some other ship. More push hands.

"What else draws you to interrogating an old woman?" Suka Kuri grinned.

Dan laughed.

"What form of government do we need to instantiate?" Dan asked. "That was the task Uly put before me. Something that will run smoothly when he's not around, either because he's off handling this war we've started or after he and I are too old for these sorts of things and retire."

Suka Kuri fell silent and Dan matched her. Coffee got sipped. Deep thoughts passed through the woman's eyes.

"I have heard tales of *Danumash* from the others," Suka Kuri finally said. "Aristocracy. While inherently conservative, often in bad ways, it is also one of the most stable forms of government ever created over long arcs of history."

Dan nodded.

"Inbreeding is eventually a problem," she replied. "Unless you have rules about that sort of thing, and laws that are greater than any single autocrat. However, those often assume a single species. If you marry across species, you ensure that there will be no offspring. That creates inheritance problems later."

"Fosterage has worked in the past," Suka Kuri nodded. "Both Yanouk and Hiko came to me under such programs. I could see extending that to formal adoption, in such non-viable scenarios. Or even in general. The more people that have experience with other cultures and other species, the better they tend to get along."

"What about the *Auga Empire*?" Dan asked.

"They conquered," Suka Kuri said simply. "My homeworld is not part of the Empire, but many of them are. Travel across the border used to be a matter of filling out the right forms."

"Used to be?" Dan pressed.

"Someone started a war with the Empire," Suka Kuri grinned wickedly. "They might eventually start closing such things down, fearful of spies and saboteurs sneaking in to damage them from within."

Dan nodded.

"If we had a thousand times the current resources, it might be worth doing," she noted.

"Or you might hire a ship to merely trade inside the Empire," Suka Kuri replied. "Gather up what general news is available, then bring it to the outside."

"Worth considering," Dan agreed.

"As to inheritance, the *Auga* are the only aristocracy," Suka Kuri continued. "They rule, and everyone else is reduced to taking orders. Non-*Auga can* get rich Can accumulate political power, even, but the planetary governors are always *Auga*. Their mental powers give them enough of an edge that they cannot be easily challenged."

"The Third Eye," Dan remembered. "What can it do?"

"Their actual powers, I suspect, are less than the media claim them to be," Suka Kuri nodded. "They can do a form of astral projection that allows them to see as if from outside their body, but I've never heard of the range being more than kilometers for even the strongest, instead of the light-years that some claim. They are also highly empathic, in the context of being able to read emotions at very short ranges. They cannot, as I understand it, read actual thoughts, but knowing someone's emotional state is generally helpful in negotiations."

"The ones I saw were amazingly beautiful," Dan said. "Short, broad, and powerful, too."

"They genetically engineered their species in the early days," Suka Kuri said. "Standardized themselves, if you will. Shorter than Humans, but just as massive, so compact. The third eye, plus a pair of hunting eyes. Their culture venerates science and scientists. However, I believe they had fertility issues as well."

"Why is that?" Dan asked. "Wouldn't that be something you fixed?"

"The powerful standardization work was millennia ago," Suka Kuri said. "They don't want to keep doing it, believing themselves to be perfection today. However, there are rumors of demographic decline. Fewer *Auga* born each generation, though at present there are perhaps trillions of them, spread out across thousands of worlds."

"So nothing that will impact our work today," Dan said. "And nothing that I have to plan for, even in the long term of a few generations."

"I would tend to agree," Suka Kuri said. "What does Uly want? What does he need?"

"He needs political stability," Dan said. "He wants to not have to become the dread overlord in order to create and sustain it, but understands that those are choices that he cannot separate into component parts."

Suka Kuri nodded.

"How does *Batyr* handle such things?" she asked. "As you only have a handful of such folks with you, I've not really gotten a chance to delve much."

"The *Institutional Republic of Batyr* is run by The Industrial Protectors Party," Dan said. "Folks join the party at some point, and can work for political power. Every five years, the *Batyr* Congress is held. Twenty-four hundred delegates, split into two groups. Local and regional deputies and specialist technocrats. It doesn't have much power, except that it, in turn, elects the Presidium, which is a standing body of around sixty folks that hold the real power. Ministers and important Agency heads are usually members of that group."

"Sixty is an unwieldy number," Suka Kuri pointed out.

"Agreed," Dan nodded. "From those sixty, twelve or so are selected as a Political Bureau, also called the Secretariat. Something of a High Council, with the Party First Secretary really in charge. There is a President of the Republic, but that tends to be a sinecure position filled by some Hero of the Republic type who has little in the way of actual power, except public relations."

Suka Kuri nodded.

"How long has the Party run *Batyr*?" she asked carefully.

"Four centuries, give or take?" Dan replied. "History wasn't my strong subject in school. There used to be other parties, but they went away. Presumably The Industrial Protectors Party subsumed them, but I'd have to have a book to give you those details."

"Good enough," Suka Kuri nodded. "Stable enough, I think, though I worry that a single demagogue might rise and overthrow everything."

"Usually, those get sucked into the mass and rise, become part of the Dodecarchy," Dan replied. "Or disappeared, if they are perceived to be too great of a threat."

"How are delegates to the Congress selected?" Suka Kuri pressed.

"Elections," Dan said. "With party members running against one another for support from their district."

"And you must be a Party member to run?" Suka Kuri asked.

"Yes, but anyone can pay their dues and join, if they choose," Dan nodded. "That and pass a series of tests on civics and citizenship knowledge. Really only important if you want to become a power. About half of all folks back home don't bother, and can't vote as a result. Don't seem to care. I never did, but I presume Uly might have. Actually, no, I take that back. He joined the navy, so probably didn't because the Party demands that the military be non-political that way. Folks can join after they retire. And often do, but can't while on active duty."

"And the technocrats you mentioned?" Suka Kuri continued.

"Experts in certain fields, identified as important," Dan said. "You, for instance, would be welcomed with open arms, were you interested. And if *Batyr* had something like an Exemplar of the Arts."

"Perhaps you should consider something similar in structure, then," Suka Kuri stated. "A wider congress of some sort, possibly sending delegates from each planet loyal to Uly based on population. Then bring that down to a smaller group of insiders, before reducing again to people like you and Uly who will actually run things."

"I feel like we'll need representation of every species, as well as every planet," Dan noted. "Places like Lacium don't have that much permanent population, but are central to Uly's plans. And have a wide mix of species. Taeli has almost no population, but should be represented as well, if they choose to follow the Corsac Fox."

"We have time," Suka Kuri said. "And you are a smart woman. Merely by asking these sorts of questions, you will be in a position to provide justice and equality to the widest number of folks. Especially those that intend to resist the *Auga Empire*."

Dan considered it. Noted the truth of the old woman's worlds.

And Uly would trust her to build something stable, even while he worked his charm on various worlds. Not all of them would have to be conquered. Some might willingly join, if the benefits were good enough.

"Thank you," Dan said. "I have much to consider."

"And friends who will help," Suka Kuri reminded her. "Remember to ask Nasrin and Katya how their respective cultures handle interstellar civilization. Ciah, too, but you also have Rabiu to tap."

"I shall," Dan said.

She rose and Suka Kuri did as well, towering over her.

"We need to build something that will last," Dan said.

And she had a few ideas.

FIFTY-NINE

Uly had met with Harald Perzi a few times. Conversations more than interrogations. Uly had already spent time with various Ononguli sailors on his crew, learning their culture in greater depth. Plus the time spent originally with Lukyan and Maks before.

And not least, Lukyan had seemingly prepared the Ononguli Elder for things.

Vahid had indeed gone all in on dinner. They'd even gotten some fresh seafood from another ship in port. One with a massive aquaponics facility aboard.

Then dessert, where someone had whispered in Vahid's ear and they got fresh custard tarts.

It was good. It was amazing.

Uly had Perzi on his right and Dan on his left. Drew was here, and the arrival of *Workshop* had really done a number on Perzi's state of mind, as the ship was larger than Taeli *Station*. And moved.

"So, Elder," Uly said diplomatically. "You have had a chance to meet with myself, Dan, and various crew members, Ononguli and everyone else. What are your thoughts?"

As his own father might have said, "*Time to put up or shut up.*"

And Anselm Fortier was an operator who'd thrived on bureau-cratic warfare.

He watched the man share a glance with Lukyan, seated next to Dan across the table. It was a knowing thing, but Uly had spent enough time around the conductor to see layers of meaning.

"This is an entirely new situation, Uly," Perzi said.

At least he had stopped saying Conductor Fortier. Or Corsac Fox.

"I am aware of that," Uly replied. "That does not make it a bad thing."

Perzi nodded.

"Part of my mission was to invite you to visit Rayzian," Perzi replied. "Once we had met and I had determined that the Horde really didn't have the sort of automatic hold on you or your crew that we do with Ononguli vessels."

Uly smiled.

"Can I travel under diplomatic immunity, Elder?" he asked.

Perzi nodded.

"That's the easy part," Perzi replied. "More complicated is your status as something of a foreign nation, however removed from the Sphere, that has active Ononguli members."

"All species are welcome, provided that they behave," Uly reminded him. "I'd even go so far as to extend that to the *Auga*, but I doubt any would take me up on it. I will not categorically deny anyone, though."

Perzi seemed amazed by that, but Uly understood. The Ononguli kept themselves aloof from everyone else. The Sphere was their realm, and few were allowed to live there. Or welcomed.

Something else Uly would have to break down. Too much of the galaxy was wrapped up on all the wrong mindset.

"How do we foster greater ties between the Corsac Fox and the Horde?" Uly asked.

"Honestly?" Perzi asked, pausing for Uly to nod. "You need to travel to Rayzian under a safe conduct. I'll arrange that, traveling back with *Compass Rose*. You give us a week to settle in and arrange things, then we'll have a ship at the border to escort you. The Vatazhko needs to meet you, and do so on even terms."

Uly was amazed. Shocked, even. But then he saw the faintest nod from Lukyan, mostly to himself.

Lukyan had been working on the Elder, probably all the way out here, breaking down some of the barriers.

Making this possible.

"What I cannot tell you at this point is how Anna might solve this conundrum," Perzi continued, gesturing to Lukyan. "Chayka has told me—as well as anybody who would listen—that we needed to make you an honorary Ononguli. I have no idea how that might unfold, but I think everyone should approach it in an open-minded manner."

"I am more concerned with making friends with the Horde, Elder Perzi," Uly offered. "Every culture, every species, will handle that in a different manner, and I appreciate that I am doing something completely new here. At the same time, it is necessary. The Trade Factors of Z'Gosza were initially hesitant, but came to see the greater profit from not having piracy problems. I haven't eliminated them, but the *Corsac Fox* has reduced them tremendously, both by driving some folks to operate elsewhere as well as by taking their ships away from them and turning those into gendarme forces instead. And profits are up for those Khet to the point they are actively buying or building their own warships and hunting pirates, when in the past they were busy funding such folks, either as protection money or to convince them to prey on other corporate entities."

"That will be an interesting thing to explain to the Horde." Perzi laughed. "Lukyan assures me that he'd told you how most Ononguli ships operate in peacetime."

"He has," Uly agreed, nodding to Lukyan. "Pirates. Except that I might have a challenge to put before all those conductors."

"Oh?"

"The line between pirate and privateer is a thin one, Elder Perzi," Uly noted, smiling. "The former operating purely for profit, with the latter seeing profit, but operating under acknowledged rules of warfare, against an enemy nation. In my case, *Corsac Fox* was hunting pirates for the Trade Factors of Z'Gosza."

He paused and waited for the elder to nod, catching up with his logic.

"What if the Vatazhko, the Lord of the Endless Plains herself, ordered all those pirates to begin preying exclusively on *Auga* shipping? They still get to be pirates, because heaven forbid they stop that sort of thing immediately and start acting civilized. At the same time, they materially damage the Horde's primary enemy, as a prelude to the next war, which everyone I've been able to consult assures me is already overdue, as those things are calculated."

"What would the Corsac Fox be doing during this time?" Perzi asked.

"I just blew up an *Auga* watchtower," Uly reminded him. "Stole or destroyed six defenders, then took away the cargo beast we call *Workshop*. Dan said it correctly when she told the folks at Ixtin that the war had begun. The Corsac Fox's war on the *Auga*, and on empire as a concept. The Empire is just a larger version of the *Combined Crowns of Danumash*, who were already my enemies. I'm merely extending this to a larger theater of operations."

"Uly, would you be interested in helping plan and lead a raid?" Lukyan asked.

The whole room dropped to sudden silence. Lukyan flinched, then drew a breath and continued.

"The Vatazhko might be much more amenable, if you were there, leading us in, as it were," he said. "There have to be places you might hit profitably."

"There are," Uly agreed. "Several, as a matter of fact, though all are far removed from this portion of Sector Fifteen. Too far away and too well defended for a single interceptor to be able to do anything about them. A squadron, however..."

He let that trail off, eyes locked on Harald Perzi now. Challenging the Ononguli Elder to put up or shut up.

Perzi sensed that.

"I'll talk to Anna," he nodded. "She might even agree, but I make no promises."

"All I ask is communications," Uly replied. "I'm already committed to my war."

"With or without the Ononguli?" Perzi asked, shocked.

"The Ononguli aren't involved now, save for my current crew,

Elder," Uly reminded him. "You can choose to join later and be welcome. Any Ononguli will be, provided they are joining my forces and operating under my command. Otherwise, they are just pirates. I do not accept piracy as an acceptable solution. Make them privateers, instead."

Perzi nodded. Uly smiled.

At least they understood each other.

SIXTY

Maks studied the newcomers around the big table. He knew Conductor Tkachuk from *Ironhorn*. The man had delivered mail more than once, all the way out to places like Lacium.

The weird part was watching Tkachuk sit next to an older Mazhin gentleman and share inside jokes like two old drinking buddies.

A year ago, he would have been aghast.

Before he met Haydar, Piruz, Nasrin, and the others, all of whom reacted very similarly to Uly.

Relaxed.

The three Khet ambassadors that *Ironhorn* was transporting were almost an afterthought, and Anna had had meetings with them under more formal settings.

Then she'd ordered him to meet with Tkachuk and Abbasi to more or less pump them for news.

Helped that he'd been there already. Knew Uly. Had felt the man's charm envelop a room and transform everyone.

"So what are your plans from here, Conductor Tkachuk?" Maks asked, in his role as chairman of the room.

Or something.

A dozen of Anna's advisors, including her niece, all but deferring to Maks Sobol, who still hadn't bothered putting any rank tabs on his lime uniform.

Might not, at least until he figured out what Anna Shevchenko planned for him. Or ordered it.

Maks had no doubts that he was a piece on her game board. At least until she sacrificed him for something.

"Originally, I was hired to haul those Khet to Rayzian," Tkachuk replied. "Technically, since the Vatazhko herself is here, I'm done. Dunno past that. Might end up escorting *Ahmadi* in anyway, just because it's been a while since we've been home and that's still the best place to let my crew have a week or two to blow off steam."

Maks nodded. Most ships were like that. Krilic, where they were right now on the border, was a border world, in every sense of the word. Raw and rough, when you could sail on to Rayzian or one of the other core worlds for so much more, if you could manage it.

"What about Ixtin?" Chervonya asked from a spot on a side of the large, square table. "You had notes from that Zuath ship that was at Taeli when you passed through with the Corsac Fox."

"Uly was going to sail over and crack heads together," Tkachuk replied. "Seemed to think it wouldn't be a problem, but he sent us on and made sure we took a different route, so that was the last I know."

"An *Auga* incursion, though?" Chervonya pressed.

"Uly didn't tell me what his plans were," Tkachuk replied in a grimmer voice, growing a little annoyed with being questioned.

Maks kept his grin inside, seeing the prototypical Ononguli male response to things.

"Let's assume that Uly did whatever needed doing," Maks intruded before the woman spoke. And maybe got Tkachuk riled up. Unnecessarily. "He was still planning to travel this direction?"

"He was, but I'm told that *Compass Rose* was heading that way with an ambassador?" Tkachuk asked.

Maks nodded, without mentioning who that person was. Didn't need to spook Conductor Tkachuk.

"Then, with any luck, they ran into each other somewhere like Taeli," Tkachuk replied. "Corsac Fox operating that far forward from

Z'Gosza meant that they could find each other pretty quickly. Dunno what they'd do from there. Shouldn't need long to find out, though."

Maks agreed, then turned his attention to the mass of tentacles sniffing everybody much closer than most of the Ononguli in the room probably understood.

Omid had said something along those lines at one point, demonstrating how much more they saw and sensed than anybody else in range.

Jamsheed Abbasi studied him back, tentacles starting to point his direction like snakes.

Maks thought friendly thoughts and tried to remain perfectly calm.

"I have an inventory of your cargo," Maks told the man, somehow still in charge with assistants, when he was supposed to be the assistant.

Wasn't he?

Abbasi nodded.

"What are your plans after you deliver everything and make a stupid amount of profit from it?" Maks smiled, skipping over about three pages of questions someone with more of a customs and legalisms mindset might wade through first.

At least he caught the Mazhin off guard. The tentacles flinching gave it away.

"That probably depends on the sorts of visas we might be able to arrange," Abbasi replied carefully. "Previously, Ononguli trade tended to stop at the border itself, so we didn't engage all that much. Since we were part of a diplomatic mission this time, I gather we'll be one of few outsiders to visit the capital directly. What might we be allowed to do after that?"

As in, did we have to immediately leave Ononguli Space, or could we trade inside for a while, maybe representing something exotic?

Maks considered his words with care, wondering if this was the exact reason the Vatazhko had put him in charge, instead of her niece, who was also present.

"Would remaining inside the Sphere to trade be of interest?" Maks asked, volleying it right back into that ball of snakes adroitly.

"There is great potential," Abbasi nodded. "Outsiders, and all that. And I have spoken with the Corsac Fox about the need to better understand other species. That was part of the reason I allowed the man to recruit a block of my younger sailors off *Ahmadi* to join him for a time. Cultural exchanges, as it were, since that ship has so many backgrounds represented in a single place."

Maks nodded. Uly, working his magic, even if Abbasi might have thought it was his idea.

Silly man.

Maks glanced over at Chervonya anyway, even though she had lapsed back into silence. And none of the others with them had spoken at all. She had no response.

And he was acting like the conductor here. For what it was worth.

"I will speak with the Vatazhko," Maks said. "Ask if she will allow it, though I hope she will. As you said, understanding one another better. I think that we will only remain here for a bit, then return to Rayzian, and thus nothing has to be finalized before then."

"Thank you, Conductor Sobol," Abbasi nodded. "Perhaps we will be able to host you aboard *Ahmadi* at some point. And even the Vatazhko, were she of a mind, though I do appreciate that she is a busy woman."

And thus, might turn you down for reasons not discussed in public. Maks understood that. Abbasi seemed quite sharp at the political side of things, where everything was often couched in possibilities.

"I would like that," Maks said honestly. "And look forward to meeting your crew in relaxed settings. For now, let me convey things to the Vatazhko that she might be able to move as quickly as she desires."

He rose first, and everyone was up a moment behind.

Maks even found himself starting to lean across the table to shake hands, which he had absolutely picked up from Uly.

Weirdly, Tkachuk did the same thing. Then Abbasi.

Maybe Uly had worked enough of his magic on those folks as well.

SIXTY-ONE

Chervonya accompanied Maks Sobol into a smaller meeting room. All of the others that had been with them to meet Tkachuk and Abbasi drifted off, but they'd been available to answer technical questions, had any arisen.

Or rescue Maks, had he started down a rabbit hole or over-spoken.

He'd handled himself better than even Chervonya had expected. And that after spending several meetings where she was paying more attention to him than the outsiders being interviewed.

Anna was seated when they entered. She gestured both of them to grab coffee and join her. Chervonya noted that it was just the three of them.

Maks flinched a few moments later when he came to the same realization. Still, he got coffee from the flask and even poured her a mug.

Chervonya was still getting used to an Ononguli male who was friendly and polite even when he didn't seem to be immediately interested in romancing her.

Alien, but in a good way.

They sat across from Anna, forming a triangle with a chair between her and Maks.

He looked like he needed that extra bit of space. Man still twitched the slightest bit when she got within reach of him.

Afraid of her? Or just Anna?

"How did it go?" her aunt asked, looking at Maks to speak.

"Good," he said simply. Nothing flowery. Nothing complicated. "*Ahmadi* would like to explore the option of trading in Horde Space for a while. I told them I would put in a good word, but that was your decision. *Ironhorn* intends to travel with them, or at least head on to Rayzian, then take crew downtime. I have an open invitation to dine aboard *Ahmadi* when they get home. You do as well, but I hedged that with various deflections that let you accept or reject without offering offense."

Then he fell silent. Chervonya kept her jaw from falling open.

Exactly precise, and nothing more. And no male ego involved, either. Professionalism.

But that was the thing he'd said about the Corsac Fox more than once when asked. Professionalism that rose to excellence. Check your ego at the door and get the job done.

Because Uly got shit done.

More and more, Chervonya found herself looking forward to meeting this alien warlord.

This other alien, rather, because Maks was a breath of fresh air, compared to most of the men she met, who saw her as a way to gain access to her aunt's power.

Maks wasn't afraid of either of them. Nor worshiping them. Simply doing the job Anna had assigned him.

Chervonya caught her aunt's quick glance, conveying something along those lines. Chervonya nodded.

"What would a Mazhin trader working Horde Space benefit us?" Anna asked.

"Allies, over the longer term," Maks replied crisply.

He didn't mention the Corsac Fox, but the name hung in the air.

Anna's eyes prompted Maks to speak more. Obviously, she was used to having things explained to her by some man, even when she knew more.

"Mazhin don't want to settle anywhere," Maks reminded them.

"They live their whole lives aboard ships, moving back and forth as they meet others. Plus, from the list, someone told them exactly what to bring from Khet space for the most profit. Not too certain, but you might benefit, both personally and as the entire Horde, by encouraging more Mazhin to trade internally. And maybe others, as long as they didn't think they were going to be allowed to settle anywhere longer than putting down a trade mission office."

Anna turned to Chervonya again. Her eyes commanded words, so Chervonya considered what to add.

Maks had spoken with utter concision. No dross at all. Nothing.

"Trade with the Khet of Z'Gosza and that region of space would strengthen our entire spinward flank," Chervonya said. "Perhaps drawing a line that would confound the *Auga* over a much longer arc of history."

"How long?" Anna asked.

Chervonya turned to Maks to answer first.

"Few ships would choose to sail that long distance regularly," he said, obviously speaking from experience. "More likely, they would haul goods between two points on the longer chain, such as we do now when ships like *Ironhorn* bring news and mail from home, back when Lukyan and I were out beyond the fringes of the map. More trade means that those stations that exist now might need to turn into places. Colonies, both producing and consuming goods."

"Political implications?" Anna asked.

Chervonya flinched when Maks turned to her to answer that, an expectant look on his face.

It took her a moment to gather her wits back up.

"The Ononguli Sphere is a place," she said. "Our borders are currently well-known and tightly held. What Maks is suggesting might necessitate the Horde starting an active colonization effort to our right, when looking at the *Auga*. Alternatively, encouraging natives in that zone, mostly Zuath and Khet but with a dozen or so others, to expand from single systems into small nation-states."

"It forms a chain across the expected line of expansion the *Auga* have no doubt mapped out somewhere," Maks added. "Perhaps, depending, it might turn into a wall that keeps them out. That's Uly's goal over a medium term, I suspect. I mean, he hasn't confided such in me, but the implications are logical, when you stop to consider what happens."

"Do the *Auga* allow it?" Anna asked.

Maks laughed.

"I doubt it," he grinned. "But they move so slowly that they might not notice before it happened. Then they'd have to *undo* it. Which means that they'd have to shift significant resources around from our frontier and others, in order to knock that wall down. What is the Horde doing while that happens?"

"What makes you think the Horde would be doing anything?" Anna asked sharply.

Not hostile. Chervonya had heard her aunt angry.

This was a razor blade in her hands.

"Do we intend to merely sit back and let the *Auga* eventually push us out of our worlds?" Maks asked.

His voice had no emotions behind it, which just made it worse as Chervonya listened. She'd automatically expected male bluster. Rage. Heat. Something.

Maks was asking clinically. His own blade, wielded just as expertly.

"As opposed to?" Anna demanded.

"As opposed to joining forces with the Corsac Fox and seeing if he can assemble a fleet of allies sufficient to maybe push the *Auga* back," Maks said. "That is his stated goal, but he was intending to work from those spinward reaches around Z'Gosza to build up a place that could hold the line against the *Auga*. What could he do with the Horde pushing from our flank as well?"

Anna fell silent. Chervonya felt like Maks had just punched her in the stomach.

The audacity of it.

Worse, Maks seemed calmly convinced that his Human could pull it off.

What was a Human, that he'd made Maks Sobol believe?

Chervonya found that she didn't know, in spite of studying everything that Maks and Lukyan Chayka had brought to the Vatazhko.

Maks also seemed to also be possessed of near-perfect comedic timing, because he let that hang for two beats, then nodded to both of them.

"What are your orders, Vatazhko?" he asked simply. "And what should I convey to *Ironhorn* and *Ahmadi*'s conductors?"

Boom.

Who the hell was Maks Sobol, and why hadn't anybody understood this man better before today?

Except that Chervonya had read those bits in the file. Or rather, the things known about Lukyan Chayka, and why he had chosen to live, as Maks had said, beyond the fringes of the map for so long.

Chayka could have risen well in the Horde, had he been of a mind. Instead, he had taken *Compass Rose* and gone sailing, with one Maks Sobol eventually rising to be his first officer, then being promoted by the Corsac Fox to conductor of a ship that had carried home such a precious prize.

Fortier had seen it in Sobol. Chayka must have as well. Nobody else had.

Chervonya turned to her aunt, watching the woman recover her aplomb a beat slower than she should have.

"We'll gather up the squadron and sail to Rayzian," Anna said firmly. "Do you wish to remain on *Storm Crow*, or transfer to *Ironhorn* as my representative?"

That visibly rocked Maks back a mental step. Payback, Chervonya presumed, since Maks had done it to Anna in the first place.

"Given the choice, I might ride home on *Ahmadi*, if it could be worked out," he replied, volleying it right back at the Vatazhko.

"Why?" Anna asked.

Not demanded. Confused.

"Because they want to be our allies," Maks nodded. "Want to trade with us. And they've come from the spinward reaches most recently, so I might be better suited to helping them understand the Sphere better than anybody else you have immediately at hand. *Ironhorn* will be fine without me."

Again, Chervonya clenched her teeth to keep her jaw from falling open.

Draw a straight line with any Ononguli male conductor at one end. Any pirate. Illya Tkachuk off *Ironhorn*, or Klyment Gavrilyuk from *Storm Crow*. Extend that line down towards *Alien*, but mark the line before you completely vanish.

Maks Sobol stood on that point. And the Corsac Fox was out there beyond him somewhere, upsetting everything?

Anna turned to her for...something.

"I think that would be beneficial," Chervonya found herself saying. "And I might ask to join him, if the Mazhin would allow it. For the same reasons, but looking the other way."

Maks turned to study her with hard eyes that held no emotions at all.

"The other way?" Anna asked, but Chervonya was staring back at Maks.

"We need to understand our potential allies," she offered ambiguously, wondering if she was really looking at another ambassador from the Corsac Fox, instead of an Ononguli conductor.

Maks shrugged after a moment, then nodded, turning back to Anna without a word.

"What are your commands?" he asked.

"You've given me much to consider," Anna said.

Chervonya recognized it for a dismissal, so she was already coiling to rise.

"We will speak on this again later," Anna continued, sending them on their way.

Maks got out the door, then stepped to one side and stopped in front of her.

Chervonya studied him from close enough to dance. Maybe to breathe on. Neither of them stepped back. Neither of them spoke.

After a moment, he nodded at something and smiled, turning quickly to walk away.

Chervonya let him go.

What the hell had she been thinking, offering to go aboard an alien ship and travel with them, when she had *Storm Crow*?

But Chervonya wanted to know how Maks Sobol thought. And who the Corsac Fox was.

She'd have to get close to both of them to understand.

TRAVELER

SIXTY-TWO

Uly nodded as *Workshop* disappeared into warp, without Drew aboard it this time. The crew and agents they'd hired at Lacium were handling things, understanding that Uly had already sent notes to Z'Goszan folks to come bid on the monstrous ship, so they would be waiting when it arrived.

He turned his mind back to Taeli, then the various travel and trade routes that ran off like spokes from here. Some large, like the run back to Ononguli Space that *Compass Rose* had taken yesterday. Some small, slipping off to small colonies and semi-forgotten worlds in the nearby darkness.

With as many ships as traveled around here, despite not staying long, folks could find one to carry them somewhere, if they demanded it. Thus, Uly presumed that many of these worlds nearby might be filled with more folks who didn't want the larger galaxy to intrude on their lives.

It was unfortunate, then, that galactic geography had put them in a bad spot, at least on the grandest of scales. He couldn't see the *Auga* doing much more than eventually building new bases in the area and informing all those locals that they had new taxes and identity cards to deal with.

Presuming nobody attempted to resist at that point sufficient that they were made examples of in the process. The *Auga Empire* had been known to bomb hostile worlds into submission first.

Evil, when there was nothing the people on the ground could do to resist ships in orbit killing them.

At the same time, he might be drawing them all into a war they didn't want.

Uly had to focus on not just being some lesser evil in the process.

He looked around. All the usual troublemakers were on the bridge with him. Dan in her spot with Nasrin and Katya on either side. Suka Kuri had joined them, in stations specifically installed for her, Yanouk, and Anari on her far side from Katya. Ethir and Piruz opposite the ladies close to Rabiu.

Sterling had sensors and guns. Yuriy on communications. Drew piloting. Haydar typing something and frowning at the results, but that tended to be normal when he was trying to invent some new system and hadn't worked out all the kinks.

Roshan had such a long lead at this point that Haydar had almost given up, and instead had worked on creating specific tools that Uly would need, instead of just making better control software and hardware for various devices.

It was good.

Haydar must have smelled Uly's attention, because his head came around to make eye contact, instead of merely pointing tentacles toward him.

"What's out there?" Uly asked in a grand way that wouldn't settle for pedestrian answers, even as the ship was poised to do...something.

Haydar paused, pupil slits narrowing.

"*Auga* that way," he said, pointing with one hand. "Ononguli over there. Khet behind us. Zuath kinda all around us, but they're only barely the largest group. Humans way the hell over there."

Uly nodded. He'd be willing to plot those tentacles on a map and expect perfect accuracy, in spite of the ship drifting as they hung in space.

"What's over there?" Uly pointed.

Haydar paused. All his tentacles curled inward.

"I have no clue," he finally admitted. "Rabiu? Ethir?"

"Middle of nowhere?" Rabiu offered.

"And then some," Ethir added helpfully.

On the map in Uly's mind, the *Auga Empire* was a blob in the middle. Sector One, plus the first ring of Sectors out from that, then portions of the rings beyond that. Humans were at the bottom, around one hundred and seventy degrees. Z'Gosza was west at two hundred and thirty. The Ononguli were a band across the top from three forty to maybe zero twenty.

Then there was a blank spot at three hundred. Nothing, once you got beyond a band of known worlds close by that he had inherited from the navigational databases of various ships he'd captured.

"Does nobody live out there?" Uly asked rotating his head back and forth to look at everyone on the bridge.

Shrugs greeted him.

"Someone must," Ethir finally offered. "They just don't talk much about it. Why?"

"Because it is about to be in the middle," Dan spoke up. "And we will wish to control the center, as is always necessary in close combat."

Uly nodded to her.

Up until now, Khet space largely centered to the north and eastwards from Z'Gosza had been his zone of operation. And he was hopefully drawing the Ononguli into a broader alliance.

But every map he could remember had lines connecting those two like blood vessels, and nothing out there. It all just petered out.

"Sterling, I need your help," Uly said simply.

"Sir?" the young man squeaked as he spoke, then blushed furiously.

Uly smiled.

"You are one of the best stellar cartographers I've ever met, Mr. Huff," Uly reminded him. "And one with a gift for understanding how other species think that kept you out of trouble in the *Danumash* days. I need to tap that now."

He watched Sterling draw a deep breath.

"Okay?" Sterling replied, voice settled and eyes sharp.

"Out there," Uly gestured. "Drew, plot me a course two eight zero from our current heading. Calculate verticality to keep us close to the center of the galactic disk for now. Sterling, I want you to study the data we have, then refine Drew's course. There have to be people out there. Find them for me."

"What about the Vatazhko?" Haydar asked.

"We'll take a loop," Uly nodded. "Sterling, you and Drew need to get us to Krilic seven days after *Compass Rose*. You have my permission to fly hard and fast between now and then."

"*Wren* will never keep up," Drew noted.

"Understood," Uly acknowledged. "Rabiu, have them head directly to Krilic from here, with expectations that we will rendezvous with them at that point to take on supplies. Am I missing anything?"

He looked around.

"We're loaded for travel," Haydar replied. "Ship is in good shape. *Wren* will be traveling on a generally safe path, as there have been a lot of warships passing that corridor recently. Are we stopping anywhere?"

Uly considered it. Turned to Sterling.

"Lieutenant Huff, you will take command," he announced, putting the young man fully in charge for now.

At least as much as a semi-civilian vessel like this handled such things.

Sterling nodded, then gestured for Bello to take his own station, even as he moved to Uly's.

"Yuriy, we'll be dropping out of warp regularly," Sterling announced, voice suddenly firm and calm. Adult. "I want all sensors prepared for a wide sweep of our forward cone when we do, ignoring the sides for now because we can always come back later. Locate me worlds emitting significant signals intelligence that Mr. Ramezani can collate. Mr. Roscoe, stand by for warp."

Uly nodded.

One of these days, **Conductor** Huff might be calling this ship his own, though they'd probably have to rename it again to avoid further mistaken identity.

But he could see the shape of a new thing ahead of him.

"All hands, are we ready for flight?" Sterling asked as Uly moved over to stand close to Dan. "Mr. Roscoe, take us into warp."

Uly smiled. It had begun.

SIXTY-THREE

Dan and Nasrin often combined dance, close combat, and conversation in their training classes. Dan supposed that at this point she probably fell around the middle for overall mastery. What some instructors back home would have ranked as about Fifth, on a scale of perhaps ten senior belts, where everyone started as black.

Nasrin was at least a black belt. After this long, all of them were, with the possible exception of Katya, and she was quickly catching up, having Ciah as another person helping train her.

And Suka Kuri instructing all of them from her vast depths of wisdom.

Tai Chi Chuan. Sunflower Fist. Ciah was teaching them a Khet form that translated from some older tongue into something like Terrible Gaff, focused on a Khet's large eyes and sensitive gill slits. Boxing a Human's ears or punching Mazhin tentacles would produce a similar effect, so all of them were learning it.

Expanding their repertoire of deadliness.

Dan and Nasrin came to rest in perfect synchronicity. Paused. Saluted the west wall, because Sunflower Fist finished with the setting sun.

"You seem distracted," Nasrin said in the sudden silence.

Only a Mazhin might notice, and then only this close, and concentrating so closely on the form, so Dan grinned.

"Break," Dan decided, moving to a table along a wall and grabbing a towel for her sweat and a bottle of lightly salted water. Nasrin did the same, then they ended up straddling a bench and facing each other.

"Been talking to people," Dan began. Nasrin nodded. "About the future of the Corsac Fox, and whatever it is he will be creating."

"Wondered when he'd get serious," Nasrin grinned.

"He's been serious," Dan countered. "He put me in charge of designing it for him, because he has too many other things taking up his attention."

"Interesting," the woman said. "But not surprising. It's Uly."

"It's Uly," Dan agreed. "Already, he *Speaks* for the Mazhin portion of the crew, replacing Haydar, who never wanted it."

"Blackmail is a terrible word," Nasrin grinned. "Roshan knew something and threatened to tell everybody if Haydar didn't step up. Plus, he was the oldest person, and we're supposed to venerate age and wisdom."

"Supposed to?" Dan pressed, eyeing the smiling Mazhin woman.

"Survivorship bias," Nasrin laughed. "Back home, Omid would have been the most likely candidate, but she is absolutely not gregarious enough to enjoy it. Plus, those shits at *Danumash* expected a male to be in charge, because that's the civilization they have created."

"But Uly came along and you took a vote," Dan noted.

"It's Uly," Nasrin nodded. "Not that hard to see that he was going to be something incredibly special. If he lived long enough."

"Indeed," Dan agreed. "But I wanted to ask you about the Convocation."

Nasrin paused. Sobered appreciably.

"*The Clan Lords in Congress Assembled,*" she quoted after a moment, voicing taking on a storytelling tone that Dan felt starting to penetrate the depths of her mind like a needle. "That's the Hall of Souls, where everything important gets decided by the matriarchs in charge of the major clans. Additionally, you have the Hall of Voices, where everyone else is represented and anyone can be elected. Mostly, they handle technocratic issues, never dealing with the military budget or interstellar relations."

"And the Speaker for the Convocation?" Dan asked.

"Usually the most powerful, dangerous female," Nasrin nodded. "I could see them electing Uly to do it for a short time. Like, say, a war. All he'd have to do would be stand up on that platform and talk for twenty minutes, letting all the Mazhin in the audience smell him."

"You think they'd accept an outsider like that?" Dan asked.

"It's Uly," she replied simply. "I'm sorry you are so limited in your sensory apparatus, to not be able to see him like we do. I've known a lot of Humans over the last several years, as well as dozens of other species. Uly comes across as sincere in ways nobody else ever does. Most folks have the level of what they actually speak out loud, where they sand off the rough spots and sharp edges, not realizing that Mazhin can generally smell that, for lack of a better verb."

"And Uly?"

"There is almost no distinction," Nasrin replied. "If he likes you, that's present on all levels. If he grudgingly respects you while wanting to nail your skull to a wall, like that one Ononguli that killed Thorley Eldridge, that's there. Uly utterly loathed Eldridge, but was still willing to tangle with that killer. And still intends to find him and hang him, Dan. We could smell it. Can smell it. I've never met anyone like that, including Mazhin."

Dan nodded. That man was special, no two words about it. And doing something special.

"He needs our help," Dan said simply. "Given the wide range of geography that Mazhin ships cover, I want to go deeper into how you do things, to find those elements that I can use to build Uly's new government. Lacium was a good start. And might become a major port later, but I suspect that he wants to do something off in this darkness around us.'"

"Middle of nowhere?" Nasrin asked smartly.

"No bad habits to undo, unlike places like Lacium," Dan nodded. "Bring in people to build a thing, instead of forcing them to change how they've always done it."

Nasrin nodded, tentacles going like they were in a stiff wind.

"If each species was represented as a Clan, the Hall of Souls model works," she finally said.

"And each planetary system sending folks to the Hall of Voices?" Dan asked.

"It has value," Nasrin said. "And, if I understand how *Batyr* works, you can pull exceptional people out of the Voices and plug them into Souls. Ministers, Advisors, Bigshots, in addition to the Clan leaders themselves."

"The Industrial Protectors Party model," Dan nodded.

They'd spoken of such things.

"You'll want more than just one species representative each anyway," Nasrin agreed. "Sixty or one hundred people would bring a lot of expertise and experience to the table. And that's what Uly needs. A place for folks to belong. Too many nations and systems tend to be dominated by a single species, and everyone else ends up something of a second-class citizen. It's as much an *Auga* and Ononguli problem as Z'Goszan. Even *Danumash*, though they do it with class instead of shape. It was still a blood issue."

"And when Haydar flat refuses to be involved any more than he has to, are you prepared to become the Mazhin representative?" Dan asked.

She'd never actually seen a Mazhin's tentacles all stand perfectly straight at once. It was like those cartoons where some character touched a live wire and their hair went out. Nasrin's eyeslits snapped all the way open, all the way closed, then settled.

Dan waited for the woman to start breathing again.

"That looked painful," she noted.

Nasrin started laughing. It had a hint of hysterical edge, but she got it under control.

"It was," she admitted. "Not many people can ever do that to a Mazhin."

"Because you can smell it coming," Dan nodded.

"Interspecies comedy is hard around us," Nasrin acknowledged with a grin. "We can see that twist that makes the joke funny before everyone else can."

"Sorry. And not sorry," Dan smiled, taking the sting out of her next words. "But it has to be you. Haydar would do it grudgingly. Piruz might be another choice, but he's not serious enough for it."

"Unless it involves swindling someone," Nasrin nodded. "And Omid has found her perfect place in life. I've never seen her so happy."

"We all find happiness in different ways," Dan agreed. "Can I count on you?"

"You already do," Nasrin replied. "Nothing changes."

"Thank you," Dan said.

She drank the rest of her bottle empty. Nasrin did the same. They toasted each other with the empties, as if a formal dinner.

And it was, in many ways.

Dan could see a thing taking shape in her mind, the same way that Uly looked at that blank spot on the map and envisioned a thing forming.

What could they build, with a blank slate and a lot of friends?

SIXTY-FOUR

Lukyan had been expecting trouble at Krilic, based on timing, but obviously things had gotten resolved faster than he'd figured possible.

He'd dropped out there to find *Tanis Dragon* and *Wardog Charlie* present, but not anybody else. Instead, Conductor Gross had simply nodded in passing and sent him on to Rayzian, without any clue what he would find there.

They were home again. Such as it was, back to the planet where he'd been born. Come back to all the usual orbital traffic he hadn't missed in being gone, but had tolerated for a few days.

Helped that *Ironhorn* was close to the main station. And *Ahmadi* as well. Uly'd given him the full update on everything.

And Harald had looked at him over coffee when they'd arrived.

"You're coming down with me," Harald had said, accepting no other answers.

So Lukyan was on the ground. Again.

In his head, he flipped a coin, and decided that he would see what kind of trouble he was in, before he contacted his brother and made arrangements to spend the night at the palace.

Of course, they'd have heard the news, so there might be a room waiting.

If he wanted to face that on top of everything else.

Lukyan still wasn't sure.

Right now, he was following Harald through the Vatazhko's palace, looking up every once in a while in surprise at skylights.

Too many years on a ship. You didn't do skylights on a warship.

Harald didn't notice. Nobody else seemed to, either.

Groundpounders.

They got led to a conference room. Long, rectangular table in the middle. Chairs around the outside. Coffee and tea station in one corner.

Anna Shevchenko on the far side in the middle. Maks seated on her right, with a young woman between them that bore a passing resemblance to the Vatazhko. Other folks at the table, including two Elders that Lukyan knew by picture and reputation, but had never spoken with. Folks Harald had gossiped about. Aides around the edges of the room, plus a couple of obvious goons, in case he or Harald got frisky.

Lukyan was too old for bar fights.

And a little grouchy at the gruff treatment everyone had been subjecting him to.

Instead of sitting, he moved to the station and fixed coffee for himself and Harald while the elder took up a spot across the table from Bakhtiar Teke. One of the ones Harald had described as a fire-breather.

Ononguli who hated everyone else. Considered them lesser than the Horde.

Unwilling to bend.

Lukyan popped his neck as he sat.

Felt like a day to bash horns together. Good thing it wasn't a Tuesday.

"How's Dan doing?" Maks asked before anyone else could speak, throwing Lukyan entirely sideways from the good grumble building up to argue with elders on their home turf.

Lukyan speared his closest friend in the galaxy with a hard glare, then relented.

It was Maks. Likely up to no good, but he had a reason for taking everyone sideways, right out of warp.

Looking across the table, the Vatazhko and the woman between her and Maks were the only two that hadn't flinched when Maks spoke.

"She's good." Lukyan even managed to sound casual, when it suddenly felt like a game of Good Cop/Bad Cop unspooling. "They recruited a Khet woman to her combat team. Tiny. Dangerous. Piranha in a bathtub. And added enough Mazhin and Khet crew that the ship felt full finally."

Maks nodded and took a sip of his own coffee, like he'd merely been curious and gotten in before everyone else. Lukyan didn't believe it for a minute.

Maks was up to something.

Interestingly, all four of the Elders present had been bounced even more sideways than Lukyan had, though Harald and Anna seemed to be handling it better.

But Maks could be a sneaky shit when he wanted to be. Part of the reason he'd been First Officer, and later gotten *Scavenger Angel*.

Lukyan sipped his coffee and waited for the fireworks.

"Welcome back," Anna began, smiling at them at least as much as a woman like her might.

Lukyan nodded. Harald did as well.

"What news?" Anna asked.

Lukyan put the mug to his mouth to keep from talking. This was Harald's gig now.

"Uly is seven days behind us," Harald said simply. "That's time to brief you and sort out if there were going to be any issues with him traveling directly on to Rayzian."

"Why would there be issues, Harald?" she asked.

"Because I offered him diplomatic immunity to travel here and meet with you and the rest of the Lords of the Endless Plains," Harald said. "No questions asked about himself, his ship, or his crew."

Lukyan was ignoring Teke to watch the other elder. Stefaniya Baran. Ally of Anna, according to Harald. Matronly, in the same way a battleaxe was somehow lesser than a greatsword.

Just a different way to get yourself killed.

Teke slammed a hand down on the table. Baran's eyes narrowed and studied both him and Harald.

There was a reason he had a mug between his smile and the woman. And it never made it to his eyes.

Hers did.

"Further," Harald continued, waiting just long enough for Teke to take a breath to wind up, "there has been a discussion about the Corsac Fox leading a raid of Ononguli ships into *Auga* Space. A demonstration of his willingness and capabilities."

Lukyan drew a breath of innocence and put his mug down for now.

"You WHAT?" Teke demanded.

Lukyan leaned forward. Not much. Just enough. Harald glanced over before taking the bait. Which was probably what Maks was up to in the first place.

"According to both Uly Fortier and Dan Chastain, his right hand, they have declared war on the *Auga Empire*," Lukyan informed the room calmly. "They attacked a new base being built at a place called Ixtin, destroying it and hauling off *Auga* ships and cargo as loot. Harald suggested that he might invite a group of Ononguli ships and conductors to join him on a similar raid, putting Uly in command and going after somebody larger and more important. You know the *Auga*."

Then he leaned back. Baran was still studying him with a scowl on her face and a smile in her eyes, but Lukyan had no idea what she was up to. Or really even who she was.

Clan Elder. Dangerous one, to be in this room and one of the Lords of the Endless Plains.

Stranger otherwise.

"He is not Ononguli!" Teke growled. "Why are we tolerating this behavior?"

"Because he's already fighting them," Anna said in a conversational tone.

If the conversation involved a length of high-strength pipe upside someone's head.

Teke almost fell out of his chair, snapping around to scowl at her next.

Lukyan watched the gravity of the room change. Anna did that. Harald had warned him.

"About that," Harald tossed into the conversation. "How do we make him one of us?"

Bedlam. Utter, freaking chaos.

Lukyan had time to grab his mug and drink some more. The Vatazhko had exceptional coffee. Shame to let it go cold.

Everyone was arguing loudly with everyone else. Except Maks. Anna was watching everyone, but not really speaking. Baran and Teke and Perzi were trading insults like old friends.

Lukyan slid his chair back and stood up.

The sound fell to silence like he'd shot someone. Probably Maks's fault.

"I'm out of coffee," he said, moving to refill.

Sound didn't come back up. He'd wondered.

Maks had set him up, but in a good way. Lukyan wondered if anybody had caught on to that.

Anna had. And the woman next to her.

Nobody else, save maybe Harald. Maybe Baran.

He got more coffee in that ugly silence, humming to himself and taking time to adulterate it slowly and carefully.

Just because.

Then he wandered back to the table.

Tempers had cooled. Or evaporated sideways, like losing half your gyroscopes to a power failure and not shutting everything else down fast enough to handle things.

Shit like that never happened on a planetary surface, except during earthquakes.

Lukyan preferred ships.

He settled. Sipped. Smiled indulgently, like he and Maks had worked out a comedy routine when nobody was looking. Maybe. You work with a guy for a decade and things happen.

Anna was studying his face as closely as Baran. Teke was chewing nails.

Maks had a hint of a grin, but he'd started it.

"Are there any precedents for an alien to become a member of the Horde?" Lukyan asked innocently, aiming his question at the woman between Anna and Maks.

She felt dangerously smart. Looked it, too.

And was sitting between Anna Shevchenko and Maks Sobol today. There was no way that was accidental.

Not in this room.

"There are not," she said quickly.

Like she'd already given this a lot of thought. One of Anna's people, obviously. Insider.

"Pity," Lukyan offered, nodding vaguely.

Then to be a shit, he turned to Harald, pulled out a One Ducat Coin and handed it to Harald, like he'd lost a bet.

Maks's eyes lit up with humor. Old joke.

Harald, at least, caught on quickly, putting it on the table between them like he was showing off how he'd won a bet, instead of distracting folks with it.

"How do we fix that?" Harald asked, looking from Anna to Elder Baran, then Teke.

Baran stirred.

"*Why* should we?" she asked in a bored tone utterly at odds with her eyes.

"How soon until the *Auga* get pissed enough to declare war on us again?" Harald asked. "I presume that they haven't offered to trade Adrian Sobol and his people home yet?"

"They have not," Anna confirmed.

"So, at some point, the ancient war starts up again," Harald nodded. "I note that Maks Sobol is in uniform, as is Anna, though the rest of you have not yet woken up to the fact that we don't have long. **We don't have long**. *Auga* will gather up ships and go do something. Anybody who is old enough remembers the last time. And everyone learns about it in school. It's coming. Uly already started it. We either declare war on the Corsac Fox and eliminate him **for the *Auga***, or find a way to side with him with what we all know is coming. Anna, you sent me to meet him. To take his measure. I'll back up what Lukyan said. The man is effective. And fearless. Let's take advantage of that and kick the *Auga* in the shins first for once. They've already issued a *casus belli*. Anything we do at this point is justified."

"But inducting an alien into the Horde?" Teke demanded hotly. "That's never been done!"

"And we've usually lost planets in every war we've fought with the *Auga Empire*, Bakhtiar," Harald snapped.

Lukyan watched over his coffee, ready to jump up and punch someone if Harald or Maks needed it.

Anna wouldn't need it. Lukyan was pretty sure she could take anybody in the room if she got angry enough. Including him.

Best not to tempt fate.

"Then why start one now?" Teke growled.

"It's already started," Maks pointed out, in that deadpan, droll way he did.

Upended the room.

Like going for more coffee.

"What?" Teke demanded, rounding on Maks now, though he had to lean out to look down the table around the women in between.

"The *Auga* ordered the Horde to do something about the Corsac Fox, under penalty of something," Maks continued quietly. "**Ordered the Horde** to do it **for them**."

Lukyan couldn't hold back his grin. Everybody had danced around that topic, apparently. Ignored the *Auga Empire* issuing ultimatums to the Ononguli Horde to do something.

Everybody suddenly remembered.

Room tilted again. Harald.

"So you have the Corsac Fox, already attacking *Auga* systems," Harald pointed out. "Ixtin was his third significant strike on the Empire, by the way, after first stealing *Iron Wasp*, then *Wren*, and now a cargo carrier that had hauled all the parts for one of the regular *Auga* watchtower stations they like to build everywhere. Meanwhile, the Horde is reduced to watching from the sidelines. I'm certain that there are at least a few conductors who might be interested in helping Uly instead of hunting him **for the *Auga***."

Low blow. Rude. Effective, watching people recoil physically instead of just mentally.

Lukyan sipped coffee and tried not to laugh as faces around the room got greedy.

War meant piracy. Profit. Glory.

The lifeblood of any conductor worth his salt.

"Conductor Chayka," Anna suddenly spoke in that ugly silence. "Would you be interested in joining the Corsac Fox on such a raid?"

"Yes, Vatazhko," he replied. "Unfortunately, *Compass Rose* is mostly a small raider. Really an oversized Ultra-Bomber configured for long-range operations. Not a combat vessel, unless you meant me to help haul off loot later."

"Understood," she said, looking pensive.

Lukyan didn't trust the way she looked at Teke, then Baran, then Harald, before cycling over to Maks and the woman between them.

Then back to him.

"We'll just have to find something more dangerous to put you in, then, won't we?" she asked.

Well, shit.

SIXTY-FIVE

Uly had everyone on the bridge, having adjusted sleep and watch patterns today. Just as they had done before arriving at Krilic, the acknowledged border of Ononguli Space.

Rayzian. The Ononguli capital world, going back many centuries, though apparently not their original homeworld. Merely the one with the perfect climate for those Endless Plains that called to them at a fundamental, cultural level.

Like oceans called to most of the Humans that Uly had ever known.

"Captain, we're being hailed by a vessel orbiting near the main station. It identifies as *Fire Diamond*," Haydar announced, so he'd been monitoring comm channels instead of Bello or Yuriy. Or in addition.

"Put them on the main screen forward," Uly decided. "Let's see who we're dealing with today."

He wondered how an Ononguli conductor would deal Uly's bridge crew. Lukyan and Maks had gotten over their shock quickly. Even Tkachuk had managed.

But *Corsac Fox* was over the Ononguli capital world, and *Fire*

Diamond looked like another heavy interceptor, comparable in mass and firepower to Uly's ship.

He wasn't prepared for Lukyan's smiling face to appear.

"Greetings, Corsac Fox," the man said innocently. "Welcome to Rayzian. There have been developments."

Uly grinned back. Sounded like an understatement. Especially as there were a number of similar ships nearby, as well as larger ones, both Strikers and a few massive Devastators. None close or threatening, but still more firepower handy than any world Uly had visited yet.

"Good news?" Uly asked, remembering the Second Law of Thermodynamics and how it might apply to this situation.

"Exceptional, even," Lukyan nodded. "Harald was successful in his mission, and I've been working up a new crew, comprised of most of the gang from *Compass Rose* plus some recruits. You've been invited to meet the Vatazhko at her palace, with timing hinging on when you actually arrived. Additionally, the Lords of the Endless Plains would all like to take your measure. You and Dan and her women, plus whoever else you needed."

Uly paused before replying. Harald's mission had been to convince the locals that they should meet with the Corsac Fox on a peer level. And that maybe he could recruit raiders to go hit some *Auga* world as a way of making a statement.

Was that why Lukyan was in another Interceptor that looked maybe more heavily armed than *Corsac Fox*? A squadron of such Interceptors would be fast and dangerous, in the right hands.

Uly supposed that they wanted to measure him as a potential Vanguard or Marshall.

A fleet commander.

So be it.

"What's the time on the surface?" Uly asked.

Planets were tied to light/dark cycles, while starships were always in motion, with someone on duty flying and commanding.

"Late morning, give or take," Lukyan replied. "I sent them a note as soon as we knew it was you, and they ought to be ready if you wanted to head down shortly."

"Do you need a ride down?" Uly asked.

"No, but I'd love to hitch one anyway," Lukyan laughed. "I'm not supposed to tell you what's coming, but it will be good."

"Understood," Uly said, catching Dan's nod out of the corner of his eye.

She was in charge of security. His as well as the ship's. She got to decide those things.

"We'll need twenty minutes or so here, then we'll cross over and get you," Uly said. "How many of your crew?"

"Just me," Lukyan said. "The rest are going to run a couple of short training flights while I'm planetside, to get used to doing things without me watching over their shoulders."

Uly grinned. He'd specifically made everyone who was qualified to sit bridge watches take command for hours at a time along the way. Especially on the flight here. No better way to learn than to train for it under someone's eyes. His, Dan's, or Haydar's, usually, but Sterling was turning into a competent Lieutenant and maybe Second or Third Officer one of these days, depending on what point Haydar finally announced he was quitting and going back to his lab.

"We will see you then," Uly said, cutting the line and turning to Dan. "Honor Guard?"

"Absolutely," she grinned. "Let's see what the Horde has for us."

Uly hoped it would be exceptional, whatever it was.

SIXTY-SIX

Dan had her new uniform, pressed and perfect. Everyone else matched her in royal blue, trimmed with scarlet and mint. And all of the combat team was armed, but nobody was holding a weapon. Even Uly had his Shadowwhip sword, but that was, as always, as much a mark of an officer in the *Batyr* Navy as a weapon.

Lukyan wasn't armed, though he had dug out the thing he had said was the military uniform of the Horde, worn only when a war was coming.

She supposed that the Corsac Fox would have that impact on people. And cultures.

Especially as Adrian Sobol was still languishing in an *Auga* prison cell somewhere. Maybe for a long time.

The ride down had been pleasant, a new Khet pilot who was a specialist at small craft and good enough that she would have hired him back in the *Marshall Castillon* days to fly them after *Danumash* ships that were being boarded.

The gravity on the surface of Rayzian was about ninety-five percent of what she was used to. Surface temperature, according to Lukyan, would normally run a few degrees warmer than Humans generally preferred, to the point he'd complained about being cold around them a few times.

She could sweat a little today.

From the starport, a smaller shuttle had taken them to an estate outside of a major city, isolated somewhat and with a few trees. And backing onto one of those Endless Plains of grasslands the Ononguli loved so much.

They arrived at the front door. Maks Sobol led a small group of locals, all in the lime green uniforms of the Horde, though Maks had no rank tabs, for whatever that meant.

Maks smiled as they got close. Shared a hug with Lukyan that surprised the folks around them more than her or Uly. She stepped up and hugged him as well, wondering, since none of them had been that tactile before.

What had changed?

And he didn't whisper any warnings in her ear or anything. Just a hug to say hello.

Dan stepped to one side and watched a young Ononguli woman study her and her folks with serious eyes. Appraising eyes.

Dan studied her back. Felt Yanouk and Nasrin watching as well.

Suka Kuri, because she was utterly fearless, walked right up to the Ononguli woman and bowed.

"Suka Kuri, Moss School," she introduced herself, leaving off the important parts.

Exemplar of the Arts, Moss School.

Dan allowed herself a smile.

"Chervonya Borisov," the woman replied, bowing deeply back. Like she'd been warned who the elder was ahead of time. "Aide to the Vatazhko."

Maks stepped up and smiled.

"This way, my friends," Maks called now, acting as a master of ceremonies, it seemed.

Dan's team shifted around to put Uly, Lukyan, and Haydar at the center, with Maks and Chervonya Borisov leading them into the building through a door large enough for Emro women to move comfortably.

Dan wondered if they'd picked this place out specifically for that. Good sign if they did.

Eventually, they landed in what Dan thought of as a ballroom. High ceilings with skylights and chandeliers. Windows and glass doors along the outside wall, but leading onto an inner courtyard instead of the wilderness.

Lukyan had provided pictures, so Dan knew Anna Shevchenko on sight when they entered. Maks also walked right up to the woman and bowed in the same way Suka Kuri had. The Vatazhko hadn't been expecting that, as she blinked.

What was Maks up to?

She stepped next to Uly, on the far side from Lukyan, as her combat team peeled back. It helped that most of the folks in here appeared to be armed, though most of them with only pistols. Nothing like the omnibow slung across Nasrin's back. Or the big Squad Exorippers that the two Emro women had brought.

Mostly for show. Everyone was intending to behave.

At least Dan hoped so. The proof would be coming shortly.

"Uly, Dan, it is my privilege to present the Vatazhko," Maks introduced her, turning sideways. "The Lord of the Endless Plains herself, Anna Shevchenko. Vatazhko, Ulysses Fortier, the Corsac Fox, and his most important aide, Commander Sheridan Chastain."

Uly stepped up and inclined his head. Two peers meeting respectfully.

Dan took more of a bow, placing herself equal with all of this woman's close advisors, which apparently had come to include Maks Sobol in ways Dan hadn't been expecting.

Good for him, having gone from Lukyan's First Officer to somebody important with the Court itself, but there were hidden tides flowing that she needed to understand better.

In person, Anna Shevchenko was tall. Almost eyeball level with Dan. Probably about even with Uly, depending on footwear. Athletic build, tapering down from broad shoulders into a wasp waist then out again to strong thighs. Almost a short, red Emro, to compare the Vatazhko to Yanouk and Anari, both close by.

Rich red skin. Dark, intelligent eyes, however they glowed.

Lustrous black hair. Horns that had been polished with something to add a metallic sheen Dan hadn't seen on any of the other Ononguli she'd met.

Intending to make an impressive entrance.

Dan made a note to talk to ways to enhance Uly's look for such things in the future. Maybe a fancy sash or something that took him that next fashion step up the ladder.

Because everybody needs a fancy sash.

Shevchenko smiled warmly and looked over the group, including up at the three Emro women who towered over everyone else in the ballroom.

"Lukyan, thank you," she said to Chayka. "Exceptionally well done."

Again, messages with layers that Dan couldn't parse without more background, but she suspected that Suka Kuri would be able to fill her in later.

Little got past that woman's eye.

Dan glanced around and picked out Harald Perzi, standing off to one side with a group of older Ononguli. Perhaps more Lords of the Endless Plains?

Many pistols. A few melee weapons. A lot of attitude, but little of it hostile at present.

"Corsac Fox, be welcome at Rayzian," Shevchenko continued.

Because she was looking that direction, Dan saw the older male Ononguli next to Harald stir, but contain himself.

One of the fire-breathers, no doubt, as Harald had identified them.

"And Dan," Shevchenko said, drawing Dan's attention back to short range. "I look forward to meeting your combat team and hearing about such a thing."

Dan nodded and pivoted in place. The Ononguli were more sexist than *Batyr* or the Mazhin. Less than the Khet. Roughly equal to the *Auga*, at least as far as she'd learned.

"Nasrin Monfared," Dan introduced them. "Yanouk Miyoshi. Anari Supasei. Katya Zehlennko. Ciah Dambe. And this is Suka Kuri, Exemplar of the Arts."

Nearby, Dan caught the flinch as Borisov reacted.

Maks hadn't told them that? So there were limits to his trust, at least so far. Or he was holding back a few things for emotional value. That actually sounded more like the Maks she'd talked at length with, back at Lacium. His smiles made more sense, seen that way.

"All of you, be welcome," Shevchenko announced, arms out to even include Haydar, who'd somehow managed to move in such a way that most of the crowd probably overlooked him.

He could be like that around strangers.

"Thank you for hosting us," Uly replied. "We look forward to making your better acquaintance and learning how we might work together for a more prosperous future."

That seemed to be the right thing, as the crowd began to melt and approach. Dan smiled as Harald and an older Ononguli woman stepped close. Around her, the combat team relaxed some, and she watched Lukyan and Uly step right up to Shevchenko.

Around them, things turned into more of a cocktail party and less of a confrontation. She caught Maks's smile and wondered how much of this was his doing.

SIXTY-SEVEN

Uly scowled at the Vatazhko, seated across the table from him in a smaller office. Her and her aide/niece Chervonya Borisov. Him and Dan. Everyone else still outside, enjoying finger foods, beverages, and companionship.

"What's in it for me?" he countered her offer bluntly.

"What do you mean?" the Vatazhko asked. Not angry. Not friendly.

Negotiating a business deal with more emotion than the Khet who Uly'd been working with before. And without Haydar in the room. Or Ethir and Piruz.

Maybe negotiating a treaty between nations, but he didn't say that, either. The Horde was a known power that had managed to keep the *Auga* mostly at bay, slowly losing ground over centuries when other stellar nations had merely vanished within *Auga* imperial lines.

"You've suggested a raid into *Auga* territory," Uly replied. "Offered several small, fast, dangerous ships to accompany us, presumably willing to take orders from an alien conductor. We'd likely be able to materially damage whichever of three targets we decided to go after, at least with the depths of surprise I imagine we could arrange. That's all well and good. It likely comes as a serious surprise and disruption to the *Auga*, as they are only slowly building themselves up mentally to have another go at the Horde. What's in it for me? Personally? Why should I become involved?"

"It is a way to establish better alliances between us," Shevchenko countered.

"I'm not Ononguli," Uly reminded her. "Not one of you, nor subject to your laws and customs. This attack is far outside my normal operations zone, so damage to regional *Auga* forces won't improve my personal situation. Why do I care?"

He left it at that. Watched the Vatazhko glance at Borisov.

Wasn't that he wasn't interested, but from where he sat, it looked a lot like him taking all the risks, and the Horde gaining all the benefits.

"Would you be interested in becoming a member of the Horde?" Borisov asked.

Chervonya. That was her name. Aide and niece. Smart woman.

"Hard to do, as I'm not Ononguli," Uly reminded her. "Harald and Lukyan both brought that up, as have several others. At present, you have defined yourselves and your forces by species, with an exclusivity unique anywhere, as far as I've been able to identify. Are the Ononguli going to open their current legal systems to include other species as equals?"

He watched the Vatazhko's eyes grow hard and angry for a moment, but Uly was willing to push a little right now. They were alone and the conversation was limited to the four of them. And he could trust Dan explicitly.

It was the two strangers he didn't know.

These people reminded him of *Danumash* in a few, unfortunate ways. Species exclusivity here instead of class, but a similarity where all others were second-class citizens, except that outsiders were exceptionally rare, as the Ononguli didn't welcome aliens at all.

His mission of sending *Ahmadi* and a whole batch of Mazhin to trade would be years in bearing the kinds of fruit Uly wanted to eat.

"Plus, if I'm to become a member of the Horde, you would need to expand that to include my people," Uly added, kind of piling on, but doing so in private. "Dan and her combat team. My Mazhin crew.

The Khet and whoever else I recruit. Rude if I'm accepted and they continue to be held at arm's length. Yes?"

Shevchenko nodded and Borisov leaned back out of the conversation.

"I've talked extensively with Maks Sobol," Shevchenko injected. "Learned about the contracts and treaties you have with the Z'Goszan oligarchs and the colonists at Lacium. The Corsac Fox is becoming a sort of multispecies polity, if I understand the implications."

"Few Humans at present," Dan said. "We've had to recruit like-minded individuals to our cause. That started with some of the Humans, then the Mazhin. The Ononguli came later, and then the Khet. All will be welcome, when Uly finally announces where he will build his fortress and capital."

Uly liked the way both Ononguli women caught that hint and leaned in. He sat still and let Dan have them.

"Not Z'Gosza?" Shevchenko asked. "Or Lacium?"

"Those are existing places," Dan nodded. "We're looking for a world where Uly will be in charge from the very founding. Where we don't have to conquer any restless natives in the process, but can instead welcome all folks who believe in the bigger thing that is the Corsac Fox."

Uly felt that wave wash over him again. The one where he got separated into two entities. Uly Fortier, former Ensign with the *Batyr* Navy turned survivor. The Corsac Fox, warlord founder of...something. Someplace. Maybe out in that darkness where Sterling had been so busy surveying on the flight in.

The Ononguli were not expansionary, so they wouldn't be pressing against his flank. Maybe in a generation he would be large enough that he would be pressing on theirs, assuming that they'd forced the *Auga* back into Sector Eight in the meantime.

"We're planning trade with that chain of worlds emanating out of Z'Gosza," Shevchenko replied. "The Corsac Fox has been operating at that end, beyond—I believe the world is Taeli?"

"Taeli," Dan agreed as Uly watched. "For now."

"For now?" Borisov asked, leaning in. Shevchenko leaned back, so the two top aides were discussing things now, instead of the bosses.

He wondered if Shevchenko trusted her niece anywhere near as much as he trusted Dan. That put a smile on his face. She matched it after a second, but they remained silent.

"For now," Dan repeated. "There are other worlds we have been inspecting. Clockwise from Z'Gosza in regions currently not heavily occupied by major powers, though we have hints of many smaller worlds out there."

"The Spinward Reaches," Borisov nodded.

Uly perked up at that term. *Spinward* made perfect sense. *Reaches* suggested that the Ononguli saw it as empty as well. Outside where they cared. And had left it alone. Non-expansionary.

Warlord of the Spinward Reaches? What an interesting title to consider.

All three woman noted his response with curiosity. Only Dan's would be assuaged any time soon, though. He gestured for them to continue and settled again to listen.

"What if the Horde took it upon itself to reduce piracy along that trade corridor connecting Krilic with Taeli?" Borisov asked, glancing over at her boss and getting a quiet nod.

"As I understand it, a significant percentage of the pirates in those regions happen to be Ononguli," Dan pointed out with a cold smile.

"And they would listen to an order to clean up their acts," Shevchenko interjected. "Especially if we expected greater amounts of trade to be flowing around that rim of *Auga* Space. Such as, headed towards Z'Gosza or the Spinward Reaches."

"Are you proposing to become something of a law enforcement force along those corridors?" Dan asked.

Uly could hear the surprise in her voice, but doubted that the other women could. You had to know her as well as he'd come to.

And it was rather rude, challenging Ononguli pirates to become the good guys.

But hadn't he convinced both Lukyan and Maks?

Could he convince the Vatazhko?

SIXTY-EIGHT

Haydar found it informative that the Mazhin of *Ahmadi* had been invited to this party. The lady in charge obviously wanted to make friends with Uly.

He wondered if the Ononguli really understood how much his kind could communicate without ever speaking out loud.

Uly had figured it out quickly. But Uly. Dan and the others had learned, once Haydar and Nasrin trusted them enough.

The Horde was an entirely different conversation.

Thus, he glanced over and noted how Nasrin was escorting Suka Kuri around the room, while Anari was standing guard with two Ononguli at a door where the four principals had gone to talk.

Haydar meandered over to where Jamsheed Abbasi was chatting with some Ononguli civilians. Best if he be seen actually talking, lest someone accuse his kind of telepathy.

Wasn't far off, as Humans and Ononguli understood it, but they were all blind anyway.

"Ex-Speaker Ramezani," Abbasi nodded as Haydar got close.

Haydar made a rude comment with his tentacles that the locals wouldn't be able to read. Abbasi laughed back, all of it organic semaphore.

"Ex-Speaker?" one of the horned folk asked, intrigued from the tone of his voice.

"Before my clan met the Corsac Fox, they chose me to *Speak* for them," Haydar offered, throwing another raspberry at Abbasi for making him explain all this YET AGAIN. "Once we joined with his clan, it was obvious to one and all that Uly should *Speak* for the combined whole."

"So you are all one clan now?" the man followed up. "But you are different species."

And Haydar understood what Abbasi was about. Even sort of apologized. Kind of.

"Clan is the thing a group of like-minded individuals come together to create," Haydar offered in an august, lofty tone that didn't sound entirely like a pile of bullshit.

As long as you were upwind of it.

"Truly?" the other of the two asked.

Haydar noted the fine fabric on both. Gray on one. A kind of dark sand on the other. Stood out as civilians with all the bright green uniforms on the Ononguli and the blue that he and his kind were wearing.

His kind?

His kind.

"Truly," Haydar nodded. And apologized to Abbasi again.

This was an opening to break down the specism of the Ononguli, if done correctly, and that old horse-trader had seen it. Set it up.

Maybe wasn't as backwards and insular as Haydar had supposed.

Abbasi's tentacles laughed and laughed and laughed.

"How does the clan perpetuate?" the man asked, tied up in lines of progeny, which was how they saw clans in the first place.

"Humans can breed with other Humans," Haydar said. "Similarly, the other species are contained, though to date none had. Instead, the Corsac Fox has created a place, and invited folks to join him. To become part of the clan and nation that the Corsac Fox intends to build. And you will note that nearly sixty Ononguli have taken him up on that, including one woman who is part of Dan Chastain's inner circle."

He nodded and used half a dozen tentacles to pick out Katya in the distance. Heads turned to follow. Abbasi grinned.

Recruiting more? he asked.

None of them have impressed Katya yet, Haydar replied. *Trying to find her a boyfriend worth his salt.*

Abbasi nodded and merchants looked back, eyes dancing with the same thoughts. Put a husband into the top ranks of the clan, at least by marriage? Ononguli were good about that sort of thing, even if they were blind to letting aliens participate.

"Eventually," Haydar continued, "the many Ononguli men we do have will also hopefully locate and convince mates to join our clan, thus setting the stage for continuation and expansion."

He wondered idly if he'd turned into some sort of pimp, if you wanted to be crude about it. But Uly would need a stable population. More Mazhin women than the two he had—not counting the newcomers—only one of which would likely ever bear children. More Khet. More Humans. More Ononguli.

He had lots of men. Not nearly enough women, though the ones he had tended to be impressive as hell.

These two merchants let their minds be guided into the same path, looking beyond mere goods and making lists of people that might be exceptional enough to join the Corsac Fox.

First mover advantage, Jamsheed noted silently. *And thus, top quarter instead of bottom. Not that the pirates you got were bad.*

No, Haydar agreed. *Merely pirates. Uly needs a solid middle to turn into bureaucrats and conductors eventually.*

And Mazhin? Jamsheed pressed.

Got more kids to send? Haydar asked. *Uly wants Ahmadi to continue trading in Ononguli Space as long as you can make money. Maybe send word to the rest of the Convocation?*

Have, Jamsheed agreed. *Lots of profit that wasn't here even two years ago.*

The galaxy is changing, Haydar told him. *Time to make money before war gets serious.*

"Where would we contact the Corsac Fox?" one of the merchants pressed.

"Taeli, Lacium, or Z'Gosza, once he leaves the Ononguli Sphere," Haydar replied. "We'll also have regular contacts with Speaker Abbasi here, so he'll be able to provide better information. Now, if you gentlemen will excuse me?"

And he backed away, watching the two each try to pounce on Jamsheed instead.

Abbasi sent a rude gesture at him for it, and Haydar laughed. Then set off to see what other trouble he could cause.

SIXTY-NINE

Lukyan found Maks at one point.

"You're out of uniform," he growled, smiling.

"Her decision," Maks replied. "Lime green, but no rank tabs. Says that it make people second-guess who I am and how much power I have."

"There's a reason she's in command," Lukyan agreed. "How have you been?"

"Second ring out from the pinnacle," Maks offered. "I have seen a lot of things I can't tell you or even my family about, but little of it fills me with dismay. We got lucky to have her as Vatazhko when all this broke. Daryna Kravchenko would have told Uly to piss off."

Lukyan nodded. Kravchenko had been a hardass, in all the bad ways.

"So I take it you don't want to come back with me and take over as First Officer on *Fire Diamond*?" Lukyan teased.

"Got a better offer here, sailor," Maks laughed, then sobered. "And I do."

"Gonna be a staff officer when the war breaks out?" Lukyan pressed.

"That's up to her," Maks answered. "Right now, she's picking my brain on anything and everything. My job is generally to brain dump on her or Chervonya. That one is likely to be Clan Leader in another generation. Maybe one of the Lords of the Endless Plains."

"Vatazhko?" Lukyan asked.

"Maybe," Maks replied. "Smart enough. Cunning enough. Haven't met the others she's competing with, but Anna has her here. That should say something."

"It does," Lukyan nodded. "Just sad you won't be with us. *Fire Diamond* is a whole lot more dangerous than *Compass Rose* ever considered being. Comparable firepower to Uly, though we're not as dangerous on the combat side."

"Nobody is," Maks smiled. "Humans, pal."

"Humans, yes," Lukyan agreed. "There will be more soon. Or at least eventually."

"The Vatazhko even thought about sending me long ways around the *Auga* to see if I could find some," Maks offered. "Decided that she needed me here more right now. Might send you or *Ironhorn* though."

"Tkachuk would never go for it," Lukyan pointed out. "He'll be right back out there raiding as soon as he's done here."

"Might be too late for that," Maks said carefully, eyes glittering with unspoken knowledge. "Especially if he's going to take a month to goof off around here before he gets ready to sail again."

"Oh?" Lukyan asked, but Maks remained mum.

Lukyan nodded instead.

That suggested that the Vatazhko was serious about raiding with Uly. Or sending *Fire Diamond* and a few others. But if *Ironhorn* wasn't going to be able to sail back out into the darkness later, that meant that she might be putting the Horde on a war footing.

Word would go out for ships and crews to return to the Sphere. More vessels like *Fire Diamond* would be hauled out of storage and refurbished for combat.

And you needed crews at that point. Warm bodies to run those ships.

Lukyan grinned.

"What?" Maks demanded quietly.

"War breaks out and piracy goes down, not up," Lukyan pointed out. "We'll all be here, instead of out raiding on the fringes. Combined with all the things Uly has been doing in Sector Fifteen, you might actually see piracy eliminated as a viable threat, at least on that reach. Dunno about the other sides, though Twenty-Five will probably calm, too."

"Normally, I'd say happy coincidence, but it's Uly," Maks agreed. "You suppose he knows that? Planned for it?"

"No clue," Lukyan offered. "Wouldn't put it past him. Might ask him or Dan at some point."

Maks nodded, then his head snapped around and he pointed with a horn.

Lukyan turned to see the Vatazhko and her aide emerge from that office, with Uly and Dan already out.

Uly was smiling, so it must be good enough.

Time for war?

SEVENTY

Uly looked around the ballroom. Noted Lukyan and Maks chatting off to one side. Saw all his people in little clusters of locals, hopefully doing deals and making friends.

Anna Shevchenko nodded to him and smiled. They'd done a deal. Pretty good one, even if he hadn't had Haydar, Ethir, and Piruz working the corners of the language for points and edges.

Uly wasn't trying to rob the Vatazhko blind. Merely lay the groundwork for her assistance in founding a new star nation in the so-called Spinward Reaches.

A new thing, largely unseen in the galaxy, at least as far as her and Chervonya were aware, and that was sufficient for Uly.

A nation where everyone was welcome. And equal. Anna had expected the fire-breathers to balk and pitch a fit, but a successful raid into the *Auga* interior would mollify them for now.

Maybe even convince a few of them that they were wrong, but even Anna hadn't been that bold.

Not yet.

Still, it was a start. Promising enough to draw him into a deal with her.

Faces watched from all directions. Uly caught Lukyan's eye and nodded him closer.

"My friends, there will be an announcement soon enough," Anna called to the group. "For now, let us enjoy ourselves this afternoon. There will be a formal dinner in a few hours."

Uly slid to his left, even as the woman walked forward. Dan stayed close. All her women were paying attention, but not reacting yet.

Suka Kuri found him at the same time Lukyan did.

"Good news, bad news, Conductor Chayka," Uly began as Lukyan got close.

Around them, a bubble was forming, leaving them some privacy. Maks was talking with Anna and Chervonya over in the opposite corner.

"I'm not going to like it, am I?" Lukyan asked.

Uly laughed.

"It's not Tuesday," he reminded the Ononguli pirate. "But it is news. The Vatazhko and I have come to an agreement. She's sending *Fire Diamond* and four other Interceptors with me to go hit an *Auga* outpost. I'll review the intelligence before we decide which, which will allow a certain level of operational security."

"Do you know who the other four conductors are?" Lukyan asked, face twisted a little sideways with concern.

"No, and you won't either, from what I understand," Uly agreed. "I expect four hungry young commanders, eager to prove themselves up in front of the rest of the Horde."

"Lovely," Lukyan grumbled. "Fire-eaters instead of fire-breathers."

"Something like that," Uly said. "But I'd rather they be too aggressive than not angry enough."

"And all Interceptors?" Lukyan pressed.

"Fast hitters," Uly said. "All a match for *Corsac Fox* in sailing and combat, which means we can go in as a single attack squadron, rather than maintaining any sort of escort formation. And all heavy enough to manage some fighting, when even *Compass Rose* would have gotten her ass kicked."

"Are those conductors here?" Lukyan asked. "I'd like to take their measure."

"No," Uly replied. "Same, but we'll have to see what they are like in battle and sailing. Not optimal, but I had to strike a balance and preferred to hit fast, instead of training for a month first."

"You expecting spies?" Lukyan was aghast.

"There are always spies," Dan spoke up. "Someone will be disgruntled at someone. Maybe at Anna Shevchenko. Maybe at working with aliens. Some of the hardest specist shits here might be willing to send the *Auga* a note, just because species purity might be more important to them than losing a war. I've seen it happen."

"Really?" Lukyan asked.

"I am not the *Batyr* ideal of skin coloration, Lukyan," she growled quietly.

Took him a moment, but Uly understood. The Ononguli didn't have anything like the skin variation Humans did. Almost nobody did, whatever that meant.

Suka Kuri could be invisible when she wanted, in spite of her size. She moved and Lukyan nearly leapt sideways in surprise.

"Do we trust those four conductors?" she asked simply.

"Yes," Uly said. "I told her I wanted hungry ones. Angry enough at the *Auga* to take orders from an alien. Don't know how far I can push, so I settled for ones I could aim and then get out of their way."

"And the mission?" she asked. "A simple smash and bash, considering your associates, or something more subtle?"

Uly smiled up at the woman, imagining what she must have been like much younger. Except that she'd said more than once that both Yanouk and Anari had the potential in them to reach her level in another few decades.

Truly fearsome. And fun.

"I have some thoughts," Uly grinned. "Based on some of the things the Corsac Fox has done in the past, and how they might be repeated, at least until the *Auga* finally figure out how to stop us. If they can."

She merely nodded sagely in that way she did, understanding that they were surrounded by folks who didn't need to know anything more.

Uly would review the files Anna had promised. Then see if he could pull it off.

RAIDER

SEVENTY-ONE

Uly looked around the bridge. Sterling and Drew at their stations, both with several other folks trained and ready to take over for them, if not quite as sharp or good at what they did.

Dan and her team were all below, getting ready, though Suka Kuri had remained here to observe. Or whatever an Exemplar of the Arts did.

Study command and starship tactics, that she might add that to a Moss or Sabre School curriculum for later?

That was a thing that could be utterly frightening. Even Sabre School tended to be about personal arms, rather than warships. Expressing the trained perfection of the Emro body.

But an Emro pirate conductor of the Sabre School?

Uly smiled. She smiled back at him as if reading his mind.

The galaxy wasn't safe if that happened.

Best make sure they were the good guys, then.

"Haydar, how are we doing with the squadron?" he asked.

"*Fire Diamond* is on our starboard flank," Haydar nodded with his tentacles. "*Starlight Relentless* is in the van, as they demanded, with *Sergiy Korolyov*, *Obsidian Nebula*, and *Granite Harlequin* all nearby, chomping at the bits, if I understand your Human vernacular."

Uly laughed. He presumed that Haydar knew the tongue better than he did, and had learned all those weird idioms from *Danumash* folks along the way.

Uly couldn't remember ever seeing a real horse in the flesh.

And he wasn't as smart as Haydar.

"Go ahead and connect me to the other ships," Uly ordered. "Main screen camera, to remind them how many other species are participating today."

"Coming live in three, two, one, now," Haydar said.

The screen showed Lukyan, with placeholder icons for the other four, but Uly wasn't offended. Those conductors were all used to operating solo, and, like Lukyan, had recently upgraded from smaller ships to something with more firepower, as the Vatazhko got her troops marshaled for the coming war by breaking vessels out of long-term storage.

"In the distance, scanners have confirmed that Nyri doesn't appear to be prepared for what we are about to do to them," Uly said simply. "As a reminder, every ship we damage today has to be repaired later. Every person we frighten must be calmed down and convinced to return to battle tomorrow. Lastly, this is not a war base. Most of the people we encounter today will not be *Auga*, but Zuath, Khet, Thogin, Guezal, and maybe Yousses. Mostly civilians, doing a job and unprepared for Nyri to be the front lines again, after centuries as a regional capital safely in the rear. Damage things, but don't stop and spend all your time trying to actually destroy anything. And be prepared to run when we have accomplished our mission. Any questions?"

He paused, but nobody answered. Lukyan merely nodded, but they both understood that the other four ships were going to go on a rampage, attacking everything that moved or could move, without putting a lot of thought into their tactics or ramifications.

Young fire-eaters, as Lukyan had said, back on Rayzian.

At least he could count on *Fire Diamond*.

"*Starlight Relentless*, you have the lead," Uly said. "All ships, stand by to launch into warp immediately after they do, and I will see you on the far side."

That vessel disappeared even before Uly finished, so he simply cut the line and watched the others go, until it was just *Corsac Fox* and *Fire Diamond*.

"Mr. Roscoe, take us in," Uly said. "Mr. Huff, stand by on all weapons."

Nods, then the blink into the warp tunnel, riding high and to the left from the others, so that *Corsac Fox* didn't stumble over their generator signal and get kicked out too soon.

He wasn't here to attack stations or blow up small ships. At least not initially.

Instead, Corsac Fox dropped back out of warp in only a few minutes, but on the far side of Nyri's orbit from *Starlight Relentless*. Hopefully, everyone was looking the other way at this moment.

"Haydar, what's our perimeter?" Uly asked as they came back into alignment with the rest of the universe.

"On target and true, as one would expect from Mr. Roscoe," Haydar replied.

Uly watched Drew blush. Didn't happen often.

"Stand by," Haydar continued. "Mr. Huff, you will have two small search and rescue vessels off our port bow. Neither appear to be armed at present."

"Neutron Omnipulsar teams, stand by to engage hostile Probe vessels," Sterling announced. "Wavebolt teams stand down."

Uly nodded. And approved. The Omnipulsar itself might actually manage to hurt one of those ships at this range, but Uly doubted it. It would, however, chivy both of them out of range quickly, when they realized that Sterling could have put a pair of 1dm bolts downrange and annihilated them before they could react.

Casualties could be kept at a minimum today. At least here. *Starlight Relentless* was probably going home after this battle without any wavebolt generators left to fire, from what they'd indicated earlier.

Nothing Uly could do about it.

"Where's *Fire Diamond*?" Uly asked.

"High and back," Haydar replied. "They confirm overwatch."

"Drew, take us in."

Uly watched on his own screen as *Corsac Fox* began to nose down and point at another one of those enormous snowflake stations that the *Auga* liked to build. Where they could stash ships that weren't immediately needed for the long term.

He'd stolen *Wren* originally thus.

Today, he had something even better in mind.

"Mr. Ramezani, is the station reacting?" Sterling asked.

On the screens, two Probes were point down and accelerating for the atmosphere of Nyri below, where presumably they could land and repair places where paint had gotten blistered.

"Negative, Mr. Huff," Haydar replied. "Automated channels are challenging us and warning us about fines for violating navigation rules. Nobody is actually bothering with things over here, considering what is happening opposite us."

"Add it to my tab," Drew called out to general laughter. "I'm good for it. Promise."

Uly smiled. He couldn't remember ever being on a ship with morale this high. At the same time, they'd been successful, even in failures that had gotten them captured twice and chased off a few times.

The *Auga* were implacable. Impossibly enormous in terms of resources, be they planets, people, or even fleets.

At the same time, that size worked against them when Uly was willing to use speed and Human savagery.

Violence, in a manner that nobody, including the *Auga*, had really understood previously.

They would need it.

SEVENTY-TWO

Lukyan was still getting used to a real warship. One where everything worked correctly and all the screens and keyboards were clean.

You didn't get that on pirate ships.

And he'd specifically asked Uly to launch his attack on a Saturday. Stay away from Tuesdays, and all that silliness.

Sometimes, however, the gods have a dark sense of humor.

Dmytro caught his eye.

"What have you got?" Lukyan asked.

"*Starlight Relentless*, living up to his name," Dmytro replied. "Went straight in, firing at anything he could see. Other three went with him. We missed something on a scan. Or somebody just arrived. Something. Got a Striker down there that just unmasked. Heavy one. Putting a shit-ton of wavebolts into the sky and *Starlight* is going to get their horns ground off if they aren't careful."

"What about the other three?" Lukyan asked.

"They're pouring fire in, too," Dmytro nodded. "Problem is, everybody is firing their wavebolts defensively at other bolts. Not a lot of damage being done, after that first salvo."

Lukyan grumbled under his breath. Normally, he'd say it served them right. Aggressive was the risk you took. And the chances that someone could smash you in the mouth.

However, this raid needed to make a splash. A big one. Enough to get the Horde on Uly's side.

He turned to Oskar.

"Get me Uly," Lukyan said simply.

The Warlord was there a moment later.

"That Striker?" Uly asked.

"Trouble," Lukyan nodded. "I think we need to do something before *Starlight* gets stomped on."

Uly paused and looked down for five seconds. No doubt reviewing everything and plotting something.

Six Interceptors were enough to chase off a Heavy Striker. Probably.

Except that you might expect to either lose one entirely or have three in a repair dock for six months.

Uly looked up. Lukyan watched something change in the Human's eyes.

Something really, ***really*** scary took up residence in that moment.

"*Fire Diamond*, I'll have Drew transmit you an intercept course shortly," Warlord Badass Uly announced. "I'm going to launch my team a little early, and we'll need to make sure that we keep everyone focused over there while things happen. That means we probably take *Starlight*'s place in the firing line. I'll need your forward defensive tubes ready to keep the *Auga* ship busy. Do you understand?"

Lukyan turned to Oskar and got a grim nod.

Fire Diamond was actually heavier than *Corsac Fox*, in terms of wavebolt mass. A pair of single 8dm turrets located fore and aft, where Uly had a twin 6dm forward. The same 1dm single turrets on his rear corners, but forward they were twins. He could drop four 1dm wavebolts defensively in a hurry.

Sounded like they would need that.

Uly was up to something.

However, it was Uly, and he got shit done.

"We're good here, Corsac Fox," Lukyan replied. "Standing by for your orders."

He turned to Dmytro, Slava, and Oskar. A look to remind them that all hell was about to break loose.

At least they were on the right side today.

Now, they had to make sure it was the winning side.

SEVENTY-THREE

Dan had her combat team settled and ready, just like at Taeli. Same folks. Same groupings. More training in weapons and small unit tactics.

And her squad leaders were turning into unit commanders.

"Dan, I have a problem," Uly said, echoing out of all helmets as folks still had their faceplates open. "The ship will need to transit lateral and engage a Heavy Striker that is bedeviling our associates. I'm going to launch you now, early, then you'll be on your own, because I don't think we'll be able to come back and escort you out. Especially if we end up having to lead that Striker astray chasing us off. Are you ready for launch?"

"We are," Dan replied, looking around.

She was back to the old days. The *Marshall Castillon* days, when her and a group of folks would rush over in a shuttle, board some barely surrendered enemy ship, and fly it someplace safe.

There were engineers handy, as well as some folks Drew had trained up to a level he felt was acceptable for flying a big ship.

And Drew's standards on doing things were almost as high as hers and Uly's.

"Flight deck, launch now," Uly called. "Then get clear quickly so we can move to warp."

Around her, Dan felt the shuttle lurch, then gravity fell to nothing as they were in flight.

Dan looked around, but everybody had learned to strap themselves down for these things. Nobody was squawking and floating.

"Flight deck, what is our ETA?" she asked.

"Calculating," the Khet pilot replied. "I'll have you to airlocks in two hundred and forty seconds, sir."

"Cut corners if you have to," Dan ordered him. "And damage to the shuttle is acceptable, as we can always steal or buy one somewhere else. Get me to that airlock *now*."

"Roger that, Commander," he called. "Leaning into it now."

Dan felt the gentle acceleration and hoped it was enough to get them there faster. Four minutes sounded like an eternity in combat, and nothing in the greater scheme of things.

SEVENTY-FOUR

Sterling could hardly remember the old days, when he'd been a kid on *King Hewitt II*, training to someday be an officer under a captain he was willing to admit had been a loudmouthed, drunk bully.

Uly was what you were supposed to grow up to be. And had made sure Sterling didn't slack in his training, mentioning more than once that one Sterling Huff would be a conductor on his own ship, one of these days, if he kept up his studies.

Today felt like a pop-quiz thrown into what should have been a normal lecture.

Luckily, he'd stayed up late last night reading his notes instead of drinking. Unlike the old days.

"Mr. Roscoe, stand by for warp," Captain called over the quiet of the room. "Mr. Huff, we're facing what appears to be one of the heavier *Auga* Strikers. What can you tell me about our opponent?"

Definitely pop-quiz.

"Armaments range from 8dm up to 12dm, depending on class, sir," Sterling replied. "As a heavy, I would expect the ship to have twinned 12dms in turrets. Probably two turrets forward, stacked, and one aft, all with at least two hundred and seventy degrees of firing arc, assuming nobody rolls to present a flat deck. Four to eight neutron omnipulsars, in squares, stars, or hexes depending on class."

"What about the 12dm should we know?" Captain asked, voice lecturing.

"Our Neutron Omnipulsar won't stop it, sir," Sterling nodded, checking how his gun teams had laid all their barrels as he spoke. "A 1dm might damage one, but won't stop it. You need a clean hit from a 2dm or better to generally disrupt. Or multiple strikes from 1dm wavebolts. They should be able to overwhelm three Interceptors. A fourth balances things, somewhat, but then it becomes a matter of training and skill of your crews on both sides."

"Excellent, Lieutenant Huff," Uly announced. "Gold star. Make sure your teams are ready, and loop *Fire Diamond* in under your overall gunnery command."

Sterling gulped at the enormity of what Captain had just said. Him, in charge of both ships?

At the same time, that gave him more turrets and barrels to engage. And the ability to plan overlapping fire.

Pop-quiz.

Sterling made eye contact with Uly and nodded.

"Mr. Roscoe, take us in," Uly ordered. "Lukyan, join us for a dance?"

Sterling caught the first part of Conductor Chayka's laugh before the bubble spun up and they dropped into their own pocket universe.

Same thing they'd done at Lacium. Hopefully, the *Auga* hadn't heard. Or didn't believe it. Or maybe just didn't understand.

You could pull a stunt like this, if you were ready. And willing.

Loop up, out, and around, dropping back in on someone, possibly from a blind side if they've already moved to engage *Starlight Relentless* and his friends.

Corsac Fox dropped out of warp and Sterling got a chance to see how the *Auga* built Heavy Strikers.

Not as big as a station. Just as intimidating. Huge, compared to the *Fox*, though. Eight or maybe ten times the crew, from the looks of it. Two big turrets forward, currently pointed away and shooting at

Starlight, who was in too deep, out of position, unable to maneuver well, and firing everything they had into salvos of four 12dm wavebolts that would leave the Interceptor looking like an aluminum can someone had stomped if any connected.

Nearby, *Sergiy Korolyov*, *Obsidian Nebula*, and *Granite Harlequin* were pouring in defensive fire as well, throwing the occasional bolt at the Striker while trying to keep *Starlight Relentless* alive.

Sterling studied the whole for a long moment, then nodded.

"Forward teams, give me two into the target on this vector, as fast as you can fire," he ordered. "Defensive turrets forward, one each of the same. Mr. Roscoe, flare our tail up and out so the rear turrets have a better firing arc."

Already, the first 6dm was downrange, but he'd trained his teams to fire quickly when they needed to. And the 1dm teams had caught his meaning and launched as well.

A moment later, *Fire Diamond* appeared on a flank, exactly where Drew had put them.

"*Fire Diamond*, hold all fire for defensive shielding," Sterling ordered them in a sharp voice. "I'll want one 8dm into their first 12 coming inbounds, then dual shots with your small ones into the other. Match any 1dms he fires with one of your own, then maneuver your rear turret to engage. At that point, I want one barrel defensive and one offensive until told otherwise."

He'd heard part of a squawk over the line. Sounded like the Gunner over there, Mr. Deville. Conductor Chayka had cracked a verbal whip on the Ononguli, though, so silence for now.

The *Auga* ship was just a string of numbers and letters on his screen, because they didn't give ships names. *Striker* was good enough for Sterling.

It fired a pair of 12dm wavebolts in rapid succession, both aimed at *Corsac Fox* because that had been the target they'd seen first. Aft, Sterling felt more than heard as both defensive 1dm turrets fired. Not much, but any damage to a 12 was necessary. Similarly, the Neutron Omnipulsar teams went to work, though it was like trying to cut down a tree with a pocket knife.

Patience and determination, which was all he asked of those folks. The bolts were moving too fast to actually die that way, but anything to reduce the force at impact. If it arrived.

Fire Diamond had something to say on the topic, launching a pair of 8dm bolts, along with two pair of 1dm from the front corners.

Sterling started to snap an obscenity at *Fire Diamond* for ignoring his orders, then saw what Mr. Deville had done and smiled.

"Sterling?" Captain asked.

Sterling paused to remember that he wasn't alone on the bridge.

"*Fire Diamond* is engaging as ordered, sir," Sterling almost laughed. "And put a second wavebolt into the mix as though engaging the Striker's pair. Enemy gunners are about to discover that he targeted them with it instead. Forward teams, I need a pair of 6dm bolts right now. Do not bother to set them special or aim. Put two downrange at the Striker immediately."

In his butt, he felt the double jolt as the forward turret fired. The aim was a little off, as both ships were moving on different vectors, but the wavebolt was a guided weapon, tracking down on a signal anyway.

The art of fire came from launching them in such a way that defenders had to maneuver to bring turrets and Omnipulsars to bear better.

Right now, he wanted them panicking.

A quick glance up and he noted that fire against *Starlight Relentless* had slacked. None of those forward turrets had turned to engage *Corsac Fox*, but the minds behind them had.

Surprise is a terrible thing.

The Corsac Fox had just surprised that *Auga* captain. As had the *Corsac Fox*.

"*Starlight Relentless* and *Granite Harlequin*, give me a salvo on this vector," Sterling ordered, transmitting a line that he wanted impressed on that Striker's captain.

More surprise, because Captain had told Sterling more than once that the second best time to kick a man was when he was already down. The best time was when he wasn't looking in the first place.

Wavebolts from both friendly Interceptors. The Striker's fire paused again. Minds stopping to figure out what the crazed Ononguli had done now.

Except that it wasn't an Ononguli attacking.

The Humans have joined in, and you are not prepared for us. Captain had told him that, too.

Auga thought they were tough, because they had numbers and patience. They did not understand going for someone's throat.

"Mr. Huff, I believe we are about to see our enemy hit by an 8dm bolt," Mr. Ramezani announced.

Sterling nodded. Smiled. Or something. Pulled his cheeks back. Captain matched it, so he understood.

"All batteries, give me two bolts as fast as you can reload," Sterling ordered. "All ships, maintain your defensive fire as much as necessary, but hit them now. Hard."

Panic is infectious. Sterling could almost smell it wafting through the life support systems on that Striker, as *Fire Diamond*'s 8dm wave-bolt impacted, however badly degraded by everything those defenders had done to prevent it at the last minute.

Minds snapped around as the hull flexed. Not much, but it would ring like a bell. Sterling could testify to that, having been at the safe end of *King Hewitt II* on that day the *Batyr* Navy had put a 6dm bolt through the ship's bridge.

On his screens, the four friendly ships downrange let loose with everything they had.

The tables had suddenly turned.

The Striker was forced defensive now, engaging 6 and 8dm bolts with his 12s. And not firing them at friendly ships. 2dm defensive bolts, paired in four turrets. Eight flashing out to stop heavier bolts impacting. The ship was at the center of a maelstrom, so they had everything firing every direction, without obstructions.

Then Sterling saw his opening.

"Drew, cut me across his bow," Sterling called as the Striker began to turn away from *Starlight Relentless*. "*Fire Diamond*, keep up as we cross to port and down, shifting to defensive fire only. Forward turrets, go for broke, firing as fast as you can reload until you are out of containers."

Sterling heard a sound, and looked up. Captain Fortier waved him back into motion, having seen what Sterling was doing.

If it worked.

Panic was a deadly infection.

The Striker's captain saw *Corsac Fox* turn to cut off his escape. He had two options right now. Stand in the middle of all that fire, hoping he could somehow hold off six ships instead of the four that would have been an even fight.

Or run.

And *Corsac Fox* was racing to get in front of him.

On a scan screen, everything is a dot, massively oversized relative to reality. Even a 3D projection makes them too big.

It is almost impossible to actually ram an enemy ship unless one of you isn't moving and the other one is trying. Space is simply too big.

But on a screen, that captain saw *Corsac Fox* big enough to box him in.

His bow started down. Away from *Starlight Relentless* and those three. Away from *Corsac Fox* and *Fire Diamond*, now pouring fire in and starting to get exceptionally close to hitting, in spite of the number of barrels and tubes the Striker could bring to bear defensively.

Down meant atmosphere. Dive in and maneuver like a pig, but everyone would be above you and you could at least escape the box that only existed in your mind.

"Do we pursue?" Sterling asked the room.

Long pause. Captain, weighing the odds. He didn't have much more experience than Sterling, but he was the Corsac Fox.

"Hound him, but do not close," Captain ordered.

"Ononguli squadron, move to this position and stand by to conform to *Corsac Fox*'s maneuvers. All ships hold offensive fire. Repeat: hold fire and reload. Maintain defensive posture. Mr. Roscoe, keep us roughly one-six-zero from his current heading and maintain this gap."

Sterling could see it in his mind, but he didn't know if that enemy captain did. Or was merely trying to get away. Get all these stinging wasps safely behind him while he got away. Something.

Sterling would let him. For now.

The box was still there. It had turned into a hollow sphere cut into layers like a cake.

Or a pond you could drown in, if you weren't careful.

That Striker was headed for deeper water than maybe he could swim in.

SEVENTY-FIVE

Dan had Nasrin and her team at the airlock when they opened. Just like Taeli. Anari was next, because they were going to abandon this shuttle and steal something better.

You didn't need to maintain a secure base when you did that.

If you were bold enough.

Or crazy.

Dan's team was third. Heaviest for firepower, in case they ran into someone, but Nasrin had Painspheres and her team were all carrying stunning weapons for now.

Civilians, as Uly had said. Employees for the most part, instead of fanatics. Send them home tonight with nothing but a bad hangover.

Nasrin paused at a major intersection. Where the trunk they were on split out into major arteries. She had a map of the exterior printed in one hand.

"Here," she announced, pointing the arm with the printout to her left.

Dan nodded and followed.

"Rear team, hold this for a bit, then follow," she ordered.

Their target was another freighter. Big one. Monstrous beast, tucked in at the base of one of the arms where it was almost impossible to get to quickly. Or get out.

Dan had looked at the layout and decided to hit them from the station side instead.

Inward they went. *Wren* had been easier, because it had been an emergency response craft, so at the end of an arm where it could detach and maneuver quickly.

This one was at the other end.

They continued inward.

Nasrin had passed another intersection and was headed down a long corridor. Anari's team had followed.

Dan caught movement out of the corner of her eye as a hatch opened.

Tall and purple. She turned and fired in a single motion, dropping whoever it was.

Whatever it was. The purple-furred body fell across the hatch. Dan stepped over it and into the room, ready to fire on movement.

Barracks, of a sort. Eight bunks, stacked in twos. All of them occupied at present save one.

Eyes opened wide as people looked back at her.

Another purple-furred biped said something, but Dan didn't understand the words. Or maybe the accent. Space was huge, and supposedly most people spoke a single tongue. Regional dialects still made things interesting.

A voice behind her answered a moment later. Dan slid to the side as the conversation woke the other sleepers, but nobody moved.

Helped that she and half a dozen folks had guns pointed at them.

Yanouk carried on a conversation with the closest one still awake, while two folks in the hallway pulled the one body into the room and slid it off into a corner.

The first one to speak held up a hand, displayed a wrist. Had a bracer of some sort on it. Blinking light. More conversation.

Dan didn't understand any of it, save that the emotions were calm enough that she didn't feel the need to open fire and put them all to sleep for a while.

The schedule was already a mess, with Uly having to dump them while he raced off to save the other ships.

"Yanouk, we don't have time," she said, interrupting.

All eyes turned towards her. Seven of the purple-furred people, plus one out cold, though not injured as near as she could tell. Still breathing regularly. Just not awake for a few more minutes.

"They claim to be prisoners, working off their sentence by doing menial, manual labor," Yanouk replied. "The one shows us her monitor that the authorities use to track where she is and what she's been doing."

The one on the floor had something similar. Dan had assumed a piece of jewelry. The creature was wearing baggy pants and a formless shirt, both in a hideous shade of dark puke green.

"And?" Dan pressed.

Yanouk said something. The one answered.

"And they'd like to escape with us," Yanouk said. "And to help us with our mission."

"How?" Dan asked.

The tone must have been sufficient, as the speaker said something long and involved before Yanouk even translated. Then it held out the bracer again for emphasis, palm inward and fingers upright.

"According to Yeong-Suk, their bracelets are programmed to automatically give them access to any ship docked, so that they can clean them as necessary," Yanouk said. "We won't have to pick or blow or override the airlock controls."

Dan considered it. Noted how nervous the other six were, all sitting perfectly still while under the guns of her killers. Stun weapons, but the intent was clear, regardless of linguistic differences.

"What species are they?" Dan asked.

"Guezal," Yanouk replied. "Originally from Sector 4, but common enough across the Empire these days."

"And criminals?" Dan pressed.

"Ethir might adopt them as honorary cousins," Yanouk smiled.

Dan snorted. That framed things nicely, as Ethir and his three cousins were hustlers, in an *Auga Empire* that didn't always reward such effort.

Too close to coloring outside the lines, which might be the single highest crime the *Auga* recognized at the end of the day.

Still, only eight of them, one who would have to be carried by two others. Unarmed. Her teams could handle them if they proved to be a problem. Perhaps terminally, if necessary.

And they might prove themselves useful.

"Bring that one," she ordered, pointing to the first one she'd met. "Any gear they want to bring can be put in Yanouk's bag. Yanouk, your team will be in charge of them. Ciah, you help as needed, but they're carrying their own."

Dan stepped out into the corridor as Yanouk spoke and bodies flowed into motion.

The clock was ticking.

SEVENTY-SIX

Uly watched Sterling conduct six warships like a symphony, smiling. And the young man had roared angrily when the conductor of *Starlight Relentless* had balked at taking orders, so those four were meekly doing as told right now.

Rage, but Uly didn't think Sterling had faked it. He had issued an order and expected these more senior Ononguli commanders to follow it. And then enforced his will on them.

Helped that the Vatazhko had ordered them to follow the Corsac Fox. And that Lukyan Chayka was happily doing what he was told.

They had fallen in, formed up like ducks flying south for the winter in an arrowhead with *Corsac Fox* second on the right and *Starlight Relentless* at the tip. Where they demanded to be.

For now, every 12dm salvo from the Striker was being met with a volley of 1dm and 2dm wavebolts sufficient to disrupt it. And Sterling was slowly, relentlessly firing back with heavier stuff, but only enough that the Striker could defend themselves.

"Sir, what happens if I score a kill on that ship?" Sterling asked. "Do the locals have anything that can haul it to safety, or am I causing it to slam into the ground at terminal velocity, annihilating anything below it when that happens?"

Ah, that was it. Human savagery had given way to tactical and strategic considerations. Moral and ethical choices. The planet wasn't that interesting, but hitting it with a starship would be bad for the *Corsac Fox*'s reputation.

"They do not, Mr. Huff," Uly said. "A kill now drops it and hits the ground."

"As expected, sir," Sterling nodded. "*Starlight Relentless*, dial your speed back ten percent and hold it there. All other ships, conform to the slower speed. We want him thinking he can outrun us and get to orbit again. Maintain current rate of fire, or slack it back randomly, as though we are running low on ammunition. Let him think he can escape me."

Uly smiled. A place where they could terminally damage the ship, and not kill innocents below.

He caught Suka Kuri's smile as well. And her nod.

She really was planning a curriculum in starship combat, wasn't she? Given what she knew, Uly found himself looking forward to taking it, if she was in the process of synthesizing everything Sterling and Drew could teach her on top of what her lifetime had included.

"Uly, I have an update from Dan," Haydar announced. "Things are moving on schedule as modified. Unquote."

He turned to the confused grumble on Haydar's tentacles. The man didn't have the sort of verbal shorthand Uly and Dan had developed. Smarter, but not sneakier, or something.

Uly smiled.

"Let her know where we are," Uly said. "And that I expect we'll bring this to resolution in about fifteen or twenty minutes, so she'll need to plan accordingly."

"Very good."

Uly watched his board. That Striker was slowly pulling away from the squadron, which would help them, at least in their minds.

12dm bolts had a much greater range that the 8s that *Fire Diamond* could loose. If the two sides were trying to hit each other, it would matter, but Sterling had the squadron defending itself well enough, while keeping the *Auga* ship honest.

"There we go," Sterling muttered under his breath.

Uly saw that ship's bow start to pitch up, as they finally decided that they had the distance to get out from under the Ononguli raiders.

It helped Uly's peace of mind that there weren't any other warships in the area worth mentioning. Or rather, there had been, until *Starlight Relentless* had caught several small ships half-asleep with a barrage of wavebolts, damaging all of them and killing a Probe.

Only the stations were armed enough to defend themselves at present, and Sterling had maneuvered the Striker into a bad position, where it didn't have any help.

At least until it got to orbit, where it could flee to safety under a station's guns, or perhaps transition to warp and get away.

Uly still wasn't sure which outcome he favored, but he'd put Sterling in charge of combat for now. He could override that later if he needed to, but Sterling had done all his homework. Exceptionally well.

"Ononguli squadron, our target is starting his run," Sterling announced calmly. "*Starlight Relentless*, draw back your bow the same angle the Striker has to maintain current separation. Up twelve. All ships conform, but maintain speed and spacing."

A giant whale, starting to surface in the distance, with harpoon-armed whalers tracking it warily.

A fitting image, though Uly didn't know what had brought that image into his head.

Slowly, the leviathan got to a higher orbit. Not down where the atmosphere was fluorescing against its shielding.

They were above now, rising to a space where the ship should take days to fall out of orbit if it lost power.

The locals would be able to attach a tug and haul it to safety at that point, as Uly would be long gone and not returning.

"All ships, stand by to accelerate and engage," Sterling called. "*Fire Diamond* and *Corsac Fox*, peel off laterally on your current elevations and go to rapid fire. *Starlight Relentless*, lead the other four in, firing as you go, but you will be on your own for defensive fire, so pay attention."

Uly grimaced, but didn't let it onto his face. Risky. Dangerous.

Hopefully, Sterling had seen something that gave him confidence, because that Striker could kill forward velocity right now by spinning in place and lighting all its engines, bringing all that firepower to best arc against the four whalers.

Which might be why the other two were surging forward on the flanks.

Goading him. Threatening another envelopment, which had caused that captain to flee them before.

Might even work.

The hull rang with wavebolt turrets firing as rapidly as they could cool, reload, and charge the next bolt. Slow, but faster than might be entirely safe, as you could set one off in the turret accidentally, blowing a scallop in the hull itself.

Hadn't happened today, but usually it only occurred on ships that hadn't maintained their gear properly.

Like old pirates. Not newly refurbished warships on their first raid.

Wavebolts raced inward from three sides. The Striker let loose with every turret and Omnipulsar it had, but they had to focus on the biggest wavebolts, ignoring the little ones.

Uly saw what Sterling had done. And approved.

Fire Diamond had turrets at either end of the hull, while *Corsac Fox* had a pair in a single turret forward. Slightly better rate of fire and accuracy. Especially when both fire as quickly as the second can go.

That second one snuck through, because someone hadn't been paying attention.

It slammed into the flanking Electroshield Array, but had been tuned as a lance instead of a fist. Like a shiv slammed into someone's kidneys, though the *Auga* wouldn't recognize that image.

The entire ship rocked once, like a stone that had been kicked loose from soil. It even started to tumble, suggesting internal damage somewhere that was worse than it appeared.

"One of their Omnipulsar mounts just ceased firing," Haydar announced.

"Power cut inside," Sterling replied. "May have just lost half of his gyroscopes as well. All ships, one more full salvo then hold for defensive fire only."

Uly caught himself short of intervening. That Striker didn't look like it could take a full salvo. But at the same time, it was like stabbing someone to death with icepicks, regardless of all the vids where a starship suddenly exploded every which way like a Roman candle.

Four bolts got through, because all the turrets on Uly's side of that ship stopped moving. Stopped firing. Stopped.

The ship was wreathed in multicolored fire for several seconds.

When the flashes of light cleared, Uly could see a tumble developing. And most of the exterior lights on his screen had gone dark.

Plus, plasma was venting into space like yellow fog.

"*Nyri Station Prime*, this is the *Corsac Fox*," Sterling said firmly. "You will immediately launch all search and rescue equipment. We're done and won't bother them again, or you, so they will be safe. On my honor. However, time is of the essence. Ononguli Squadron, come starboard to zero-four-zero and elevate ten. Cease all fire save defensive engagement and stand by to rendezvous for departure."

"But we could kill him," an angry voice came over the line.

Uly didn't bother trying to see who had transmitted. All of them probably felt that way.

"*Starlight Relentless*, we just did that," Sterling announced in a cold sneer. "That vessel will require extensive repair work to ever possibly fly again. At this moment, they will have to work at keeping it from falling out of orbit and impacting the planet below. We are done here. Unless you feel like disobeying orders?"

Uly didn't remember teaching Sterling that particular tone of voice. Must have learned it from Captain Winter, back on *King Hewitt II*. Or his mother, catching him with a hand in a cookie jar. Not normally appropriate, but this situation wasn't normal.

"No, sir," the man replied. "Maneuvering now."

Uly nodded at Sterling when the young man looked up and seemed to come back from some high, distant place, eyes suddenly growing huge as he reviewed what he'd done.

He'd gone to war. And treated it like a professional, instead of the usual Ononguli raider berserker.

Like, say, *Starlight Relentless*.

Uly approved. He would need conductors like Sterling Huff.

And whoever else Suka Kuri might train up for him.

SEVENTY-SEVEN

Dan kept the Guezal prisoners in front of her. Her team kept guns vaguely aimed at them, regardless of how polite the seven were being.

They were in the corridor leading to the big ship Uly had wanted her to steal. Nobody else had appeared, but Yanouk had relayed that each of the six major arms only had one group assigned for cleaning duties. Someone would have to cross the center, and nobody on this station was armed.

Or suicidal.

"We're here," Nasrin announced as she came to an airlock. "Yanouk?"

The female apparently named Yeong-Suk walked right up to the airlock and tapped her wristband against the control mechanism with a thunk. A moment later, the airlock slid open, revealing the corridor inward.

Nobody home. Shouldn't be anybody on the ship. Had they moved quicker, Dan figured that they might have not seen anybody, save for the one man who had awakened in the middle of his night and needed a potty break.

Luck, but Dan wasn't sure if it was good or bad yet. Yeong-Suk probably wasn't sure, either.

Dan would let Ethir sort the Guezal out when she got them to Uly.

"In," Dan ordered, but Nasrin was already leading her team down the long corridor.

The ship was so big that they'd had to telescope an airlock arm nearly fifty meters merely to connect, despite the way it had been docked and snugged up against the side of the station itself.

Intended for long-term storage, perhaps measured in years. Because the *Auga Empire* was like that. Prepare relentlessly. Build and stage resources. Move everything slowly and deliberately into position.

Attack.

Uly had said that they didn't understand jazz. Dan was finally starting to understand what he meant by that observation.

And how Uly intended to take advantage of it.

At the far end, Yeong-Suk opened the next hatch, then said something to Yanouk.

"According to her, that's it for primary security she can help us with," Yanouk relayed. "The ship is in a low-energy state, with engineers that monitor things from the primary station instead of locally, and only visited monthly for more advanced maintenance. It is, however, supposedly extremely automated."

"Let her know we just stole an identical copy not all that long ago," Dan smiled.

Ahead of them, Nasrin had boarded and taken control of a mud room. Or whatever the *Auga* called that space where you stored life-suits and exterior gear. Lockers filled with tools. And suits of every size, though none of them would have the sorts of armor Dan required on her team for combat operations.

Good enough for workers.

"Okay, people," Dan announced. "That airlock should have set off an alarm somewhere, so we do not have long before someone notices. Everyone to your stations. Yanouk, you and Katya swap places and bring your team and friends forward with me."

Bodies got into motion. Soon, the ship would be in motion.

Then the Corsac Fox would be in motion.

SEVENTY-EIGHT

Ciah was glad that she had inherited a group of Khet men that Dan had already broken in for her. Back home, her lack of stature would have almost guaranteed that at least one of them would challenge her for her right to lead.

At the same time, every one of these men was at least a half-decade older than Ciah. Sometimes more than a decade. Old veteran troopers.

She had caught a few knowing glances of those sorts that meant breaking in a young new officer, which really did describe the situation. But Dan didn't allow any hazing, and all these men were professional volunteers.

"In motion aft," Ciah ordered.

She'd left her faceplate open in spite of how dry the air in here was, so she'd turned the mister on to intermittent to keep her gills happy. And let her smell and taste the air as they moved.

Not as good as a Mazhin. Nobody was as good as that, but Khet were probably the closest second place. Not counting Uly. He was kinda scary at times.

She started to jog, for no other reason than it would force all those

339

long-legged men around her to do the same, when she frequently had to churn her legs to keep up with them.

And she was on point, because she'd moved before ordering. In the rear, Katya's team was still adjusting, as they'd planned on storming the empty bridge with Nasrin and Dan.

Ciah led.

This ship was simply enormous. Two kilometers long, and most of that was those tremendous cargo bays. She went through an open hatch and marveled at the thing she saw, then realized that it was one of the plates to make up an *Auga* watchtower station, seen edge on.

And a meter thick, with twenty-odd meters of curve at the center, where it would assemble into a cylinder.

HUGE.

Well organized, though. The *Auga* did that. And did it with the efficiency of an accountant, which was what her parents had wanted her to be when she grew up.

Worse, she'd finished a degree in business with an accounting sub, but not gotten around to taking the certification test yet because you had to have so many years of practice as a bookkeeper first.

And all her spare time had been at the dojo, when her classmates had all been working part-time gigs to earn their hours.

Ciah figured she'd come out ahead. Dumb luck, but she'd lived up to the name she had taken when she was old enough to legally do it.

Troublesome Warrior Child.

She grinned. Behind her, the men had all fallen into a stomping rhythm as they matched her pace. Rear-facing cameras showed two lines of three each, quick-marching like this was a parade.

Ciah continued to grin and held her pace. They matched her.

For those veterans, it was a form of acceptance, because they'd apparently decided she knew what she was doing here.

And seven guns were pointed forward as they crossed, looking for the engine room.

SEVENTY-NINE

Yanouk had taken Yeoung-Suk and her cohorts under her wing. They spoke an obscure, regional dialect of *Auga* Common that Yanouk only understood because Suka Kuri apparently spoke everything and had insisted that she and Hiko speak it, too.

It was not impossible to learn from someone you shared no common language with, but it did make it complicated and make you prone to missing important sub-text.

Pantomime only got you so far, as Yanouk had learned.

And asked the Guezal a few leading questions, then sat back and listened to Yeong-Suk answer, as well as the five men and other two women.

Ethir would absolutely call them kin when he got to know them. And not in a bad way.

Mostly.

You never knew with Thogin, though *The Cousins* were Yanouk's only exposure to the species in person. Books generally painted them as everyday folk, leading humdrum lives.

The Cousins had gone off for fortune or fame. And run into Uly eventually.

Like the Guezal might.

Purple fur, generally about a centimeter thick, though she recalled from somewhere that it might double that and grow an undercoat in cold weather on a planetary surface. Long-limbed bipeds of a fairly standard design.

She also remembered that they came from a high-gravity, barren, mineral-poor world that had many moons and was known for its archaeological wonders. The species had risen and fallen several times in ancient history, then been absorbed by the expanding wavefront of the *Auga Empire*, who had looted the antiquities for display in their own museums, even while treating them like second-class citizens of their own homeworld.

"How did you end up at Nyri?" Yanouk asked as she walked next to Yeong-Suk and in the middle of the others, with her team around that and Dan's team trailing and watchful.

"They wanted the troublemakers as far from home as they could get us," Yeong-Suk laughed. "The time served wasn't going to be all that long. The problem was that after that, they'd drop us on the planetary surface and expect us to work. Or pay our own way home to Sector Four."

"So a form of exile?" Yanouk asked.

"They're good at that," Min Choe spoke up, one of the older males in the group, though only barely thirty if Yanouk had gotten names and ages memorized correctly.

Yeong-Suk seemed to be the ringleader, though she was younger than most of the other seven. Smarter, too.

"Oh?" Yanouk turned to the male.

"Third time for me," he nodded. "At this rate, I might see the entire Empire before I'm done."

"We're leaving the Empire," Yanouk told them.

And watched all eight perk up, as well as a dozen armed killers around her watching the newcomers. Prisoners? Something.

"Where?" Yeong-Suk asked. "We originally thought you were pirates, hiding on some missed *Auga* world."

Yanouk turned to Dan and got her nod before proceeding to explain it.

"We are leading an Ononguli raid to Nyri," she said. "Then returning to that space for a brief time. Then elsewhere."

All of them got big eyes, watching her.

"But we are so far from Ononguli Space," Yeong-Suk whispered. "How? Why?"

"We belong to the forces loyal to the Corsac Fox," Yanouk told them. "He is Human, like Commander Chastain here. His fleet contains many species, working in concert to thwart the *Auga*."

"I'm in," Min announced. "Tired of forced exile. Tired of *Auga* shitheads, too."

That drew a round of agreements from the Guezal, all of whom turned to Yeong-Suk.

She seemed to be in charge of them, in spite of being young.

She did have the force of personality that the others seemed to lack. Leader, when the other seven were followers.

"All other species?" she asked.

"Even renegade *Auga* would be welcome," Yanouk assured her. "Look at Commander Chastain's combat team leaders. Human, Mazhin, Ononguli, Emro, Khet."

These Guezal looked around with new eyes and some astonishment, but Yeong-Suk locked eyes with Yanouk.

"We could finally be free?" the Guezal woman asked quietly.

"Yes," Yanouk assured her.

"I'm in," Yeong-Suk nodded.

Yanouk smiled.

EIGHTY

Dan looked around the bridge of the ship she was about to cut out of storage. Drew had sent Yaqub Zobo with her to fly it, the young Khet having been originally trained on big cargo freighters before running off to a life of piracy at Lacium, then deciding he didn't want to be a pirate after all.

At least, not like that.

His last name apparently referred to the purple petals of a Khet flower, so he always had a stripe of purple tape somewhere on the outside of his suit. Like now. And one across his back let her know who was in the pilot's station, rapidly and precisely clicking things and making adjustments.

The air in here wasn't stale, but had a metallic taste. Blowers on minimum. Heat down to the point she'd brought her own suit's up for now. Maybe six degrees above freezing water. Coat weather, if she was in her usual uniform.

Dan made a note to talk to Omid about adding a heavy jacket to the usual uniform, for cold weather operations on a planet. Or for dress occasions.

Too much time on a ship, where you controlled the temperature at all times.

One more thing for her to make a decision on, so Uly didn't have to think about it.

Chief of Staff.

"Yaqub, where are we at?" she asked after a few moments.

Yanouk had gotten all her people off to one side and seated facing inward, with instructions not to touch anything. The rest of the raiders were scattered about. Ciah and Katya had a group of engineers with them in case there were issues aft.

Yaqub was in charge of handling everything at this point.

He kept clicking things, then finally looked up.

"Nobody has noticed us boarding," he said. "At least, nobody has asked what's going on. That will change in a few minutes, when I trigger the docking locks to disengage and we start elevating out of dock. I'm taking a bit to get everything fully warm, instead of just running like hell with half my systems still off."

"Wise choice," Dan nodded. "They are hopefully all distracted by Uly and those ships."

"My thought as well, Commander," Yaqub nodded, then went back to his board. "Engineering, how long?"

"Three minutes and the generators will have stabilized fully," someone replied from aft. "Engines are warming up and we're running a test cycle on the Variable Pulse Spatial Generator before we activate it. Figure they have to see that happen and start asking questions."

"Engineering, I don't show anybody on this side of planetary orbit with guns," Yaqub said. "As soon as the engines read green, let me know and then bring the Spatial Generator to full operations and charge it. Either it works, or we have to ask the Corsac Fox to come rescue us. Pretty embarrassing at that point."

Dan grinned. All of them were professionals, and Uly had impressed on them that professionalism was the highest state of a navy. Let the Ononguli go be crazy. Or the Khet be business sharks.

Uly wanted you to do your job as well as you could, with an expectation that you'd figure out how to top that tomorrow.

Like he did.

And she was in command of yet another starship, in spite of

hardly knowing anything. But she had the right people, one of whom was technically out of uniform because he couldn't resist the purple duct tape.

Yaqub made up for it. Especially when he looked up at her.

"Sir, we're ready to move," he announced, looking for her to give the actual order.

"Unlock and engage thrusters," Dan ordered, only because she'd stopped to look up what a captain was supposed to say at this point.

Wasn't second nature, like with Uly or Drew.

But she was learning.

And none of them were any good with firearms or close combat. Though maybe she needed to work on that, too.

The entire hull rang as locks disengaged like an antique zipper opening. Her grandmother had liked to use such strange tools when sewing.

"Engine Room, stand by for thrusters," Yaqub called. "Straight up in three, two, one, now."

Dan didn't feel anything, but she looked over Yaqub's shoulder as the ship seemed to slowly start drifting, like a balloon set free on a calm day.

"Engineering, I show greens on all the places I need them," Yaqub said a few moments later. "Please confirm."

"Engines show good, bridge," someone answered. "Generators are holding nicely. Spatial Generator passes all tests and is ready to come on line when you give the signal."

"Stand by," Yaqub said. "Station Prime just noticed troubles and asked if we were joining in the search and rescue operations. What the hell are they talking about?"

Dan had been listening to the main squadron frequency in one ear, mostly to feel the rhythm of things.

"*Corsac Fox* just ordered all ships and stations in system to launch S&R ships," she told him. "That Striker has suffered a complete systems failure and might have to be towed before it falls out of orbit. The squadron is moving off to let the *Auga* folks rescue people from the wreck."

"Wreck?" Yaqub asked, bewildered. "But that's an *Auga* Heavy Striker."

"Past tense, sailor," Dan replied. "Sterling Huff has reduced it to a navigational hazard."

"Shit," he whispered. "Okay, I'm sending them a note that we're coming to help. Lying, of course, so everybody strap yourselves in for maneuvering."

Dan joined the others laughing as she settled into the captain's station and brought things live.

The Corsac Fox had struck again.

EIGHTY-ONE

Uly studied the scene. One *Auga* Striker, badly mangled, with mobs of smaller ships swarming around it, picking up sailors and bringing repair crews to stabilize the hull. One massive cargo ship, undocked and moving like an iceberg as it got far enough into a clear space that it could transition to warp.

As with the former *Workshop*, it moved slowly. Same size. Same class. Same engines.

Same cargo. Full this time.

This one, however, would have a six-ship escort back to Ononguli space, picking up a couple of cargo ships with food and supplies as they went.

"Ononguli squadron, this is the Corsac Fox," he announced on the main line, leaving it unencrypted for now so the locals would hear as well. And referring to himself as THE Corsac Fox to indicate a singular person, instead of the ship.

Not the time for mistaken identity. He wanted the *Auga* to know who had done this.

Uly paused to draw a breath.

"We have attacked the anchorage at Nyri successfully," he continued, knowing that Imperials would record these words for later. And be utterly pissed. "We have badly damaged a Heavy Striker, though we showed mercy to the sailors aboard when it became clear that the ship was no longer a threat. We have damaged several patrol vessels stationed at Nyri, rendering them unable to threaten me or the Ononguli who are my allies. Finally, we have stolen an *Auga* vessel that we will keep. The *Auga* will be appalled and angry, but we have begun to draw a line on a map. They can stay on their side of that line and be good neighbors, but I do not expect that concept to take hold, so we will engage them every time they cross, pushing them back. Maybe, in time, it will be necessary for us to push them farther back, and look to liberate former Ononguli worlds lost in previous invasions. The Emperor of *Auga* must decide which of several futures he wishes to embrace. Thank you for your help in doing this thing. People of the Nyri System, the war has begun, and today you are on the front line, because of the choices of the *Auga* in charge. Ask them why this day was necessary."

Uly cut the line and listened to the snickers around him. Ethir and Piruz he was expecting. Suka Kuri was a surprise, but her face held a great joy.

"You are an evil person, Uly," she chortled. "But I approve."

He nodded to her.

The Corsac Fox had to be larger than life. Had to make pompous pronouncements like that.

Had to jar the very foundations of the *Auga Empire*, if he wanted them to change into something better. Something nicer to all the folks who didn't have that third eye.

Or he'd *make* them change.

Uly turned to Drew and smiled.

"Mr. Roscoe, take us home."

EIGHTY-TWO

Lukyan was just glad to be home.

Back to Rayzian orbit, anyway. Looking across the squadron, now plus-one with a ship that weighed more than all six Interceptors combined, he wondered if he'd be staying in command of *Fire Diamond*, or going back to *Compass Rose*. And everyone had known they were coming, because *Obsidian Nebula* had raced ahead with reports from Uly.

Scary reports.

What would the Vatazhko say?

Oskar looked up and caught Lukyan's eye.

"Message from the palace station," the dork said.

Lukyan cringed. Couldn't help it. They'd sailed in on a Tuesday, in spite of everything he'd tried to do to prevent it.

Ship that big simply moved on the pace it wanted, and that got everyone home on the wrong day.

"I'll take it in my office," Lukyan decided, unbuckling and rising.

He paused for coffee on his way, but didn't dawdle.

Palace meant serious business. And he was the conductor over these yahoos.

Especially on a Tuesday.

The screen came live.

Maks?!?

Lukyan's face must have been something, because the guy just grinned.

"I'm on the station with the boss and a few of her people," Maks said immediately. "We knew when you were coming in. Sorry you picked the wrong day of the week."

Lukyan shook his head. Maks laughed.

"What's the news?" Lukyan asked.

"*Augia Governor* at Nyri sent a high-speed courier about six hours after you left," Maks said. "All the usual complaints, threats, bluster, and bullshit. Threw in a couple of jibes about how the Ononguli seemed to be siding with the criminal they had demanded be arrested, and how badly the Emperor himself would look upon such reckless actions."

"My, they are pissed," Lukyan laughed. "Gonna round up twice the usual suspects or something?"

"That's my guess," Maks agreed. "Boss was more interested in what Uly did to that Heavy Striker."

Lukyan nodded.

"Do not underestimate that kid Huff," he told his best friend. "I'll play you the tapes and walk you through everything, but you're buying the beer."

"Deal," Maks said, then his face grew a little concerned. "However, it won't just be the two of us."

"Oh?" Lukyan perked up.

Tuesdays, ya know?

"I'd say double date, but that's just what it looks like on the surface," Maks nodded, way more serious.

Lukyan hated it already.

"And?"

"You and me," Maks continued. "Plus Chervonya and Anna. Just us four. Neither lady really thinks that the other four conductors can add anything useful, short of the normal bluster and hype you get from any young officers who just raided an *Auga* system."

Lukyan nodded at that. *Starlight Relentless* was the perfect ship to put on point, because they thought that charging madly into battle and shooting every which way was the right answer.

Didn't matter what the question was.

Sterling Huff had given Oskar and Lukyan a university-level class in tactical maneuvering and combat operations of a small strike squadron.

Lukyan still woke up in a cold sweat occasionally, remembering that Sterling Huff was young enough to be his kid. And Uly hardly older.

What would they look like in a decade, assuming they survived?

"What are they looking for?" Lukyan asked warily.

"I don't think they expected Uly to succeed."

Lukyan snorted. Maks nodded.

"Sure, blow shit up," Maks continued. "But they took down a Heavy Striker, Lukyan. Not just beat it, but bashed it into submission, then ordered—ORDERED—Search and Rescue teams into motion to save it. No Ononguli conductor would have done that."

"And stole a cargo ship," Lukyan added.

"Yeah," Maks said. "What the hell is he doing with it, anyway?"

"Building a base of operations, Maks," Lukyan replied.

"Where?"

"Dunno," Lukyan said. "Asked him on the way home, since we had so much time lollygagging while it crept along. They don't know, near as I can tell. But they have a full *Auga* watchtower base, unassembled, that they can put up somewhere. That thing turns into Base Prime for the Corsac Fox going forward."

"What about Z'Gosza?" Maks asked. "Or Lacium? Taeli? What the hell are Uly and Dan up to?"

"Building something bigger," Lukyan said.

"What?"

"Uly called himself *Warlord of the Spinward Reaches* over dinner at one point."

Maks's eyes got big. Lukyan nodded.

"There's nothing out there," Maks whispered.

"Yet," Lukyan corrected him. "That's going to change."

EIGHTY-THREE

Maks was still recovering his wits after talking to Lukyan.

They'd all underestimated Uly.

Again.

And he should know better.

Should have.

Anna and Chervonya were waiting for him when he got to Anna's office.

He paused to fix himself a mug of coffee before he sat, feeling almost pink in tone instead of his usual scarlet.

Chervonya caught it. Her eyes got big.

"What did Lukyan have to add?" she asked carefully as he settled.

"They captured one of those massive freighters that the *Auga* use to build forward bases," Maks said, watching both women nod warily. "Fully loaded, too. Apparently, Uly is only planning to stay put here long enough to be polite, then he is going to gather up his forces and sail off into that darkness known as the Spinward Reaches and locate a spot to assemble that thing and build himself his first major base."

Maks felt deflated, just speaking the words aloud.

The two woman gawked. He couldn't think of a better word to use.

"And we don't know where, do we?" Chervonya asked quietly. Nervously.

Maks had noticed that Anna let her speak much of the time. Plausible deniability later, most likely. Things that she hadn't said, and could deny.

If anyone was stupid enough to maneuver against her like that.

"We do not," Maks nodded. "And that zone is simply huge."

"He cannot move quickly," Anna spoke up, causing Maks to snap around.

"Ma'am?"

"Those things require a huge crew of workers to assemble," she nodded. "Uly has always been shy on crew. At least until recently. He'll have to find a spot, then truck in a thousand workers and all their supplies. That will take time. Then feed that many people. Plus, I cannot imagine that he simply withdraws into the wilderness like some fairy tale character for years, building his strength."

"He might," Maks offered, causing both women to lean in as well. "Nobody knows what's out there. Everyone is always focused on their own local region, and the *Auga*. Even we call it the Spinward Reaches, because we don't know if there is any nation currently sitting quietly out there not bothering anyone. Could he recruit folks there, instead of getting them from us or the Oligarchs of Z'Gosza?"

Maks sipped his coffee and tried to remember anything he'd heard in a decade of sailing with Lukyan on *Compass Rose*, but even his old boss had been at a loss on that one.

Everyone working that distant region had pretty much sailed the same three courses, eventually ending up at Taeli or Lacium, depending on how far from Rayzian you decided was safe.

None of the trade routes he could remember went north from Lacium any distance on any map.

None.

Maks didn't trust it.

"Maks, how committed are you to returning to your own command station?" Anna asked after a pregnant pause.

"As opposed to?" he volleyed carefully.

This was the woman who could make him. Or break him.

Simple as that.

"Going with Uly when he leaves, aboard *Corsac Fox*," Anna said. "As an ambassador from the Horde."

Maks was just glad he was sitting down, or he might have fallen over. Almost dropped his mug anyway, but Anna always got the good coffee, and that would be a criminal waste.

He did blink. Felt like his brain rebooting or something.

He bit his lip, deep in thought.

"I might have a better idea," he offered hesitantly.

"Oh?"

He turned to Chervonya to speak, but that was him including both of them.

"What if you were to offer Uly some resources in the way of a ship filled with skilled workers to help with the assembly?" he asked. "And sent me in command of said ship. And sent Chervonya as your ambassador instead. That way, it is a much more serious, *public* commitment on our part. Uly appreciates that sort of thing, so it would earn us points later, and keep him engaged with the Horde more directly."

"Would he go for it?" Anna asked.

"If he didn't have to pay for people?" Maks asked. "And they were mechanics we'd picked out for expertise on this sort of construction? Yeah, I think he would. After all, we kind of blackmailed him into hitting Nyri for us in the first place. This is a way of paying him back. And keeping him friendly. We all know the *Auga* are going to lose their shit at some point, and we want somebody like Uly willing to help when it happens."

Maks paused there. Sipped coffee. Wondered at the audacity of pretty much demanding that the Vatazhko give him a ship anyway. And send him on the mission.

Maks Sobol was never going to be a player in Clan politics. He knew that. And didn't want to have to answer for whatever shit Adrian had brought down on himself this time. Or why he wasn't going to get traded home anytime soon.

Better if Maks could sail off into the darkness, too.

And get Chervonya away from her aunt, so he had a chance to

figure out which of those signals she'd been putting out were personal, instead of merely political.

Like touching him on the arm more than strictly necessary when talking.

Maks wasn't dumb. Or blind.

And only *occasionally* clueless.

However, he was swimming in dangerous waters with these two women. Best to keep them friendly, too.

Anna's smile told him that she was reading him like a book, but that was okay. He was her agent. And knew she was using him. At least he could get something out of it when she was done with him.

She turned to her niece.

"Thoughts?" Anna asked as Maks held his breath.

He was, after all, kind of blackmailing both these women, however slightly.

Chervonya smiled at him in that same way Anna did. Knowing.

"I think we should ask Uly," she said.

"Ask Dan," Maks interrupted automatically.

"Chastain?" Anna asked.

"She's his Chief of Staff now," Maks nodded. "Get her off to one side and see what she thinks."

Chervonya nodded.

"I'll handle that," she said. "Maks, what kind of ship?"

He paused, juggling things in his head.

"A troop transport, maybe?" he offered. "Except that those tend to be extremely austere, and we want folks happy."

"What if we pulled a cruise ship out of commission and hired it instead?" Anna asked.

Maks didn't contain his goggle. Both women smiled indulgently at him.

"Not as sexy as a warship, Maks?" Anna teased.

The Vatazhko. Teasing him.

HIM?

"Maybe," he managed.

"It will prepare you for what you might do with *Scavenger Angel* after the war," Anna said with a knowing nod. "Or maybe you build out a whole fleet of such ships and make stupid amounts of money in the process."

"Those profitable?" he asked.

"Maks, you have no idea," Anna laughed. "*Scavenger Angel*'s first annual operating statement will knock you on your ass when it arrives. Trust me, I've been reviewing monthly numbers so far."

He nodded.

"Cruise ship, huh?" he asked, trying to envision himself.

Those folks always seemed to be wearing bright, pretty colors, almost at odds with how pirates did things.

But wasn't that the whole point? Impress folks with money? Like, say, Anna Shevchenko?

Shit, it would work. And Uly and Dan would probably go for it.

He'd miss the fighting in the near term, and have to settle for making money instead?

Something in Anna's eyes made him nervous.

"You own such a ship, don't you?" he asked.

Her laugh was like a bell on a clear day.

"Yes, Maks, I do," she said. "And I'll have to sell you a small percentage so you become a partner in the enterprise. Sweat equity. I'm sure you'll sweat for it. Plus, it lets my ambassador travel in style. Does that work for you, Chervonya?"

"Whatever you need, Anna."

Maks nodded.

Not the most impressive thing on a resume. At least for pirates.

Still, he suspected that Uly and Dan would approve. And that was what really mattered.

EIGHTY-FOUR

Suka Kuri studied the young woman. Guezal, which she hadn't been expecting to encounter in this stretch of *Auga* space. They were normally found mainly in Sector Four.

A long ways from home. But weren't they all?

Yeong-Suk did not fidget, but it was clear she wanted to. Nerves, being confronted by an old, Emro woman other folks held in high esteem. Which just showed that most of them were fools, as well.

Still, *Exemplar of the Arts* brought with it certain operational requirements.

Reading Yeong-Suk's mind might be among them, even though that wasn't how she was doing it.

Reading her soul, perhaps.

"More tea?" Suka Kuri gestured to the pot, steeped with the good stuff and refilled once as they had spoken of many irrelevant things.

"Please," Yeong-Suk nodded, placing her mug just so on the table between them.

Suka Kuri had chosen a small lounge. Two chairs, both facing the same direction towards an artificial fire with good graphics and the ability to output heat as though real.

A low table between them with her tea service. Even a plate of sweet pastries she'd asked Vahid to produce for this interview.

The Guezal had been with them for nearly a month now. The long sail back from Nyri.

Long enough for all of them to have picked up the Ononguli dialect. It helped that their culture tended to be linguists. Almost social chameleons, for all that purple fur made them stand out physically.

Suka Kuri filled the cup and watched the young woman sip.

Younger than Dan. Older than Yanouk. Perhaps close in age to Anari and Katya.

Wicked smart and charismatic in ways that had her, like Ethir with his cousins, something of a ringleader.

"You have had time to understand what the Corsac Fox implies," Suka Kuri informed her, leaping over many intervening conversations that were unnecessary because Yeong-Suk was smart enough to follow her path. "You now face a branching."

Yeong-Suk nodded, sipping, eyes and mind deep in contemplation.

"We could, were we of a mind, turn back now and find a way to cross back into *Auga* space along a less energetic border," Yeong-Suk stated. "A few might prefer that outcome, but will not argue strongly for it if the others disagree."

"I concur," Suka Kuri agreed, having taken the measure of the other seven.

Followers, as Yanouk had indicated. Only one leader among them.

"Or we might take passage laterally, following new trade routes that eventually bind Ononguli to the Khet at Z'Gosza," Yeong-Suk continued. "Our exoticness would probably be in our favor, especially as we could tell people we were rescued by Uly and Dan."

Suka Kuri noted how quickly these newcomers had picked up the language.

Everyone spoke of the Corsac Fox as the overall military and business enterprise, but when referring to people, they said Uly and Dan.

She approved. Already, that young man had bound them to his

legend, without possibly even realizing it, as he'd been busy with other things and most of his meetings with them perfunctory.

Suka Kuri was weighing her soul.

"Or we could remain with the Corsac Fox," Yeong-Suk added. "I believe that there are four strong votes in favor of that outcome, though I have not taken any sort of poll."

"Because they will follow your path, once you determine what it is," Suka Kuri noted.

Yeong-Suk flinched, then nodded, accepting that logic, though she may have never spelled it out, even to herself.

"They will," Yeong-Suk agreed.

"What path will you seek?" Suka Kuri asked.

Yeong-Suk turned her torso and leaned back some, until they were staring at one another. Guezal were tall among the medium-sized species. Emro were much taller than everyone.

"I note that Dan's combat team seems to fill several roles, beyond simply professional violence," Yeong-Suk said.

Suka Kuri nodded. The young woman had seemed smart enough to pick up on those things.

"What other roles are inherent?" Yeong-Suk asked.

"Species representatives," Suka Kuri replied. "One woman, at least, from each such group Uly encounters, in a position to advise the woman who will make many of the day-to-day decisions about his life and legend."

"And both Moss and Sabre Schools, though I note that neither seems purely devoted to one," Yeong-Suk said.

Suka Kuri nodded and smiled.

"Both have it in them to achieve the level of Exemplar," she told the youngster. "In fact, all of the women on Dan's team do. Each of them also brings a perspective unique to her species."

"All of them?" Yeong-Suk asked.

Suka Kuri nodded sagely. After all, she was a sage. Whatever other silliness she got up to notwithstanding.

"How does one join such a thing?" Yeong-Suk asked.

"Commitment," Suka Kuri said simply. "Getting up each morning and announcing that you will be better today than yesterday.

That nobody else will outwork you towards your eventual goal. It is a lifetime of such daily decisions, compounded."

Yeong-Suk nodded. Paused, deep in thought.

She had many options open before her. Only one had been sufficient for Suka Kuri to invite her to a private tea. And then, only after a month of surreptitiously studying the woman. Watching how she handled herself and her people in a new culture. A new place.

Outsider, in almost every way.

Almost.

"Those women are Dan's inner council," Yeong-Suk mused. "The ones she goes to with questions and needs. The ones who help her shape things, because she trusts them."

"Indeed," Suka Kuri agreed.

"How do I get there?" Yeong-Suk asked.

Suka Kuri smiled.

"You must learn how to fight," she told the young woman. "And to think. Most importantly, however, you must learn how to dance."

EIGHTY-FIVE

Dan studied Maks and scowled prodigiously at him. He bore it well.

"Why do I feel like you are up to no good, Maks?" she asked.

They were alone in her office. On board the *Corsac Fox*. He had finally added a rank tab to the collar of his lime uniform. Rose gold circle. Conductor.

When he'd been without such a rank indicator this whole time. Even as everyone else she met in Ononguli service was extremely specific and diligent about such things.

"Because I might be," Maks agreed. "Or rather, the Vatazhko needed a thing. And a person. And I was handy."

"I get the feeling she learned she needed the thing when you mentioned it to her," Dan noted.

Maks shrugged.

"It made logical sense, once we figured out what Uly had done," he said with a quiet grin. "Those bases are huge. And require a lot of folks to assemble. Hordes of experts, if you want it done in any sort of hurry."

"So you convinced her to charter a cruise ship, stock it with just the folks we need, and pay their wages for a year?" Dan asked.

Maks's grin got bigger.

"Don't forget the part where I'm a junior partner in the profit-sharing," he said. "And Chervonya is coming along as Anna's ambassador, instead of me."

"You don't feel safe in the role?" Dan asked.

Maks sobered.

"Uly surprised the shit out of everyone, Dan," he said. "Again. Including me. I'd rather those sorts of fuckups land on somebody else's horns, thank you very much."

Dan laughed. Maks hadn't changed all that much, for all he seemed more comfortable around her and confident in himself.

"Which of you is the spy, then?" Dan pressed.

"Probably all of us," Maks shrugged. "And I'll send home reports with ships bringing supplies. Chervonya will have official stuff. At the same time, I doubt that Uly's doing anything that threatens the Horde, except where he pissed off the *Auga* enough that they move forward their next invasion a few years."

"Somebody just stole the ship that they might have used to build a new forward operating base," Dan reminded him.

"Twice," Maks laughed. "Don't forget Ixtin. They gotta replace all that before trying something new. Uly probably bought himself and everybody else two years of peace, depending on what he does next. Which brings me to the really important question I have to ask you."

Dan nodded.

Where were they going?

"I have guesses, but haven't gone deep with him yet, Maks," Dan nodded. "We have maps. We have people to talk to. We have friends. If you're coming along with mechanics and supplies, that means we can get started sooner, and finished sooner. But I don't know where."

"Good enough," Maks nodded back. "Anna's great concern was that Uly disappeared for five years and nobody knew where he was or how to find him when the shit with the *Auga* started. Didn't think he'd want to miss the war if it did, but years is a long time."

"It is," she agreed. "And a lot can happen. Who is Chervonya Borisov?"

"Trying to determine that myself," Maks said. "She flirts a lot, but

I don't know if it is professional or personal. Getting her off by herself maybe lets me figure it out better."

"Put Suka Kuri on the case," Dan suggested. "She's good at reading minds."

"Would she, though?" Maks asked.

"Lots of reasons," Dan nodded. "The formal Ambassador to the Horde makes her important, so Uly needs to know who she is and what she wants from us. Especially if she's going to be your girlfriend at some point."

Maks blushed. Turned almost as black as his hair. Dan laughed.

"So Uly will be okay with all the shit I'm trying to do here?" Maks asked.

"None of it threatens him, Maks," Dan informed him. "That's the starting point that matters. Plus, the Horde is putting its money where its horns are. Eventually, I think Uly needs a bigger vessel than the *Fox*, but that's part of building out a fleet for when he goes after the *Auga* personally."

"How big?" Maks asked.

"Flagship," she replied. "With all that implies. One of the first tasks after the base itself is complete is to acquire or build a drydock capable of repairing and later building new warships of a more Human design."

"How do Humans do it?" Maks asked, suddenly nervously curious.

"More firepower," she replied. "Better internal structure. Better Electroshield Arrays. Things designed from the ground up to sail into combat and pound on other ships, like a brawl in a bar. Most of your pirate vessels are lighter than the equivalent Human hull. That Striker we killed at Nyri only had three turrets. A *Batyr* Heavy Cruiser would have had four. Maybe five, if they were a Command Cruiser."

"Wow," Maks whispered. "You folks really are different, aren't you?"

"Violent enough to start a war with the *Auga*, Maks," she nodded. "And expect to win it, scale be damned."

She watched him blink several times.

Recalibrating. Yet again.

Nobody understood Humans, and those who watched them only saw saw Uly, who could be violent, but always in a calm, professional manner.

"*Starlight Relentless*, for attitude problems," Dan continued. "Now multiply that by a species, Maks."

Yet more blinks.

He muttered something under his breath that she didn't pick up.

"What was that?"

"Lukyan was right," he repeated louder. "Better to be on Uly's side than the losers."

Dan nodded.

Maks was entirely correct.

EIGHTY-SIX

Uly had taken a day off from various meetings with various Ononguli discussing various things.

Detail work, but things that he needed to touch. People he needed to meet with personally, because the Corsac Fox was a totem that moved them into action, even as Dan was meeting twice as many people and getting lots more done.

Little of it would draw headlines. All of it was probably more important than him having coffee with merchants wanting to get into the Z'Goszan trade.

He was in the wardroom, drawn by the smell of muffins fresh out of the stove. Vahid, experimenting with Ononguli grains and fruits, looking to see how things worked.

Uly would call them purpleberry muffins for now. He was considering going back for a second when Dan found him, so he stayed put with a mug of coffee and watched her walk. Move.

Dance.

Idle daydreams. And not so idle.

She settled across from him.

"You're smiling," she began.

"You're here," he replied.

Then watched her blink once and blush ever so quietly under that dark bronze skin.

His grin got infectious, so they sat and smiled at each other for a moment.

Then the rest of the galaxy intruded on his mind.

Uly sobered and came back to a place where he wasn't sitting across from a beautiful, competent, deadly woman.

Not just.

"How can I ruin your day?" he asked, just to watch her blink.

"Probably ruining yours," she said. "Or something."

"I doubt it, if it means I get to spend more time with you."

They were alone. He could say these things to her, at least quietly.

More blush.

"I need a vacation," Uly announced.

"Then I have good news," she smiled.

"Talk to me."

"I've been dealing with Maks, and through him those two women."

Uly nodded. Almost as dangerous as Dan was.

Almost.

"We have a deal, whereby Maks and a crew of mechanics in a cruise ship accompany the ship we've been calling *Watchtower*," she said. "*Wren* will be packed full of supplies, also at their expense, then we're on the hook for resupply after that, but I expect that the Fox can swing down to Taeli, pass along a message for Z'Gosza, then race back into the darkness and find a spot we want to settle, leaving marker buoys along the way for our merchants and trailing fleet to follow."

Uly felt a weight slide off his shoulders. It let him sit up straighter.

She smiled, noticing.

"Thank you," he said simply.

More blush, but he honestly couldn't do any of this without her.

"Do we know where we're going yet?" she asked.

"Sterling has a list of stars he wants to visit," Uly told her. "Not a lot of them had signals, but that works in our favor, if we can move in like neighbors. Assuming they are friendly enough to strangers moving into the neighborhood."

"And if they aren't?"

"We move on," Uly nodded. "This is a major project, and at this point, I'm measuring things in a generational scale because I honestly don't ever see us going home. Or if we do, taking everyone with us to meet the various kin and blow open the blinders that have been keeping them ignorant of the wider galaxy. I certainly was, and I was on a warship."

"We didn't talk about it to outsiders," she nodded back. "And you'd been with us for all of three weeks at that point, so you were probably a year from being fully initiated into the secrecy, knowing Captain Savatier."

"I still wonder how much fun it might be, sailing a fleet of Devastator-class boats to Gralbo and saying hello," he laughed.

"Endless amounts," she agreed. "The Mazhin would freak them completely out."

Uly nodded again, sobering back to reality.

"For now, we go build something where we can be safe," he said. "Then we figure out what we want to do when we grow up."

"Thirty-one felt old, two years ago when this started," she agreed. "Now, I see what we're doing and wonder where we'll be at forty or fifty."

"Or more," he said. "This will take lifetimes, if we do it right."

"Is it necessary?" Dan asked, watching him closer now.

Him, and not the Corsac Fox. They were back to people, instead of concepts.

"I think so," he told her. "The *Auga* have a plan to eventually conquer the entire galaxy, however many millennia it might take them. They need to be stopped now, and forced to change into something that can live with the other species, instead of just conquering everyone they meet. And yes, that takes precedence over my personal happiness, even though I have your support. What do you want from all this?"

"I'm doing it," she said quietly. "You've empowered me to create an entire new civilization, and do it the way I think is correct."

"You are the best person I know for that," he told her, watching yet more blushes. It was fun, seeing that. "You have ideas, you listen to people, you adapt. You build."

"Sounds like someone else I know," she grinned.

Uly shrugged. She was not wrong. It was part of why they were such an effective team. One plus one equaling three, or maybe even seven.

"So what can I do to help?" he asked her.

"Believe in me."

"Done."

They shared a moment of smiling silence.

Tomorrow would be here soon enough, with all those new problems that would crop up.

He'd be off, on the next phase of building that thing he called Warlord of the Spinward Reaches in his head.

And he had her help.

Uly figured he could do anything, when Dan believed in him.

ABOUT THE AUTHOR

Blaze Ward writes science fiction in the Alexandria Station universe (Jessica Keller, The Science Officer, The Story Road, etc.) as well as several other science fiction universes, such as Star Dragon, the Dominion, and more. He also writes odd bits of high fantasy with swords and orcs. In addition, he is the Editor and Publisher of *Boundary Shock Quarterly Magazine*. You can find out more at his website www.blazeward.com, as well as Facebook, Goodreads, and other places.

Blaze's works are available as ebooks, paper, and audio, and can be found at a variety of online vendors. His newsletter comes out regularly, and you can also follow his blog on his website. He really enjoys interacting with fans, and looks forward to any and all questions—even ones about his books!

Never miss a release!
If you'd like to be notified of new releases, sign up for my newsletter.

http://www.blazeward.com/newsletter/

Buy More!
Did you know that you can buy directly from the KRP website?

https://www.knottedroadpress.com/shop/

Connect with Blaze!

Web: www.blazeward.com
Boundary Shock Quarterly (BSQ):
https://www.boundaryshockquarterly.com/

ABOUT KNOTTED ROAD PRESS

Knotted Road Press publishes dynamic fiction set in exotic locations and unique non-fiction voices in genres such as autobiography, business, cookbooks, and how-to. Our authors cover a wide range of genres including science fiction, fantasy, mystery, literary, and poetry, appealing to all readers. We offer both DRM-free ebooks and print books for a global readership.

Knotted Road Press
www.KnottedRoadPress.com
www.KnottedRoadPress.com/Shop